PARANOIA BLUES

BOOKS BY JOSH PACHTER

The Tree of Life
Styx (with Bavo Dhooge)

As Editor
The Beat of Black Wings: Crime Fiction Inspired by the Songs of Joni Mitchell
Only the Good Die Young: Crime Fiction Inspired by the Songs of Billy Joel
The Misadventures of Nero Wolfe
The Man Who Read Mysteries: The Short Fiction of William Brittain
Amsterdam Noir (with René Appel)
The Misadventures of Ellery Queen (with Dale C. Andrews)
The Further Misadventures of Ellery Queen (with Dale C. Andrews)
The Great Filling Station Holdup: Crime Fiction Inspired by the Songs of Jimmy Buffett
Paranoia Blues: Crime Fiction Inspired by the Songs of Paul Simon

PARANOIA BLUES

CRIME FICTION INSPIRED BY THE SONGS OF PAUL SIMON

EDITED BY JOSH PACHTER

Down & Out Books
3959 Van Dyke Road, Suite 265
Lutz, FL 33558
DownAndOutBooks.com

Cover design by Margo Nauert

ISBN: 1-64396-291-4
ISBN-13: 978-1-64396-291-7

TABLE OF CONTENTS

INTRODUCTION

As I write this introduction, I recently celebrated my seventieth birthday, and let me tell you, old friends, Paul Simon had it exactly right: "how terribly strange" it is to be seventy...

It seems like only a couple of years ago—though it was in fact more than a couple of decades!—that a teenage me rode the train from my little town on Long Island into Manhattan on what was a sunny day to pay a dollar (one dollar! outrageous!) to see Simon and Garfunkel perform live in Central Park.

Twenty years later, I was living in what was then called West Germany but felt like another galaxy, and I was lucky to score a ticket (for a lot more than a dollar, but nothing like prices today!) to join the crowd in a giant outdoor stadium for the *Graceland* concert, with Miriam Makeba and Hugh Masekela and Ladysmith Black Mambazo joining Simon onstage. That was—and remains—one of the greatest evenings of live music I've ever been privileged to experience.

Today, even after all these years, I still listen to one of Paul Simon's American tunes every year on September 14. The song is "Have a Good Time," and if you can't figure out for yourself why I listen to it on the day after my birthday, please go check it out on Spotify or Apple Music or YouTube or wherever. I'll wait right here for you...

You're back? Good! And did you spot the Easter eggs in the preceding paragraphs? Awesome! So, shall we move along?...

Speaking of birthdays, Paul Frederic Simon is exactly to the day ten years minus a month older than I am. (And I can only imagine how terribly strange it must be for him to be *eighty*.) Often thought of as a quintessential New Yorker, Simon was actually born slightly to the west, in Newark, New Jersey, although he was raised in Queens, one of the five boroughs of New York City.

He and Art Garfunkel met at the age of eleven and began singing together at thirteen...around the same time Simon wrote his first song. At sixteen, recording as Tom and Jerry, they had their first hit, "Hey, Schoolgirl." Still in his teens, Simon was writing songs and producing singles for singers signed to Amy Records under the *nom de musique* Jerry Landis, and he had several Top 100 hits of his own, both as Landis and as a member of Tico & the Triumphs.

In 1966, Paul S. and Arthur G. reunited to record "The Sound of Silence"—and the rest, as they say, is history, their story, his story.

This is the fifth of my "inspired by" anthologies—following *The Beat of Black Wings: Crime Fiction Inspired by the Songs of Joni Mitchell* (Untreed Reads, 2020), *The Great Filling Station Holdup: Crime Fiction Inspired by the Songs of Jimmy Buffett* (Down and Out Books, 2021), *Only the Good Die Young: Crime Fiction Inspired by the Songs of Billy Joel* (Untreed Reads, 2021), and *Monkey Business: Crime Fiction Inspired by the Films of the Marx Brothers* (Untreed Reads, 2021)—and this time around I decided to invite submissions *only* from authors who hadn't contributed to any of the previous books.

Some of them—Ed Aymar, Mark Bergin, Kris Kisska—are

friends from my old stomping grounds not far from our nation's capital and my new home outside Richmond, Virginia. Some—Paul Charles, Martin Edwards, Debra Goldstein, Edwin Hill, Gabriel Valjan—are people I've met face-to-face at writing conferences in recent years. Others—Eve Fisher, Cheryl Head, R.J. Koreto, Raquel Reyes, Andrew Welsh-Huggins, Frank Zafiro—are folks whose work I admire, but who I didn't *know* until I reached out to them as possible contributors for this book.

Three of the remaining five contributors are people I'd like to introduce to you individually.

Robert Edward Eckels published some fifty terrific short stories in *Ellery Queen's Mystery Magazine* in the late Sixties and through the Seventies, and he was one of the several crime writers who befriended me when I was a teenager and just beginning my own career. Bob stopped writing in 1982—but when I began work on "Paranoia Blues" I asked if he might be willing to jump back into the game...and was delighted when, just after his ninetieth birthday, he accepted the challenge. Writing "The Big Bright Green Pleasure Machine" apparently flipped some sort of switch in Bob's head, because after he completed the story you'll read in this volume, he churned out a number of additional new works, several of which he sold to *Ellery Queen's Mystery Magazine* and other publications. On May 17, 2022, I was shocked and saddened to receive an email from his wife Margaret, letting me know that Bob had died the previous day, at the age of ninety-one. Although I miss my old friend, I'm happy to have inspired him to allow Paul Simon to inspire him to resume writing crime fiction after his forty-year hiatus, and I'm eager to read more of the stories he wrote in the last weeks and months before his passing.

Tony Head—no relation to Cheryl—is new to the world of crime fiction, but he's the author of a charming memoir and a virtual friend who shares with me a love for all things Parrotheady. I hope you'll agree that, in this case, two Heads really *are* better than one!

And then there's Rebecca Jones, whose first novel, *Steadying the Ark* (Bella Books), came out in March 2022...and who has been for the last thirty-five years my daughter! Becca and I collaborated on a short story that was published in EQMM in 2009, and she translated two stories by French author Thomas Narcejac for my *Misadventures of Ellery Queen* (Wildside Press) and *Misadventures of Nero Wolfe* (Mysterious Press) anthologies, but this is the first time I've had the opportunity to include a story she wrote herself in one of my books. Hey, Bec, say hello to the nice people!

If you've already looked at this volume's table of contents, you have perhaps noticed that four of the five Simon and Garfunkel albums and all of Paul Simon's fourteen solo albums are represented here by a single story...and you've perhaps wondered why *Bridge Over Troubled Water* is an exception.

Allow me to explain.

Some anthology editors operate on the basis of what's known as an "open call," which means that they announce the project publicly and welcome submissions from every Tom and Jerry who sends in a story by the deadline.

Until recently, though, I've been working a full-time teaching job, and I simply haven't had *time* to read fifty or a hundred "over the transom" submissions for a book that's only going to include fifteen or twenty stories.

So my "inspired by" books have been open to submission by invitation only, and the authors I invite are people I'm confident can be counted on to produce quality work in a timely manner.

Much more often than not, that's turned out just fine. Every once in a while, though, I find myself in the uncomfortable position of having to reject a story that was written for no reason other than the fact that I invited its author to take the time to write it. (That doesn't mean that those stories were "bad." Mostly they've been *good* stories that simply didn't fit the parameters of the book I was editing at the time.)

Well, that's what happened here. I invited an author I know face-to-face and respect to write a story inspired by one of the songs on the *Bridge Over Troubled Water* album. As luck would have it, he wound up being the last person to deliver a manuscript—and, as *bad* luck would have it, his story—though well written and interesting—simply wasn't a *crime* story. I invited him to "crime it up" and waited several weeks for his revision...and the second version of his story still didn't give me the type of tale I was looking for.

Which meant that, with my deadline looming, I was short a story to represent Simon's *Bridge* album. I considered putting all my eggs in one basket and inviting *one* writer to come up with a story quickly...but what, I worried, if that author also delivered a story I couldn't use? That would mean I'd have to start from Square One *again*, and I'd be almost certain to miss my deadline, which would upset my publisher's schedule and probably push the book back by at least half a year.

Instead, I approached *three* authors, hoping that at least one of them would be interested in the project, would have time to write a story quickly, and would deliver one that was right for *Paranoia Blues*.

You've probably figured out by now where this is going. As it happened, *two* of the three people I approached—Tom Mead and Anna Scotti—delivered top-notch work, and when I checked the rulebook, I discovered that there was in fact nothing preventing me from using two stories inspired by songs from *Bridge Over Troubled Water,* rather than only one. (I mean, hey, it's my book, right, so I get to make the rules...)

So, there you have it: that's the slate of contributors, and you can learn more about them by reading their biographies at the back of this volume.

To learn more about the cast of characters who populate this collection of crime stories inspired by the songs of one of contemporary music's greatest singer/songwriters—you can call him Paul—all you have to do is turn the page.

So God bless the fiction we've been given, and God bless the US of A—and now, let's all have a good time, baby, reading the twenty stories in *Paranoia Blues*!

Josh Pachter
Midlothian, Virginia
March 31, 2022

PART I

THE SIMON AND GARFUNKEL ALBUMS

Wednesday Morning, 3 A.M.

Released October 1964

"You Can Tell the World"
"Last Night I Had the Strangest Dream"
"Bleecker Street"
"Sparrow"
"Benedictus"
"The Sounds of Silence"
"He Was My Brother"
"Peggy-O"
"Go Tell It on the Mountain"
"The Sun Is Burning"
"The Times They Are a-Changin'"
"Wednesday Morning, 3 A.M."

"You Can Tell the World" is by Bob Gibson and Bob Camp,
arranged by Paul Simon.
"Last Night I Had the Strangest Dream" is by Ed McCurdy,
"Benedictus" is by Orlando di Lasso,
"The Sun is Burning" is by Ian Campbell,
"The Times They Are a-Changin'" is by Bob Dylan,
all arranged by Paul Simon.
"Peggy-O" and "Go Tell It on the Mountain" are traditional,
arranged by Paul Simon.
"He Was My Brother" is credited to Paul Kane, a pseudonym for Paul Simon.
All other songs by Paul Simon.

THE SOUNDS OF SILENCE

Gabriel Valjan

Detective Joseph Burrow descended from the neon lights of Manhattan into the 14th Street-Union Square subway station. Cigarette butts littered the concrete steps. The deeper he went underground, the denser the air became: unmoving, thick, unforgiving. The scents—human and other—commingled with the stench of garbage, the dust from the trains' brakes, and the traces of ozone from the high-voltage arcs and sparks.

Sergeant Staskiewicz was in command of the scene pending his arrival, and a pair of patrolmen held back a cadre of curious commuters.

As Joe approached, a street prophet waved a sheet of paper in his face. "I'd like to talk to you about the word of our Lord and Savior, Jesus Christ."

"Fuck off," he said.

Staskiewicz shook his head.

"What?" Joe asked. "I can't say 'fuck off' to a bum, but Ford can tell the whole city to drop dead?"

"You're a ray of sunshine, Joe. You know that?"

"Never was a people person. And what sunshine? It's the middle of the night."

"You're a weatherman, too?"

"Enough foreplay. What do you have for me, Stasi?"

"Looks like our Tunnel Thief has stepped up his game to

murder. The vic is male. Asian. Late twenties, maybe—I can never tell age with them."

"Don't tell me they all look the same, Stasi. What else?"

"The Transit Authority's stopped the trains, so the clock is ticking. Follow me."

They headed into the black tunnel side by side.

"Dispatch said the 911 call was all over the place, like scrambled eggs," Staskiewicz reported. "I'll be honest, Joe, we didn't know what we were walking into."

"Do we ever? Any ID?"

"None that we could find, but we haven't moved him. He could be sitting on his wallet, or the perp could've ripped the cash and tossed the leather. We've established a perimeter, but we waited for you."

"Thanks."

Stasi looked concerned, and Joe asked what was on his mind.

"When we caught the call, we thought this mighta been another one of those Son of Sam killings, but there's no sign of a gunshot, and—"

"This wasn't Sam, unless the bastard can be in two places at the same time."

"Are you saying what I think you're saying?"

"Sam shot two kids in Queens two hours ago."

"Jesus."

Joe conveyed what he had gleaned from a detective at the One-Eleven. The couple had left a disco in Bayside and were sitting in a Cadillac actually *talking* about the killer when he'd graced them with his malignant presence and blasted them. The young lady was critical at Flushing Medical with three shots to the head, neck, and shoulder. Her boyfriend had taken a traveler, one round through his arm and into his leg.

They arrived where the dead Asian was sitting on the ground, his back against the tunnel wall.

"Stasi, your flashlight over here, please."

The wall had been tagged by local artistes of the spray can.

Joe recognized the tag *Gen II*, a talented guy who had a graffiti gallery in a tunnel beneath Riverside Park.

The artwork closest to the victim was a portrait of a black rat standing on its hind legs. It held a .45 automatic aimed at the viewer in one paw, a flashlight in the other. Next to the rodent, the letters *HoBo* were fat and white, outlined in Army green. As for the victim, he could've passed for a Bowery drunk, except he wasn't a bum, and he wasn't asleep. He was clean and looked professional.

Joe crouched down in the light from Stasi's flash and used a pen from his shirt pocket to examine the body. The sergeant told him more about the concerned citizen who'd called 911, but Joe only heard about every third word, because he was on the ground and his friend's face was above him and in the shadows.

Joe didn't like what he saw when he worked the guy's collar loose with his pen. The dead man had been garroted. Strangled.

"Interesting. The body here and that rat on the wall are a statement."

The sergeant reconsidered the rat. "Payback, as in someone squealed?"

Joe stood up. "Not payback. You said we're on a clock?"

Stasi checked his Timex. "Less than an hour before the barbarians take Manhattan."

"You have your perimeter. Get the scene photographed, bagged and tagged."

"Will do, Joe, but gimme something."

"What we have here is a tunnel rat."

"Come again?"

"Consider the victim's nationality, Stasi."

"He's Asian, so what?"

"He's *Vietnamese*, and he was targeted."

"Because he's Vietnamese?"

"Because the night belongs to the hunter. I'll follow up with you soon. I gotta go."

***

Joe thought about the case.

It'd been a typical summer so far. There was the heat. Tempers flared, subsided, and rose again. People were on edge, restless—and not just people. Joe had spotted live rats in the subway tunnel. They were New Yorkers, too. They had watched him and Stasi, unafraid and undeterred.

The summer's swelter did something to everyone. The vulgar and vital became vulgar and violent. The crime rate climbed, echoing the mercury in the thermometer. First the Son of Sam, and now this.

Joe walked the click to East 23rd Street. He covered the half mile in less than ten minutes, even though his knees were almost bone on bone and his back ached from his infantry days.

People mobbed the sidewalks and street corners. A man held an arm up high, stabbing the air and yelling for a cab. Others stood waiting, their cigarettes lit, going nowhere fast, as overhead the clouds grew gray and silent raindrops began to fall.

Joe was on his way to an appointment.

The test done, he sat and waited for the results, squeezing the tennis ball he'd "borrowed" from the empty desk in front of him. When the office door opened, he shot upright and returned the ball to its place.

"Some good news and some bad news for you, Mr. Burrow," the man in the lab coat said. "Which do you want first?"

"The bad."

"The bad news is you need hearing aids."

"And the good?"

"You can hear vowels."

"Vowels?"

"A, E, I, O, U, and sometimes Y."

"I know what vowels are. How's that good news, doc?"

"I'm an audiologist, not a physician." The man smiled, as if to accept the offered title would constitute fraud. "If you'd been *born* unable to hear vowels, that would've affected your speech. Since you're an adult, and your loss is with consonants, you can intuit words, given the context of a conversation."

Joe swallowed his anger. The guy was speaking slowly and clearly, and Joe could hear every comma. He found the carefulness patronizing, but he went with it and shrugged. "So you're saying I need hearing aids."

"Don't you want to hear the world around you?"

"Do you really want me to answer that question?"

The audiologist flipped a page. "Says here you're a veteran. Seen combat?"

"Some. Why?"

"That would explain the etiology for your condition. Even *with* hearing aids, there's the matter of occupational hazard. You're a detective with the NYPD."

"You have a thing against cops?"

"No, but your hearing loss makes you a liability in the field."

"I can manage." Joe shifted in the chair. "I have years of experience."

"I'm sure you do, but your hearing issue isn't a career ender."

"It would be to the brass," Joe said.

"What's the worst that could happen?"

"They'll put me on a desk. Do I look cut out to play office secretary, sit around and make coffee all day?"

The audiologist held up the file folder. "These results say you look like a guy who can't *hear* it unless he can *see* it. Your hearing loss isn't going away, Mr. Burrow. You could jeopardize the life of your partner or other officers on the street."

"Like I said, I'll manage."

"Because you have years of experience? This isn't the VA, so nobody else knows about your tests, but I hope you'll do the right thing here." He smiled. "Let's try something, shall we? I'm going to say one word, and I want you tell me what it is."

He held the report in front of his lips and spoke, then lowered it and asked, "What was the word?"

"I dunno. You were mumbling."

"Try again." He covered his lips, repeated the word, lowered the folder. "What did I say?"

Joe said nothing.

"If you could see my lips, you would've guessed the word."

Joe rose. "I don't read lips."

"I bet you *do*, without realizing it."

"I've got two words for *you*," Joe said. "The first one begins with an F, and the second one ends with a U. We're done here."

As he reached for the doorknob, something smacked the wall beside Joe's head. His hand shot out and plucked the tennis ball from the air on the rebound. "What the hell is wrong with you?"

"I'm proving my point."

"Which is what exactly? I heard it, okay?"

"Not until it hit the wall. And that's my point right there."

"What is?"

"You're going to have to learn to live your life on the defensive."

"I already do," Joe said, lobbing the ball back to its owner. "That's what being a cop's all about."

The audiologist raised the folder to conceal his lips.

Joe said, "Not that again."

"Have it your way." The man lowered the folder. "The word was *liability*."

Outside, Joe stopped for a pretzel from a street cart, looking forward to the tastes of warm dough, salt, spicy mustard. The vendor had a portable radio tuned to a news station and took his money without looking at him.

Later, he had dinner at his friend Duc's restaurant. While he waited for his vegetarian soup, *chả giò*, and *phở chay*, Joe called the station house so the desk sergeant would know where to find him. Duc served him and sat down with his own meal, spinach stir-fried with a generous amount of garlic and some fish sauce. As usual, they ate near the kitchen, and Duc amused Joe with his comments on politicians. Nixon was a hungry ghost; Kissinger, a goblin; Ford, the man who fell up steps. Duc considered Jimmy Carter more of a parent than a president and Americans his children, toddlers throwing temper tantrums, drunk on anger.

Ten years earlier, Duc had been the enemy. Today, his smile was at times as enigmatic as the Mona Lisa's; at other times, it was simply a smile. "What clouds your mind, friend?" he asked Joe.

"I was told I need hearing aids. What do you think?"

"Perhaps it's karma telling you that you must learn to listen."

"Don't go all Master Po on me, Duc."

"If you don't want my guidance, then listen to the silence, and the answer will come."

"I do want your advice."

"Then talk, and I will listen."

"I'm on a case, and my instinct tells me I'm up against a tunnel rat."

Duc worked his chopsticks like a surgeon closing a wound. He had himself served as a tunnel rat during the war, when the VC had made use of the vast complex of tunnels that the Viet Minh had built in their fight against the French. These tunnels offered escape routes and points of ambush, or led to greater caves and caverns of supplies, weapons, even hospitals.

The VC hid inside the labyrinth of tunnels. They set traps, which varied from sharpened sticks dipped in excrement to poisonous insects, scorpions, and snakes.

The Americans and their allies sent in volunteers—all of them men under five-six—whose task was to gather intelligence, then destroy the tunnels with C4 explosives. This wasn't just a matter of clearing a tunnel with a flamethrower. A man was sent into every spider hole. The entrances were trapdoors no more than eighteen inches wide, and the tunnels varied from twenty to several hundred feet long.

Duc said he could smell the Americans because of the food they ate. He would sit in the dark for days and nights on end, watching the GIs pass within inches of him but unaware of his existence.

Joe never asked his friend the obvious question: how many Americans had he killed? The tunnels conducted noise, so pistols were rarely used; hand-to-hand combat was the order of the day. Up close and personal, murder was never as easy or as quick as the movies led viewers to believe.

Duc placed his chopsticks across his dish. "Tell me why you think it's a tunnel rat."

"We found the word *HoBo*, with a capital H and B, at the scene. Graffiti."

"And you don't think it's your English word for a street person?"

Joe shook his head. "The artwork includes a rat with a flashlight and a sidearm."

"I see." Duc looked into his glass of water. "Ho Bo Woods."

"Exactly."

During the war years, Ho Bo Woods—thirty-odd miles northwest of Saigon—was rumored to house the subterranean headquarters of the entire North Vietnamese Army. Aboveground, it was a vast forest of rubber trees and rice paddies. Belowground, it was infested with tunnel rats and snipers. American and Australian joint operations had eradicated some of the enemy, but they cropped up like weeds elsewhere. Eventually, American B-52 bombers had reduced Ho Bo to a lunar surface.

"You see my problem, Duc?"

"Yes. Battle with a tunnel rat only ends one way."

A cook approached the table and rattled off rapid Vietnamese to Duc, who told Joe there was a call for him. Joe knew where to find the phone. He put the receiver to his ear, expecting the desk sergeant.

"He's struck again, Joe," Stasi said. "A jogger, this time."

"Same MO?"

"Victim is male and Vietnamese. Same artwork, but there's two differences: this time, he slit the vic's throat, and—get this—the graffiti's still wet."

"Where's the body?"

"Under the Winterdale Arch in Central Park."

"Winterdale's near 82nd Street," Joe said. "He has a choice of several bus stops, but I doubt he'd take a bus."

"Why not?"

"Two reasons. One, there'll be blood on him, and he'll want to avoid eyes. Two, he prefers tunnels, they're home to him. The two closest subway stations are at 72nd and 86th. Put out an APB to all units in the area. Male, five-six or less, and tell them not to engage him. Repeat: do not engage, suspect is armed and dangerous."

Stasi digested that and said, "I'll have units in the area do a slow prowl. The whip will have to call Transit Police to get coverage in the subway. Get here pronto. The world is calling."

Joe returned to the table for his coat. He told Duc, "There's a situation. I gotta go. Have any wisdom for me, Master Po?"

"Life is uncertain. Only death is certain."

"Why break open a fortune cookie," Joe said, "when I have you?"

During the short drive from Duc's place in Hell's Kitchen to the Upper West Side, Joe remembered an enemy without weapons, an enemy who stood on both the light and dark squares of the chessboard. By day, this enemy would look at him through the eyes of a child, a young girl, or an old woman. At night, though, rifles cracked, bullets buzzed by, a rocket grenade whooshed...and men fell and died.

The Henry Hudson Parkway was riddled with potholes. From the river came what some described as the odor of rotten eggs, though it reminded Joe of fuel oil, not unlike Vaseline but ten times stronger.

He rolled up behind a cruiser on Central Park West, and Stasi opened the passenger door and slid in beside him. "About time."

Joe asked after Stasi's partner and learned he was assigning sections of the park to recruits on the force.

"I need backup," Joe said. "You want to leave him in the field?"

Stasi hesitated. "You know it's a mortal sin to leave your partner behind."

"The guy we're after isn't in the park, or on the buses, or on a subway train."

"And you arrived at this conclusion how?"

Joe tilted his head toward the open window on his side of the car and said, "What's on our left?"

Stasi suspected a trick question. "More of the city, and then the river."

"And right before the river?"

"Riverside Park, why?"

"What's underneath the park?"

Stasi understood—and froze. "An Amtrak tunnel." He studied the open window on the driver's side as if it were a painting, then looked over his shoulder at the scene behind him and back to Joe and said, "You think our guy legged it?"

"Was the body warm when you found it?"

"Yeah."

"And the spray paint was still wet?"

"Yeah."

"And the vic was Asian?"

"Yeah. Jesus, Joe, you're right. Our rat's headed for the Amtrak tunnel." Stasi seemed to accept the idea. "There's a lot of homeless folks down there."

"And veterans."

"How bad do you think it'll be?"

"Like a thorn in the eye, but this guy isn't going to stop."

"Like Son of Sam," Stasi said.

Joe shifted into drive. "Take your hat off," he said, "and cover the shield on your chest."

Stasi looked perplexed. "Why?"

Joe pointed to the nickel-silver shields on Stasi's cover and left breast. "You saw the cartoon rat. If he shines his light on you and there's glare off your badges, he'll take your head off with his .45."

The tunnel snaked the two and a half miles from 72nd Street to 124th Street, providing Amtrak with a corridor it used to run freight between Penn Station in Midtown and the yards in the Bronx and Jersey. Joe and Stasi descended a stone staircase into an underworld of passages, some narrow, others wide. They climbed up and down ladders, cut through a ventilation tube, and reached the railroad tracks. By the time they got there, they were covered in grime, and cobwebs stuck to them like cotton candy.

Rats squealed and scurried for cover. A cat yowled and dashed off. Trash cartwheeled in a subterranean breeze. The odor of dust and the acrid tang of urine were undeniable, an assault on their lungs and noses. The stench of excrement and decay invaded the darkness and almost made them gag. Joe had told Stasi not to use his flashlight, and they worked their way through the blackness, blind as moles.

When they heard the gurgle of water, they unholstered their revolvers. Where there was water, there was life. They heard the sounds of human activity. Feet. A disembodied groan.

Shadows of primitive housing came into view. Makeshift tents. Tarps. Milk crates. Dirty faces.

This was a modern-day catacomb. Here lived the dispossessed, the persecuted.

Joe saw a silhouette on the run, the profile of a short man. In that quick glimpse, he could see that the man was armed: one hand held a bayonet, the other an odd gun, not the Army's standard-issue Colt .45 or a police officer's .38. The shortened barrel reminded Joe of something Duc had told him once: American tunnel rats had carried modified .44 Magnums, because they were quiet in close quarters. A .44 also made Joe think of Son of Sam.

Stasi touched his shoulder.

"What?" Joe whispered.

"I said watch your step."

Joe looked down and saw the outline of a cinder block inches before him.

They moved forward to establish their position.

"Come out with your hands up," Joe yelled.

"Go to hell!"

"Buddy, this place will be crawling with cops soon. This won't end well for you."

"I'll take my chances."

"Nobody has to get hurt," Joe shouted.

A shot rang out, and Joe and Stasi hugged the ground. The muzzle fire gave them a good idea where the shooter was holed up.

Stasi tugged on Joe's sleeve. "Didn't you hear me?"

"What?"

Stasi said, "I have an idea. The cinder block."

"The what?"

"The *cinder* block."

Stasi pointed downwind. He turned to Joe, then back to the block, so Joe's eyes would track his. He held out his hand, touched his chest and then pointed at the stone. His fingers mimicked a spider's crawl. He pointed to the flashlight, and then at the stone. He touched the flashlight, flicked his thumb as if lighting a Bic, touched his blue shirt again, and then patted the ground.

Joe understood.

"Buy me time," Stasi said.

"I don't know what time it is."

Stasi grabbed Joe and whispered fiercely into his ear: "Buy—me—time, dammit."

Stasi moved off, and Joe counted silently to twenty, then yelled, "This is your last warning!"

"Go to hell!"

Joe aimed his revolver. "Throw down your weapons and surrender!"

Behind Joe, Stasi crept like a snake on its belly toward the concrete block.

Joe waited until Stasi placed the flashlight inside the block, turned it on, and rolled away. The plan was that the tunnel rat would respond to the light.

Which he did.

The rat fired a single shot. Joe fired twice.

Dog tags identified the tunnel rat, and the investigators requested copies of his service records from the VA. A rumor surfaced that the deceased had a history of mental illness since his separation from the Army. That was mere speculation, but what was found among his belongings was hard evidence: he had kept souvenirs from his kills.

After the incident, Stasi asked Joe how he'd managed a perfect double tap, one round each to chest and head.

"Experience," Joe said.

Asked how he felt about killing a veteran, Joe provided no official answer. Off the record—and only to Stasi—he said, "I looked into that dead man's eyes and saw myself."

During the investigation, Joe manned a desk.

He typed.

He made coffee.

He wore hearing aids.

Sounds of Silence

Released January 1966

"The Sound of Silence"
"Leaves That Are Green"
"Blessed"
"Kathy's Song"
"Somewhere They Can't Find Me"
"Anji"
"Richard Cory"
"A Most Peculiar Man"
"April Come She Will"
"We've Got a Groovy Thing Goin'"
"I Am a Rock"

"Anji" is by Davey Graham.
All other songs by Paul Simon.

APRIL COME SHE WILL

R.J. Koreto

April 5

I enjoyed the look the bartender gave me when I ordered a Glenfiddich with a little water, instead of one of those ridiculous concoctions with an umbrella sticking out of it. It was like we were part of a secret men's club, of which I was a rare female member.

"What can I say?" he said, pointing to the Hawaiian décor. "The tourists like it."

"That couple in the booth in the corner. They're not tourists."

"Nah. They're here several nights a week."

It was April, spring, when streams are ripe and swelled with rain, and everything seems perfect.

I settled my bill with cash, adding a generous tip, and carried my drink over to the corner booth. I liked its occupants' Barbie-and-Ken looks, blond and fair, more like siblings than a couple.

I dragged a chair from a neighboring table and sat down. Toned and tall, I am used to my figure startling men and women alike. My stature makes dating tough, but it's an asset in my profession.

"I'm Sienna Delahanty," I said. "And you are Angie Skipton and Tommy Brasher. You, Tommy, work in the sales department at Brasher Industries, owned and run by your Uncle William, but you aren't very good at it. And you, Angie, are an accountant in the finance department. Your company is building a new facility in Omaha, and the two of you are conspiring to skim three million dollars from the construction."

I allowed myself a moment to relish the fear and astonishment in their eyes, then downed my scotch in one swallow.

"Let's not waste anyone's time here," I said. "You haven't been exactly subtle about your plans, and, in case you haven't noticed, everything is connected nowadays. Fortunately, you haven't been found out by your employer—yet. I represent some people who *have* discovered what you're up to, and we're prepared to help out before you trip over your own feet. My people will take a million off the top, and the two of you will walk away with the rest of the score."

They listened in stunned silence as I laid out our plan. Tommy was amiable enough, not especially greedy, just a kid with a yen to live nicely without having to work hard. Angie was different: she *had* worked hard and had dreams for the future, and she was well aware that her job at Brasher Industries wasn't going to get her where she wanted to go. I found the two of them rather sweet.

"One more thing," I said. "You need to exercise a little discretion. I don't want anyone connecting the two of you. I'm not saying you can't be together. Just keep it on the down low. And leave some evenings open for me."

"Why?" asked Tommy.

"You're not my only job." I stood. "I'll be in touch. Don't do anything until you hear from me."

May 7

Stealing money from a company is surprisingly easy. But stealing it so they don't find out—at least until after you're long gone—requires finesse. Here a truckload of glass panes that aren't needed, there a construction crew scheduled for redundant work. The auditors would take months to find the dots and months more to connect them. The devil, as they say, is in the details.

Tommy and I met at a lousy neighborhood bar I'd chosen. I had my usual scotch and water, he had a gin and tonic. He was handsome and knew how to dress, with a haircut that must've cost a mint.

"So, you and Angie. Is this something long-term or just convenient for now?"

He smiled awkwardly. "It's long-term. After all this is over...we'll take the next step."

"That's nice. I'm glad to hear it. Because things are going to be stressful over the next few months, so it's good to have someone you can rely on. Emotionally, that is."

They'd moved into the May of their relationship, past the first excitement and reliably comfortable.

After his second gin, Tommy unwound a little. "At the end of the day, you know, it's wonderful to rest there in her arms."

"Tommy, I don't want to interfere in your social life. Angie's a sweet kid—but you're a Brasher. You have an Ivy League degree. You're smart. Lazy as hell, but smart."

He laughed, and I liked him for that.

"I'm just thinking, soon we're all going to have a lot of money." I ran my finger across his wrist. "Maybe you can do better for yourself..."

May 15

Angie and I met at her apartment and worked on the details. All the Brasher invoices came across her desk. She'd printed out a list, and we went over obscure places where—based on information from Tommy—we could pad expenses.

"All right," I said at last, "that's good for now. We should hit our three-million goal, maybe a little over." I let a pause stretch out for a couple of seconds. Then: "I suppose, when we're done, you and Tommy will set up house somewhere?"

"Oh, yes," she said, with a blush. She really was lovely.

"Look, I don't want to interfere. But we girls need to stick together, right? I just want to make sure you're...I guess the word is *secure* with him. I mean, he comes from a prominent family. If there's anything you want to talk about..."

She gave her golden curls a toss, as if she'd practiced the move. "Oh, I understand what you mean. We've discussed that."

"Because money changes a lot of things, a lot of people."

She looked a little uncertain at that. Good—I had guessed correctly.

"Sweetheart, I'm older than you," I went on, "and I've been down this road before. Would you mind a piece of advice? You need to look out for your own interests. If I was you, I wouldn't depend on a man."

Those lovely eyes got big.

I had been right about her.

June 10

Under my direction, Angie and Tommy were doing their part, but the stress was beginning to show—as expected. If either one of them slipped up, they'd both be going to prison, and that kind of pressure can damage the strongest relationships. By now, the cracks were showing and their tunes were changing. Sooner or later, every relationship comes to its June, when the minds are riddled with restless doubts and prowling fears.

Tommy and I were at another seedy bar—I know a dozen of them.

"I don't understand," he said, a little weepy after his second drink. "She gets all worked up, can't stop going over every little detail. I keep telling her it'll be okay, but it's like she's obsessed."

"That's the accountant personality," I said. "Add a layer of criminal conspiracy, and they get *really* wired. Keep in mind, though, Angie's just doing the numbers. *You're* the one who has to worm things out of your uncle. That's the hard job."

"No, *you* have the hard job, Sienna." He gave me a puppy-dog look. "You're the one keeping this all together."

It was inevitable, of course. You have two people drowning, grasping at each other to stay afloat, and if one of them sees a chance to lean on someone who's got her shit together, he'll take it.

I stroked his wrist the way I knew he liked. He grabbed my hand and leaned over the tiny table and kissed me.

"Hey, no PDA," I said. "And we need Angie. If she finds out about you and me, she'll come unglued. Let's be careful and wait."

"I understand," he said, but he didn't let go of my hand. We shared another lingering kiss.

"This'll be over before you know it," I promised. "Then you and I can take things to the next level."

Tommy grinned, and I stroked his wrist.

June 17

Angie was crying. We were in a quiet Italian restaurant in a forgotten neighborhood, its tables far apart. I ordered a carafe of red wine, and she drained her glass quickly.

"I can't sleep. I keep seeing numbers jumping around, and I know if I make one mistake—"

"You won't," I said. "I'm a good judge of character, Angie, that's what I'm paid for. Don't forget: you have the hard job. I'm just making lists, and Tommy only has to schmooze his uncle over prime-rib lunches."

"Thank you," she said. Women like Angie can live on simple acknowledgments. I know: that was the basis of my parents' marriage.

She took a bite of her Caesar salad. "Tommy hasn't been especially supportive," she said. "I wish he would...I mean, he's as tense as I am, and that isn't helping."

"Ivy League guys always let you down," I said. "It comes from having everything handed to them."

"There's no one I can talk to," she said. "Except you." She gave me a warm look.

I smiled. "You can always come to me, sweetheart," I said.

June 20

After we made love the first time, we lay there in the dark.

Women often blame men for not meeting their needs, but I've found it's a partnership thing. Someone who's bad with one person can be amazing with another, and this had been pretty amazing.

"This is secret," I said, when I'd caught my breath. "I mean it."

"I know." Firm, with no hesitation.

I find it refreshing to talk when you can't see the other person's face or body language. It forces you to really listen to your own voice and theirs, and that can be useful.

"We have a three-way partnership," I said, "and each of us is equally important. We can't have jealousy sending anyone off the rails."

"Kiss me again." It was half a question, half a demand.

I liked that.

July 9

I'd figured one of them would bolt, and it turned out to be Angie, who gave no warning to her flight. Of course, she had more to lose: William Brasher would be more lenient to his nephew than a mere employee.

She texted me from the road, using a burner I'd set up for her, and it took a lot of patient back and forth before I finally got her to pull off at a motel about two hours outside the city. She hadn't given notice at work, she told me, which indicated that her disappearance had been more a cry for help than a real attempt to run away—but I still needed to take it seriously.

Before I went after her, I called Tommy.

"It's my fault," he said. "I mean, you and I—"

"You didn't say anything, did you?"

"No...but I wasn't honest with her, either, wasn't *present* for her. She said we're over. You think she's found someone else?"

"What makes you say that?"

"I wouldn't have thought she'd run out on us like this unless she had some support. She's an attractive girl..."

His voice trailed away.

"Look, Tommy, she's been working nonstop. She hasn't had *time* to meet anyone new. And she's just upset, not stupid. Let's keep our eye on the ball. Things are going well. Money's pouring into the hidden accounts. Most of the deals are set up—if the company was paying attention, the alarms would already be ringing. I'll go reassure her."

"I'll come with you—"

"Oh, no, you're the last person she wants to see. This'll be just us girls, you understand? I'll give her the usual line: before you know it, things will be back to normal, with the pair of you richer by a cool two million. Look, baby, I'll calm her down, bring her home. Then you call and say all the right things. I'll give you a script, okay? I know how women think."

And you haven't a fucking clue.

"We'll be back tomorrow, and I'll make some time just for you and me, okay? I know a fantastic Hungarian restaurant. And then maybe..."

I could almost hear him drooling over the phone line.

For men, the *possibility* of sex is actually better than sex itself.

***

August 11

The business end was going great. It looked like we'd have three point two million nicely squared away: private equity funds in the Cayman Islands, a few kilos of platinum in a vault in Macao, Bitcoins floating in the ether. That was thanks to my expertise.

On the other hand, early autumn winds blew chilly and cold over what was left of Angie and Tommy's relationship. Fortunately, they didn't need to talk to each other anymore.

"A million dollars isn't infinite," I told Tommy over dinner. "You could buy a club, if that's your idea of fun. Or I could introduce you to people. I have contacts."

"That sounds promising," he said with a smile.

"I just need to keep an eye on Angie. She's fragile. No need to mess things up right at the finish line, okay?"

"Of course," he said, charming as always. "Of course."

August 12

The worst part is the uncertainty. Once it's over, you can move on. August, the end of summer, a time when relationships die.

Angie was coping.

We sat in her little apartment. She kept it very tidy and had clearly read a lot of articles about decorating and organizing a small space. It was very affecting.

"What are your plans?" I asked her. "I assume you won't want to stay on at Brasher Industries."

She laughed. "No, I'm done there. It may sound silly to you, but I want to start my own tax and consulting firm. It takes a while to get going—you have to pay salaries and rent and marketing before you even get your first client."

"Not silly at all. Admirable, in fact."

"Can I ask what *you'll* do? I mean, you're getting a nice cut of this, right?"

"I'm going to hang around," I said, not quite answering her question. "We'll talk, afterward," I said, giving her hand a squeeze. "Things will be different."

I needed her to go on believing that, just for a few final weeks.

"There's a lesson here that will stand you in good stead for the rest of your life," I said. "Be careful who you depend on."

She nodded. "Trust is important."

I shook my head. "Listen to me, sweetie. I am precise with my words. I said *depend on*, not *trust*. You will find people you can *depend* on. But you won't necessarily be able to *trust* them."

August 14

Tommy wasn't much of an actor, and I didn't want him to appear "off" when he spoke with his uncle. He seemed to like our sneaking around in expensive, out-of-the-way restaurants. We had some incredibly fresh sushi paired with Junmai Ginjo sake, of which he drank too much. He offered to pick up the check, but quickly backed down when I insisted. Fine with me. I had an expense account, and I didn't want him thinking I owed him anything.

The sex that night was fantastic.

September 21

Done and done. I was sitting in William Brasher's office with an excellent cup of coffee.

"You told your nephew?" I asked.

"I did. He threw Angie right under the bus."

I shook my head. "She's just a silly girl, really."

"I'm sure. I won't prosecute, but I *will* fire her. I'll give her a good reference, though, to avoid a scandal."

"You don't have much on her—or him, for that matter, despite my report. I'm just a PI, not a lawyer, but this whole thing smells a lot like entrapment."

He shrugged. "You're probably right. Anyway, the point was to scare the hell out of him and give me something to hold over him. I won't have any trouble with him now. He's terrified."

And, I reminded him, I'd arranged it so that Angie no longer cared for her former lover and would happily turn state's evidence if she were asked to—as Tommy well knew.

Brasher smiled at the way things had turned out.

"If that's all," I said, "I'll take the balance of my fee and go."

"Not *quite* all," he said. "There's still about two hundred thousand dollars missing."

"I warned you when we started that you might lose up to ten percent of the total amount at stake. To make it *look* real, it had to *be* real, which means I was dealing with people who don't give refunds just because we backed away before playing the final card."

"I suppose." He sighed and handed me an envelope.

I opened it to check the amount. As I'd suggested to Angie, I depend on people like William Brasher—but I don't trust them.

I wanted to say it had been a pleasure doing business with him, but I didn't think I could make that sound convincing, so I just tucked away the check and shook his hand.

His secretary saw me out.

Later, Angie and I met at a diner.

"Here's the real deal, hon. I'm a private investigator specializing in corporate fraud. This whole operation was a sting to catch Tommy embezzling from his uncle. He won't go to prison, but he's been scared straight. You are not going to be charged, but later today you'll be fired for unspecified reasons."

She stopped breathing for a moment.

"But the money," she said.

I took a check from my jacket pocket and gave it to her. "Just over two hundred and ten K disappeared during the course of the scam. I told Brasher it was gone for good and he'd have to suck up the loss. The money's been laundered, and it'll show up as an insurance payout from a company based in the Seychelles. It's not a million, but it ought to be enough to get that tax firm of yours going."

"Yes," she said, after a while. "Yes, it will be."

I could've brought up the next subject myself, but I decided to wait for her to go there.

"I'll always remember Tommy," she said, and then a shy blush colored her cheeks. "But what about us?"

"We've had fun," I said. "And we can go on having fun, if you'd like. Out in the open now, since we don't have to hide from your prick of an ex-boyfriend. Would you like that?"

"Yes," she said. "Yes, I would."

It wouldn't last forever. Both of us knew that, I think. *I* certainly did. A love once new inevitably grows old.

But that was okay with me. It was April for us now. Next we'd have our May, and we'd make that last as long as we could.

Parsley, Sage, Rosemary and Thyme

Released October 1966

"Scarborough Fair/Canticle"
"Patterns"
"Cloudy"
"Homeward Bound"
"The Big Bright Green Pleasure Machine"
"The 59th Street Bridge Song (Feelin' Groovy)"
"The Dangling Conversation"
"Flowers Never Bend with the Rainfall"
"A Simple Desultory Philippic (Or How I Was Robert McNamara'd into Submission"
"For Emily, Whenever I May Find Her"
"A Poem on the Underground Wall"
"7 O'Clock News/Silent Night"

"Scarborough Fair/Canticle" is traditional,
arranged by Paul Simon and Art Garfunkel.
"Cloudy" is by Paul Simon and Bruce Woodley.
"Silent Night" is by Josef Mohr and Franz Gruber.
All other songs by Paul Simon.

THE BIG BRIGHT GREEN PLEASURE MACHINE

Robert Edward Eckels

"You ever get the feeling somebody up there doesn't like you, Jerry?" I say, rolling my eyes heavenward. "And whatever you do, you're going to end up holding the short end of the stick?"

Jerry Thomas owns a bar and grill next to my apartment building. I make it a habit most nights to drop in for a nightcap before bed. Jerry's my best friend—in fact, my only friend. That's a heck of a note, isn't it? Thirty years old, a college graduate earning a good salary from a job I used to enjoy—and my only friend is a bartender. But at least Jerry lends me a sympathetic ear, which nobody else seems willing to do. And life in the business world's become such a drag that I couldn't make it through the day if I didn't have these little chats with Jerry to look forward to.

I think he enjoys them, too. In this part of town, a bar's business is mostly during the day: lunch hour and the five o'clock happy-hour surge of office workers grabbing a quick drink before catching the commuter train back to the suburbs and the wife and kiddies.

Anyway, Jerry thinks about my question and says, "Sometimes. Not very often."

"I wish I could say that," I tell him, "but I get that feeling almost every day."

***

My name is Henry Morris. I'm an actuary.

Most people think actuaries are the people who tell insurance companies how much to charge for life insurance, and that's true—as far as it goes. Insurance companies *do* use actuaries, but so do a lot of other businesses.

Actuaries are risk managers. Our job is to tell the folks who hire us how to avoid losing money. Of course, no matter how sophisticated your math or how accurate your statistics—and we use a lot of both—you can never be a hundred percent sure of *anything*, but all in all I think we earn our pay.

I work at the headquarters of a tech startup that's developing a new virtual-reality headset called the Pleasure Machine, which the company hopes will revolutionize the video game business. Copies of our bright green prototype are scattered around the office for anyone who wants to put them to the test, and of course our thirty-odd computers are loaded with data about our product.

There are about fifty of us in the office. Only a few are actuaries. Roughly half are clericals, mostly women in their late teens or early twenties—they do the typing and filing and all the other little jobs necessary to keep a business running. (That used to include getting coffee for their bosses, but no longer. Our corporate heads got the message early.) The others are specialists in one field or the other, about evenly split between men and women. The same is true for us actuaries, although we tend to be somewhat older than the rest of the crew.

Our manager is a guy named Fred Mayberry. He isn't an actuary or a specialist. The conventional wisdom is that *anyone* with good management skills can manage *anything*. Whether or not Mayberry possesses such skills is an open question. Even the toadies who play up to him don't like him. The rest of us cordially detest him. He's the reason I have that "somebody up there doesn't like me" feeling.

My main problem is that I just don't seem to fit in. Only Mayberry is actively hostile, but my coworkers do have a tendency to dump on me.

I'm a relative newcomer to the organization. When I started, I'd go down to the cafeteria with everyone else for coffee break, only to find the tables mostly filled and any empty seats being saved for somebody else. It didn't take long before I stopped going. Instead, I'll have a thermos filled at the restaurant where I eat my breakfast and drink it at my desk. It isn't pleasant to sip my coffee alone, but it's less humiliating than sitting by myself in the cafeteria.

A lot of my coworkers are married and, at the end of the day, go their separate ways. But most of the singles head off after work to a nearby happy hour. At thirty, I'm not too old to be a part of their group, but I've never once been asked to join them—and I'm not desperate enough to try to invite myself along.

The clerical who does my typing and filing—a teenage chatterbox named Judy—keeps me up to date on the in-house gossip. She has all the details on office romances—especially the ones where both partners are married to somebody else. But the relationships she really gushes over are those she expects will *end* in marriage. All the girls—including Judy—hope to be bridesmaids.

I wish her luck. My own love life isn't going all that well. I did meet a woman at the office Christmas party who I'd really have liked to get to know better. We talked for quite a while, and she seemed interested. I asked her if she'd care to have dinner with me some time, she said yes, and we arranged to meet at a nice restaurant the following Friday. I was on time. She wasn't. In fact, she never showed up at all.

She apologized on Monday, saying an emergency had come up. She'd tried to call, she said, but got no answer. Well, I have a cell phone I always carry and never turn off, and there wasn't a buzz out of it that Friday.

I told her I understood, and maybe we could try again another time. She agreed—but she didn't propose a date, and I never followed up. So I sleep alone while others sleep in pairs...

The day things started coming to a head began badly. I overslept, which meant I had to skip my usual restaurant breakfast and settle for toast and coffee at home. In my haste, I burnt the toast, and the coffee was tepid.

This was the day our annual activities-and-results report was due to be submitted to the Powers That Be on the tenth floor. But Mark Hansen, who was responsible for preparing the report, hadn't finished it. From my desk, I could see him and Mayberry in Mayberry's glass-walled office. Mayberry looked so furious I actually felt sorry for Mark—until Mayberry turned and glared at *me.* He pushed himself out of his chair, slamming it back against the wall, and stormed through the door, heading straight for me.

"What the hell is the *matter* with you, Morris? Have you no sense of priorities? Hansen tells me *he* couldn't finish on time because *you* were late getting your data to him. Well, that better never happen again, man, or you're out of here on your ear!"

I looked over at Mark, who was still sitting where Mayberry had left him. He lowered his head and looked away.

It was true my data got to Mark late, but only because Mark kept putting me off when I said we needed to go over it together, in case he had any questions. Time after time, he'd had "something else to do" that took precedence.

So here was Mayberry, reaming *me* out because *Mark* couldn't get it together to talk with me.

That night, when I told Jerry about it, he said, "Why didn't you tell your boss what actually happened?"

"No point," I said. "I guarantee Mayberry'd take Mark's

word over mine."

Jerry shook his head. "I guess you know what's best," he said. "But don't let it get you down. Tomorrow's bound to be better."

Actually, the next day turned out to be worse.

Normally, Mayberry was the last one out of the office, and just before he'd leave, he'd set the alarm. But the day of the reaming, he was so ticked off about missing the activities-and-results-report deadline that he left early—and, as was usual on such rare occasions, he said, "Last one out, remember to set the alarm."

And, as was usual, nobody bothered.

There's really no reason to set the alarm. The cleaning crew comes in shortly after we leave, and their supervisor turns *off* the alarm, then resets it when they're done. Even if the alarm's off when they come, he still sets it when they go.

For whatever reason, though, he didn't set it that particular night. And the next morning, all our computers and all the prototype Pleasure Machine headsets were gone.

Naturally, Mayberry blamed me. "Except for me, you're always the last one to leave, Morris. And because you couldn't be bothered to set the alarm, look what happened!"

I admit I frequently *was* the last to leave work before him, but not always. In fact, on the night in question, I hadn't been. But of course nobody acknowledged remaining on the premises after I'd left, since that would only bring Mayberry's wrath down on *them*.

Mayberry spent a lot of time on the tenth floor that day. The rest of us pretty much just sat around waiting for replacement computers to be brought from other offices. Once they arrived, more time was lost clearing them and loading them with our files from backup. Any files that weren't backed up had to be completely reconstructed.

This was a major blow, and if Mayberry convinced the tenth floor that I was to blame, it was dead certain I'd be fired.

The police were called, of course, and Mayberry brought the

two detectives assigned to the case down from the tenth floor to investigate.

I was the first one interviewed. We sat in Mayberry's office, and the lead detective—a guy named Haggerty—told Mayberry politely that he wasn't wanted. So Mayberry went grudgingly back up to the tenth floor.

For the first few minutes, the two detectives studied me in silence, as if waiting for me to start the ball rolling. I was sure Mayberry had given them his version of what had happened and not sure how much of it they believed, so I decided to leave it up to them to begin the interview.

Finally Haggerty said, "Mayberry says you're pretty much a loner. That true?"

I answered cautiously. "I'm not sure 'loner' is quite the right word, but I don't have much to do with the rest of the staff outside of work."

"Since you were the last to leave last night," the other detective said, "why didn't you set the alarm?"

"I *wasn't* the last to leave," I said. "There were three or four others still here when I took off. And anyway, there's no need for *anyone* to set the alarm. The cleaning crew does it when they're through for the night."

The detectives looked at each other. Haggerty frowned. This was obviously the first he'd heard about a cleaning crew. "You sure about that?"

"I am," I said.

Of course, they wanted to know the names of the others who had still been in the office when I left, and I had no reason not to tell them. There was too much at stake here for me to hold back anything that could help me.

"They'll back you on that?" Haggerty said.

They hadn't said anything in front of Mayberry, but I didn't think they'd lie to the police. "They *ought* to," I said. "It's the truth."

"Mayberry and some of the big brass think the competition

has a spy here, and the computers and headsets were taken for the data that's in them." He was watching me closely as he said this, looking to see how I reacted. I had no doubt Mayberry had named me as his chief suspect.

I shrugged. "Possible, I suppose. But if I was a spy, I wouldn't steal *everything*. I'd need a crew to cart it all away. It'd be easier and safer just to steal one of the Pleasure Machines. That's all the competition would need—and the way they're scattered around and not assigned to anybody in particular, one missing unit probably wouldn't even be noticed until someone called for a count."

Haggerty looked thoughtful. "That's all for now, Mr. Morris," he sighed. "We'll be in touch if we need anything else from you."

Dismissed, I went back to my desk and waited while each of the others was called in. First up was a fellow actuary named Ernst. He didn't spend much time with the detectives, and he came to my desk as soon as he emerged from Mayberry's office. He was sweating.

"I feel a lot better now," he said. "I'm sorry about not speaking up before, but—"

I held up a hand. "I understand," I said. "Speaking up now is what counts."

It turned out every one of them confirmed when I'd left the office, and they also backed me up about the cleaning crew setting the alarm, so I was off the hook on both counts.

With the police, at least. Not necessarily with Mayberry.

But I couldn't stop thinking about the robbery, couldn't understand *why* the cleaning crew hadn't set the alarm. Of course, there was nothing to show that they *hadn't* set it and someone else hadn't turned it off later. But if it wasn't the cleaning crew themselves that took the computers and headsets, who was it?

The theft had to have been planned. Our office is on the ninth floor of a ten-story building, and—once the cleaning crews leave—the building is deserted except for a couple of guards at the main entrance. So there was no way this could have been a case of someone just happening to be there when nobody else was around and taking advantage of the situation. But before anyone from outside could get in, they'd have to overpower the guards at the door, and that hadn't happened. So it *had* to be someone already in the building...which took me right back to the cleaning crew.

Maybe not the *whole* crew, but two or three of them could have hung back when the others left, loaded the computers and headsets onto one of the large carts they use to move their equipment around, and taken off with the goods. Of course, *proving* it would be difficult...which might be exactly why they'd figured they could get away with it.

I had no intention of playing Hardy Boys and confronting the possible culprits myself. Instead, I told Mayberry what I was thinking and suggested he pass the information along to the police.

"Not a chance," he said. "They get enough crank calls as it is. They don't need any helpful hints from me or you or anybody else." He shook his head. "Just do what you're paid to do, Morris, and leave playing Sherlock Holmes to the professionals. Although"—he gazed at me quizzically—"I do wonder why you're so eager to pin this on somebody else. Now get out of here and let me get back to what *I'm* paid to do."

I was fuming when I left his office, but I wasn't about to give up.

On Saturday, I drove down to police headquarters and asked for Detective Haggerty. He met me in what he called an "interview room," but I suspect that "interrogation room" would be a more appropriate label.

Haggerty listened quietly to what I had to say, considered it for a minute, then said, "Good thinking, Mr. Morris. But you're a little late."

"Late?"

Haggerty nodded. "When you've been a cop as long as I have, you get a feel for this sort of thing. Thefts like yours, where there's no obvious break-in, usually turn out to be inside jobs. So the cleaning crew was our prime suspect from the start. When we asked Cominsky, the supervisor, why he hadn't set the alarm that night, he said he was *off* that night. He'd asked one of the crew to set it, but the guy probably forgot. Trouble is, when we went looking for the guy to confirm Cominsky's story, he was nowhere to be found."

"Wouldn't *that* tend to confirm Cominsky's story?"

"As in the guy took it on the lam?"

"Something like that," I said.

"You might well think so," Haggerty said. "But that just didn't feel right to me. It was too convenient. It raised questions."

"So what did you do?"

"What we always do in this kind of case. We sent a notice to all the local pawnbrokers, asking them to call in if somebody showed up with a computer to pawn. Professional thieves have fences, but amateurs like Cominsky go to the pawnshops, and that's where we catch them."

"And you caught Cominsky?"

"Red-handed," Haggerty said, "trying to pawn five computers that matched the description of the ones taken from your office."

"Does Mayberry know this?"

"Sure," Haggerty said. "I'm surprised he hasn't already told you."

Damn Mayberry! Okay, maybe he hadn't known yet when he was shooting me down. But he'd found out quickly enough afterwards, and he hadn't had the decency to let me know I'd been right.

That did it. I was going to do something I'd never done before.

I was going to strike back.

If this was a mystery story, this would be the moment when I began thinking how I would kill Mayberry. But in real life, unless you're a psychopath or a professional hit man—and I'm neither—

"Thou shall not murder" is a tough commandment to deliberately set out to break. Everything you've been taught from childhood on holds you back. Fortunately, there are easier ways to take revenge on those who've wronged you.

Mark Hansen had finally finished the overdue activities-and-results report, and Mayberry had sent it upstairs. I had Judy pull the office copy from the files, and there was no mention of my data or any indication that any of it had been used. I would have been appalled, if that omission hadn't fit in so well with what I was planning. Even worse—or better, from my point of view—the conclusions reached were far rosier than my data indicated was really the case.

I was pretty sure Mark hadn't written it that way at Mayberry's request. Mayberry would never have let him miss the due date, nor would he have reacted the way he did when it was late if he'd been in on it from the start. No, the statistics I'd supplied were pretty daunting, and I suspect Mark was simply too lazy or too rushed to take the time to figure them out—so he just ignored them. Unlike Mark, Mayberry didn't have access to my data, but he should have caught that my work wasn't even listed as a source and refused to send the report upstairs until he knew why.

Anybody with any knowledge of the company's business who compared Mark's report with my data would immediately recognize that *something* was wrong. All I had to do was put both documents in an envelope, add a note explaining what to look for, address it to the CEO—and, when everybody else was out of the office on their coffee break, quietly slip it into the inter-office mail basket.

The results were more than gratifying: both Mayberry and Mark Hansen were fired.

No explanation came down from the tenth floor, but Judy—my harvester of the office grapevine—reported back that everybody *knew* the firings must have had something to do with the activities report.

Judy's information came from the clericals and the younger

members of the singles group. I'm convinced, though, that the other actuaries and maybe even some of the non-actuary specialists suspected that I was somehow involved. Word got around the office, and I've become a sort of hero for having engineered Mayberry's dismissal. Turns out Hansen wasn't all that popular, either, and no one seems to mind his having also gotten the axe.

They're all a lot friendlier to me now. We greet each other, they stop by my desk to exchange pleasantries, Kellogg even asked me to come to Sunday dinner at his house. I went, had a nice time, Kellogg said we'll have to do it again, and I believe he meant it—if only because his wife kept looking at me appraisingly, probably deciding which of her unmarried girlfriends I should meet first.

I'm beginning to think somebody up there doesn't dislike me so much, after all.

Bookends

Released April 1968

"*Bookends* Theme"
"Save the Life of My Child"
"America"
"Overs"
"Voices of Old People"
"Old Friends"
"*Bookends* Theme"
"Fakin' It"
"Punky's Dilemma"
"Mrs. Robinson"
"A Hazy Shade of Winter"
"At the Zoo"

All songs by Paul Simon,
except "Voices of Old People" is by Art Garfunkel.

A HAZY SHADE OF WINTER

Frank Zafiro

"The days are getting shorter," Mr. Amato the grocer said, right before Floyd decked him.

The blow took the old man by surprise. They almost always did, Floyd had noticed, even though he didn't understand why they didn't see it coming.

This was what Floyd did: he collected money from those who had it and smacked those who didn't. He'd been doing it for forty-five years, so it wasn't like these facts were a mystery. Yet the people he smacked still stared back at him with surprise and hurt, almost every time.

Truth was, Floyd's smacks weren't skull splitters. He thought of them more as love taps, since he felt like a reluctant parent forced to discipline a wayward child for the kid's own good. He didn't *want* to hit Amato. The grocer had simply left him no choice. So he gave him the love tap.

Amato buckled and sank to the floor. Floyd stared down impassively as the old man moaned and wobbled on his hands and knees.

Might have hit him too hard, he decided. Maybe he didn't know his own strength. Or else Amato just couldn't take as hard a shot as he used to. This wasn't the first time the grocer "didn't have it all today."

Floyd reached down and grasped him by the upper arm.

"Here you go, old timer. Upsy daisy."

Amato groaned and struggled to his feet. "I'm sorry," he murmured.

"I know."

The grocer's eyes were still a little dazed, and Floyd waited for clarity to seep back into them. His next words came by rote. "When I come back tomorrow, you'll have it?"

Amato nodded. Not frantic, but definitely eager.

That was good enough.

Floyd patted the old man's shoulder. Then he turned and left the small corner store.

Outside, the winter air lashed at him. He drew his coat closed and strode down the street. He walked as he always did—steady and with purpose. People coming the other direction tended to peel off to the side to make way for him. He was used to that, barely even noticed. His mind was already on his next stop.

There were fewer *of* them, these days. Family stores like Amato's were becoming the exception. More and more of the businesses moving into the neighborhood were corporate, and getting a manager at one of those uptight joints to tap into the register to pay their weekly tax to Mr. Giordano wasn't as simple as it used to be.

Not that the managers weren't willing, especially after Floyd had made his point. Intimidation wasn't hard, never had been. But corporate bureaucracy was another matter. If anything ever broke up Mr. Giordano's hold on the neighborhood, Floyd suspected it would be some kind of policy manual that finally did the trick.

Still, life finds a way. One of the chain stores had figured out they could hire him on as an assistant maintenance man. Strictly a no-show gig. But Mr. G got the forty hours of pay from the position, and Floyd got health insurance, so it worked out for the both of them.

Today, though, was for the old standbys. The neighborhood

institutions. Maybe that was what had him feeling nostalgic.

Pagliano's was a little bigger than Amato's but still a family affair. Sal, the owner, spotted Floyd as soon as he came through the door and flashed him a guarded smile.

"Floyd! Good to see you, my friend."

Floyd grunted. When he reached the counter, he stopped and waited.

"Your family doing well?" Sal asked.

It was that way with some. Social niceties camouflaged the business at hand. Floyd suspected there was some misplaced hope that this welcoming approach might bank goodwill in the event of a light envelope. It never did, and that was also usually met with surprise.

Floyd understood the pantomime but didn't like it. "Fine," he said, just to get it over with.

"And Mr. Giordano? In good health, I hope."

"Strong as a bull."

"Good, good. You want a sandwich?"

"I ate."

"Of course, of course. How about for later? Let me make you something."

Floyd didn't argue. He waited while Sal gathered together condiments, lunch meat, and cheese. "Fresh from D'Angelico's bakery," he said, patting the top of the roll.

Floyd knew the place. D'Angelico's was on his Thursday route.

Sal surreptitiously slid his envelope into the paper bag with the sandwich before offering it to Floyd. He never understood why some people felt the need to be crafty, but he'd long ago stopped worrying about the things people did to be comfortable with the way the world was.

The bag was light, but he knew the envelope wouldn't be. Sal's father, Alberto, had never once missed a week in thirty years, even when he was in the hospital after his first heart attack. For the last ten, Sal had proven to be his father's son, through and through.

Floyd left the store and detoured toward a nearby park. Despite the cold, the streets were mostly bare of snow. He passed a man ringing a bell for the Salvation Army, a cup of coffee in his other hand. He wondered briefly what path your life had to take to end up like that. Abandon all hope, or whatever.

As he passed the donation pot, Floyd removed the envelope from the grocery bag and slid it inside his coat with the others.

The park was a postage stamp in the middle of the block, a few bare trees lording it over the play equipment. He found a bench and sat. A single mother hovered over her toddler, who was trying to climb onto a merry-go-round that was strewn with brown leaves. She cast a suspicious glance at Floyd. He pretended to ignore her, staring straight ahead but watching them both in his peripheral vision.

The boy reminded him of Ray, his own son. No reason, really. Ray had dark hair, and this kid was a towhead. Throw in that his little boy was in his thirties now and probably didn't much care for merry-go-rounds these days. Never liked boxing, either.

He'd tried to bond with Ray over the sport. After all, *his* father had named him after the great Floyd Patterson—and he'd continued the tradition, naming his own son after Sugar Ray Leonard. But Ray didn't like boxing. Way it had turned out, he didn't like the sport, this city, or anything to do with his father.

What he *did* care about, Floyd had no idea. They hadn't spoken in, what? Ten years, at least.

He tried to look away from the mother and her son, but he couldn't. The woman seemed to sense his scrutiny. Probably misconstrued his interest, too. Either way, she gathered up her boy, and the two of them hustled out of the park and onto the sidewalk without a backward glance.

Floyd watched them go. The woman's purposeful stride made him think of Connie, Ray's mother. Funny that he thought of her that way. Not as *his wife* but *his son's mother*, despite their twenty-six years of marriage. None of them bad, really, except for the last one. Their time together had been mostly colorless, a convenient habit neither of them'd had the energy to break, especially not once Ray came along. Only that final year, watching her wither away with the cancer, felt real to him. Maybe he hadn't loved her—but he'd *cared*, hadn't he? At the end, surely.

"What's in the bag, old timer?"

He knew from the sneering voice what he'd see before he even turned his head. Black, white, brown, didn't matter. The cocky expression, the contempt, was the same no matter what.

And he was right. Two of them, both white. The taller one had a feral look to him, like someone whose recreational heroin use had fully transitioned to addiction. He wore black jeans and a blue flannel shirt over a white T with some band's name emblazoned on it. Floyd didn't recognize the name. He'd stopped recognizing new bands twenty years ago.

The other one was shorter, stockier, in a puffy blue jacket. The scar that slashed across his eyebrow spoke to some possibilities, but the way he stood made Floyd dismiss the thought. Punks, same as they ever were. The seasons changed, the scenery and the players changed, too, but the roles were always the same.

"I said, what's in the fucking bag?"

Floyd stared up at the tall one, unblinking. "Trouble you don't want," he said evenly.

They both burst out laughing. "Listen to this Clint Eastwood motherfucker here," the tall one guffawed. The stocky one hooked his thumbs in his belt and looked at Floyd with disdain.

A few years ago, he'd have said nothing, just waited for them to make their predictable move and then given them the beatdown that was just as predictable. Watched them scurry off, hurling insults once they were far enough away to feel safe again.

Instead, he spoke. Maybe it was seeing the kid at the park, thinking of Ray. He'd long ago stopped hoping he'd hear from his son. But hope is a stubborn weed, steadfastly refusing to die. Every so often, it shot up through the cracks in the sidewalk to confront him.

"Just walk away," he said, trying to inject some compassion into his voice, as he had with Amato earlier, helping the old man to his feet. Even to his own ears, though, the words sounded like a challenge. Long years of habit, he supposed. Hard to change gears. Even harder to start over, which is why he supposed he never had.

"We will," said the tall one. "But we'll take the bag with us."

Floyd wanted to give them the sandwich. They looked like they could use it, especially the tall one. But he knew he couldn't. Charity was one thing, but you couldn't let them *take* from you. That would be weak—and as soon as he showed weakness, his world would fall apart.

He set the bag beside him on the bench and stood.

The tall one waggled his hands. "Woooo. Scary." Then he snapped his fingers. "The sack, old man."

Floyd didn't respond. The time for talk was finished.

The pair puffed up almost in unison, chests out, trying to look intimidating. They glared at him for a full fifteen seconds.

He waited.

"Fuck this," the tall one said. He took a step forward.

Floyd struck.

A small shuffle with his lead foot, and he lashed out with his jab. The punch caught the tall one right in the beak. His eyes crossed. He staggered two steps back, hands flying to his face. A sound somewhere between a gasp and a groan escaped his lips.

Floyd pivoted toward the second man. The stocky kid was uncannily quick for his size. He pounced forward, drilling Floyd in the side with a sledgehammer blow. Floyd grunted and hunched his body in that direction. A moment later, a left hook came singing through the air.

He saw it, clear as day. His brain told his right hand to raise up to deflect. Told his chin to tuck into his chest, just in case the fist got past his block. But he felt suddenly hazy, like he was frozen in time, and his body refused to cooperate.

The punch crashed into his chin, rocking him. His vision went black, flashes of white dancing before his eyes. He staggered to his left. His right hand finally obeyed, rising to defend against the second punch that followed the first.

He shook his head, and his vision cleared. The stocky kid was sneering at him behind the straight right barreling toward his face.

This time, Floyd reacted. He twisted and moved his arm, and the punch landed on his forearm and slid off. Without thinking, he launched his own punch. He was in a southpaw stance, so it was his left that plowed forward. He felt as if he was moving through water, as if the blow would never land. But his fist connected, catching his stocky opponent at the corner of the jaw. Right on the button, as his father used to say.

The punk crumpled to the ground.

Floyd looked for the tall one, expecting an attack, but the coward was scampering away, Floyd's sack clutched in his arms, not daring to look back.

He could have gone after him. Or taken out his .32 and sent shots chasing the runner down the street. There was a time he wouldn't have even thought about it, just acted. But that was in the springtime of his life.

No longer.

He turned his attention back to the stocky one, who'd risen to his hands and knees. Floyd gave him a sharp kick to the ribs, sending him rolling away, then shuffled forward and kicked again. His foot landed awkwardly, and he felt a twinge in his ankle. But the guy let out a satisfying grunt and curled into a ball beside a patch of snow on the ground.

"No more," he murmured, covering his head with his hands.

Floyd kicked him again, just to make a point. Then he turned and left the park, limping slightly. Far ahead, he saw a flash of blue flannel.

He watched until the sandwich thief hooked to the left and out of sight.

He resumed his collections, walking slower to disguise the limp. The pain in his ankle never went past a threatening twinge, so he knew he hadn't hurt it badly. Still, it wouldn't do for the neighborhood to see any sign of weakness.

When he hit the strip where the whores gathered, Floyd could feel eyes on him. The pimps watched him warily. The women offered practiced smiles.

Sibelle, who he'd dated a few times, sidled up to him.

"Hey, Floyd, honey. You okay?"

"I'm fine."

"You're limping a little."

He slowed his pace to disguise it better. "I'm fine," he repeated.

"You feel like falling in love tonight?"

"Maybe later," he told her. "I'm working."

"So am I. I might not be, later."

"I guess I won't be falling in love, then."

She touched his shoulder tentatively. "Maybe I'll wait, huh?"

He slowed further at her touch, turned to look into her deep brown eyes. He knew the look she gave him was all artifice, a pleasant fiction that was there for rent. Still, it was a nice place to retreat to on occasion. Sibelle's pretense helped him with his own pretending, his own rebuilding of hopes that inevitably wore down, time and again.

"We'll see," he said, starting to believe that tonight the answer would likely be yes.

Yes, help me forget.

Yes, help me remember.

"I'll count on it," Sibelle said, her voice husky. She gave his shoulder a light squeeze and slid away.

Floyd walked on. Slowly. He had two more collections to make.

The first was a diner. He thought about ordering a coffee but decided to wait for something stiffer. The owner was a sour man who never met his eyes when he handed over the envelope, but he also never kept Floyd waiting.

Tucking the envelope into his coat pocket, Floyd heard singing through the service opening to the grill.

"What's up with that?" he asked the owner. "This a karaoke bar now?"

The sour man shrugged. "He's in love. What can you do?"

Floyd frowned and left, but the cook's baritone voice stuck in his mind like an ear worm. It wasn't the song itself, but the emotion behind it. He wanted to say that the voice had been full of hope, but that wasn't it, exactly. No, it had been full of *certainty.*

He'd only felt that way once in his life. Anne Marie Kostinaka. For over a year, he'd pined for her. Even took her to a movie once. But before he could screw up the courage to ask her out a second time, she'd started dating Theo Dimitrakos. A year later, they were married.

I should have told her, Floyd thought. First date or not, he should have come clean. How different would things have been? He was barely into this life back then. With Anne Marie, he could have gone a different direction. Lived a different life. Instead of a dull marriage, a son who hated him, a job as a leg breaker, he could have...could have what?

Been a good man? A caring husband? An attentive father?

Floyd thought about that as he pulled open the door to Timothy's, his last stop for the day. What was the point of looking to reorder a life already lived? But he couldn't help himself. He was like the goddamn History channel, running back the film every day.

Gary Eakin was behind the stick. A beefy man with a weathered look to him. He'd bought the place from Tim when the bar's original owner retired. When he saw Floyd, he raised his chin in greeting.

Floyd eased himself onto a stool. Some days he just took the envelope and left. Others…

"Vodka and lime," he said.

Gary nodded and began to put together the drink.

Floyd didn't know why he'd ordered a gimlet. Vodka and lime had been Connie's drink. Floyd preferred bourbon. But the words had just spilled out of his mouth, no doubt born of nostalgia. It was pretty sad, he figured. To be nostalgic for something so pale, so bland.

He looked around the dimly lit bar. There were a few customers huddled over their drinks, silent and morose. The cold weather tended to have that effect, he supposed. Warm weather, too, come to that.

He took a deep breath. A pain in his side flared slightly, answered by a pulse in his ankle. For the first time, he felt the warmth on his right cheek where the stocky kid had landed one. He reached up to touch it and was surprised to find it a little swollen.

Comes with the territory, he told himself. And it was too late to change up now.

He let his mind wander over that thought. Maybe things *could* be different. He could talk Mr. Giordano into some kind of retirement package. Find out where Ray was living and surprise him. After all this time, the boy's hard line had to have softened.

Did he have grandchildren, he wondered?

Probably. For all the pain in the ass he was, Ray was a sensitive kid. He'd be a good dad. Better than *he'd* been, Floyd was sure.

Maybe it wasn't too late to make some changes.

Never too late.

Gary set the drink in front of him. Floyd lifted it and took a sip.

"Someone take a poke at you?" Gary asked, gesturing to Floyd's face.

"There was two of them."

"Figured it had to be at least two. You okay?"

"I'm fine."

"You sure?"

Floyd tried to imagine what Gary saw when he looked at him. A battered enforcer in his sixties with a limp and a bruised face. Nothing more than that.

"You know what I heard, earlier today?" Floyd asked.

"Tell me."

"The days are getting shorter."

He tapped his glass on the bar as he said the words.

Gary nodded as if he understood. He didn't, of course, and Floyd knew it. But all the same, he slid an envelope across the bar.

Floyd put it in his pocket with the others. Then he finished his drink and left.

Bridge Over Troubled Water

Released January 1970

"Bridge Over Troubled Water"
"El Cóndor Pasa (If I Could)"
"Cecilia"
"Keep the Customer Satisfied"
"So Long, Frank Lloyd Wright"
"The Boxer"
"Baby Driver"
"The Only Living Boy in New York"
"Why Don't You Write Me"
"Bye Bye Love"
"Song For the Asking"

"El Cóndor Pasa (If I Could)" is by Daniel Alomía Robles, with English lyrics by Paul Simon, arranged by Jorge Milchberg. "Bye Bye Love" is by Felice Bryant and Boudleaux Bryant. All other songs by Paul Simon.

BRIDGE OVER TROUBLED WATER

Anna Scotti

The pandemic had worn me down. We were back on campus, albeit with masks and social distancing and handwashing, but so short-staffed that we'd pulled in grad students, retirees, and even a few unemployed parents to deliver canned lessons. Because I am credentialed, I'd been reassigned from my regular third-grade classroom to special ed at the junior high.

Two of my seven students had full-time helpers, Selena Martin used a massive motorized wheelchair, and I had a part-time aide, so space was tight. The room was as cheerful as a run to the ninety-nine-cent store could make it, with lots of bright plastic baskets and silly posters. Anything to take our minds off COVID-19. My kids ranged in age and ability from Darcy Sims, a bright African American with neatly beaded braids whose Tourette tics seemed to be her only challenge, to Paolo Miller, a frail white boy who looked several years younger than the nearly thirteen his records indicated.

After two grueling years online with my third graders, I'd looked forward to the relative independence of students on the verge of adolescence. Instead, I found myself expected to serve as an island of peace and tranquility in a stormy sea of emotional, intellectual, and physical desperation. I knew two months into the school year that, while little kids take everything you have to give, the older ones break your heart a different way.

It was Paolo who troubled me most. Many children on the spectrum are able to participate fully in school life—with a little support, some don't even need special-ed classes. But fully autistic kids like Paolo seem as though they're in a different world, a world where a simple piece of paper pushed across the floor by an errant breeze can provoke terror or inspire delight.

Paolo's green eyes were milky and unfocused. Ragged black-rimmed fingernails and pants three inches too short spoke of a tough home life. But poverty was the norm in our district.

Some of the most severely autistic kids are nonverbal, meaning they never speak. But a few—like Paolo—can sing...and Paolo did, with gusto. We'd often hear his lovely contralto as he worked a jigsaw puzzle or dabbled with fingerpaints at the art station. In September, he hummed choruses from "Knockin' on Heaven's Door" and "Summer Breeze," but by November he seemed stuck on a single tune.

"Okay, Paolo Simon," my irascible aide Julian muttered one afternoon, as the boy sang its refrain—the part about tears in your eyes and drying them—yet again.

"Actually," I told him, "that was Garfunkel singing. Paul Simon wrote it, though."

Julian looked down at our charge and tousled his blond hair with affection. "So if he can sing, Aubrey, why can't he talk?"

I shrugged. "Nobody knows, really. But maybe music can be our way in. If we—I don't know—*sing* his times tables, maybe he'll sing them back."

Julian looked at me skeptically. "Teach him to wipe his own mouth after he eats, and *that'll* be progress."

Paolo's sweet voice interrupted our banter. "Bridge over troubled water," he trilled, his blue eyes vacant, his face turned toward me. "Bridge, over truh-uh-bulled waaaater..."

"Good job," I told him. "Chelsea will be here soon, buddy. Hang in there."

I was surprised when he clutched at my hand. Paolo mostly avoided touch. But now he held my finger and seemed to be trying to look into my face, though his gaze slid past mine and over my shoulder. "When tears are in your eyes," he sang, and then, heartbreakingly, tears welled up in his own eyes as he sang the line again.

Chelsea Miller was a tough-looking high-school freshman. With a shock of blue hair and a stud in her nose, she was off-putting at first glance. But she showed up every day to walk her brother Paolo home—always ten minutes late, because it took exactly ten minutes to walk down the hill from the high school to our campus. More often than not, she'd have a brownie or a handful of graham crackers wrapped in a napkin, carefully saved from her school lunch, and Paolo would placidly munch his treat as he followed his sister out the door.

When Chelsea came in that afternoon and saw Paolo clutching my hand, her green eyes widened in surprise. "I guess he likes you," she offered.

I smiled. "That's good. Because I like him back."

Julian and I were alone in the classroom. He straightened a stack of papers while I sorted counting blocks. "I've been thinking," I ventured. "I want to talk to Selena's advocate about trying her in mainstream classes again. Darcy, too."

Julian rolled his eyes. "The mainstream kids are not gonna leave Darcy alone," he said glumly. "You weren't here last year. They thought it was hilarious to get her ticcing, usually by repeating some filthy word. She's better off here. But Selena? *Maybe*. She couldn't handle it last time, but she's older now."

"I really think we could do more for Paolo," I went on. "I've been reading about some new educational therapies that—"

Julian's eyes were glazing over.

"Look, Paolo can manipulate words to *some* degree. We know that from his singing. Do we know for sure that he can't *read*?"

Julian shrugged. "Dunno how he would have learned."

"I'll check with his mom and dad."

"No dad in sight," Julian grimaced, "and good luck with mom. I don't think I've seen her a single time this year, now that Chelsea's old enough to take charge."

"I hope she's not ill." Our teachers, students, and staff were tested weekly for COVID, but of course the testing didn't extend to parents. Though the worst of the pandemic seemed to be over, some people were still getting sick.

Julian shrugged again. "If you call being a doper *ill*."

I suddenly felt very tired. "Meth?"

"No, nothin' like that. She's an alkie on oxy is my best guess. Or benzos, maybe. Not the hard stuff. You know: sleepy eyes, slurred voice, that dreamy look."

I tried not to shudder. Only in our district would an educator refer to oxycodone as "not the hard stuff." It had been ravaging families and ruining lives for the past twenty years.

"Anyway, Paolo's better off with Chelsea in charge." Julian was still talking, but I was lost in thought, imagining a mother who'd cared enough to teach her son the gentle hits of the early Seventies, who'd given her children beautiful names. I didn't have kids of my own, but I knew, if I ever did, there wasn't a drug or drink in the world that would seduce me away from them.

And then I wondered if all the drunken, addicted parents I'd known in my years of teaching had at one time thought the same.

The only number on file for the Miller family went right to voice mail. They lived less than a quarter mile from campus, which explained why the kids walked—the bus stop was probably farther from their home than the school itself.

When Chelsea rushed in the next afternoon, holding a paper napkin full of orange slices, I pulled her aside. "I'm trying to get hold of your mom," I explained. "Is there a phone other than the one listed here?" I showed her the number.

Chelsea narrowed her eyes and ran a hand through the stiff blue bristle of her hair. "I can give her a message."

"Thanks, but I need to speak with her. I'm thinking about trying some new methods with Paolo that might—"

"Do whatever you want," Chelsea interrupted me. Her tough demeanor fell away as her eyes begged me to understand. "She's—pretty busy, y'know?"

I felt for her, but I'd need a parent's signature as well as at least minimal cooperation at home if the new therapy were to have any chance of success.

I tried Mrs. Miller a few more times over the next couple of weeks, without luck. Emails went unanswered, and eventually I gave up, figuring I'd try again in the spring. For now, it was hard enough to roll out of bed each day, cold feet on a cold floor, wondering what joy I could bring to my classroom. It seemed as though every day brought some new disaster to the national or international stage. Chemical spills. Looming war. In December, a group of middle schoolers tore the sinks out of the wall in the girls' bathroom and smeared waste on the mirrors.

The holidays passed. I don't have any relatives locally, though I adopted a stray cat for the sheer comfort of holding her on my lap in the long evenings, and Julian's mother invited me to spend Christmas Day with his big extended family.

I worried about my students. Without school lunch, some of them would be going hungry, Christmas or not. On our last day before the break, I'd handed out wrapped snacks and candy canes, and on our first day back I set out cartons of chocolate milk I'd cadged from the cafeteria.

Paolo drank three of them. He was skinnier than ever, but he seemed glad to see me, humming a little bit of what I was pretty sure was "Hello It's Me" as he put together a three-dimensional puzzle astonishingly quickly, rocking all the while.

"How's your family, Paolo?" I asked him. "How are Chelsea and your mom?"

He turned his face toward me, and his eyes caught mine for a moment before they slid up toward the fluorescent ceiling lights. I almost thought he was going to speak, but at that moment an aide pushed open the door and Selena wheeled into the room, beaming, holding a shining trophy high in the air.

"I won the Community Center spelling bee," she shouted. "Miss Aubrey, I won!"

Tomas and Ricky crowded around her, reaching for the trophy, and Darcy began to tic.

"I won, I won, I won," Darcy chanted.

Selena was too excited to take offense. "No, *I* won, Darce! Want to hold my trophy? I think it's real silver!"

It wasn't, of course, but even Darcy's jaw dropped as Paolo's sweet voice rose over the hubbub.

"Sail on, silver girl," he sang. "Silver, silver, silver girl."

He wasn't looking at Selena—that would have been too much to ask—but he was staring over her shoulder with a big crooked grin. Selena couldn't see it, but she must have felt the warmth, because she wheeled over to Paolo and tried to put her arms around him.

He squirmed away from her, fumbling, still singing.

Not everyone had received presents during the break, so Julian and I steered away from that topic. I showed the kids pictures of my cat, and one of the aides passed out paper crowns that read *Happy 2022!* It was a lovely but exhausting day.

By four thirty, everyone had been picked up except Paolo. Julian offered to stay, but I sent him home. Chelsea had never let her brother down before, so I figured there must be a test or a game or something keeping her. But at five, Paolo was still scribbling on my whiteboard with a marker, and most of the building was silent. I could have checked the boy into aftercare, but some of those kids were rough, and there were never enough supervisors.

I had the Millers' address, so I helped Paolo into his coat and asked him if he'd like a ride home. I expected him to resist, but he was curiously compliant. I offered him another carton of chocolate milk, and he followed me to my car, sipping contentedly.

The parking lot was nearly deserted. I opened the door for Paolo and tried to buckle him in, but he pushed at my hands impatiently, head turned away from the uncomfortable proximity.

"Okay, buddy," I agreed. "Just buckle up good and tight. We'll get you home, and I'll finally have a chance to meet your mama."

Paolo began to rock. "When you're weary," he sang, "feeling small."

So we were back to Simon and Garfunkel.

It might have been my imagination, but it seemed as though Paolo hunched into himself as he sang. When he got to the part about tears in your eyes and drying them, his quavering voice nearly brought tears to my own eyes.

"Does your mama do that, Paolo? Is that what you mean? When you're tired and sad, does she dry your tears and make you feel better?"

He didn't answer, just rocked in time to the movement of the car.

The Millers lived in a run-down neighborhood, mostly cement-block shanties, but I saw signs of love and life in the early evening shadows. Pink plastic hula hoops scattered across a lawn. A metal jungle gym, rusted and bent but still good for climbing.

We crossed a little culvert, and Paolo pressed his face to the glass. "Bridge over troubled water," he sang mournfully, repeating those four words over and over, singing louder and rocking harder with each repetition.

I cared for Paolo, but it had been a long day and I was about at my limit. I wondered if Darcy's echolalia was beginning to affect him adversely. That would be one more thing to discuss with his mom.

But the little shanty that bore the Millers' address was dark. There was no welcoming light in the window, and the porch light didn't even have a bulb.

Paolo seemed happy enough to be home. He jumped out of the car and went in through the unlocked front door, seeming to forget my presence, though I followed close behind him. In the living room, he dropped onto the sofa as if to watch television. But the TV wasn't on.

The lights didn't come on, either, when I tried a few switches. Both tiny bedrooms were empty, though the beds were neatly made. I went into the kitchen, which smelled of sour milk and spoiled meat. I opened the fridge, and a miasma of rotten odors suffused the air. Still, a loaf of bread, a jar of peanut butter, and a bag of chips—all nonperishables—sat on the counter. The family was eating, at least.

A roach ran over the counter, and I reacted predictably, but my little squeal was nothing compared with what came next.

I heard her shrieking from a block away, calling her brother's name as she tore across the yard, up the front steps and into the house.

Chelsea, breathing hard, stared at Paolo, who sat calm as a statue on the sofa.

"Paolo, where were you? I was terrified—I got to school, and everyone was *gone*! I'm sorry, baby, I'm sorry, we went on a field trip and the bus broke down! The driver lent me his phone, but there was no service, and—"

She gulped and calmed herself. "Miss Aubrey, why are *you* here?"

I ignored the question. "How long has your electricity been off, Chelsea?" I demanded. "And where is your mother?"

I could barely see her eyes in the darkening room.

"She's coming back soon, Miss Aubrey, I promise! She just

went to—to visit her sister, and—"

She was a tough kid, but she was only fourteen years old, maybe fifteen, and she'd had enough. She sat down on the sofa beside her brother and began to cry.

"You can't stay here without electricity," I said, "and without adult supervision. I'm sorry, Chelsea, but I have to call Child Protective Services. I don't have a choice: I'm a mandated reporter."

"You can't, Miss Aubrey," she pleaded. "You *can't.* You know what they'll do. They'll put him in one of those places. He can't handle that, and you know it."

She wasn't wrong. The idea of Paolo in a group home made my stomach churn. Funds were tight, the safety net had a big hole in it, and a kid like Paolo would fall right through.

"Does your aunt have a phone?"

Her silence told me there was no phone—and surely no aunt, either.

Chelsea had been in charge of this mess for long enough. "Here's what we'll do," I said firmly. "You two must be hungry. We'll head into town, and I'll treat you to dinner at Denny's. Then we'll figure it out. I have a friend in Social Services. Maybe she can—"

Chelsea stood, shoulders slumped. She touched Paolo lightly on the head, and he got up, humming.

Chelsea got into the back of my car, letting Paolo have the passenger seat in front. When we pulled out of the drive, he began to rock again.

"It's okay," I said, as he began to sing—loudly, almost desperately.

As we approached the little bridge that spanned the culvert, he grew more frantic, slapping the dashboard with the flat of his hand.

"Just a few more blocks to town, Paolo, and—"

"Like a bridge," the boy sang frantically. "Like a bridge, a bridge, a bridge!"

Something in his voice pierced my exhaustion, and I pulled over.

"Chelsea," I said, trying to stay calm. "Paolo got agitated when we drove over the culvert before. And now he's doing it again." I met her eyes in the rearview mirror. "I think you know that his song choices are intentional. They *mean* something."

Chelsea didn't answer.

I turned off the ignition and got out, using my phone to light my way down the slope to the drainage tunnel beneath the bridge.

Behind me, Paolo's screeching made a mockery of the song's gentle lyrics.

I think I knew what I would find, even before I saw her.

It was only her size that shocked me, her tiny figure curled into a ball, hugging herself in death. I couldn't make out her features, but her blond hair gleamed dully in the light of my phone.

I looked up and saw Paolo in full-on meltdown mode, lying on the grass by the car, screaming, pummeling himself with his own fists. I wouldn't need to call anyone now. The neighbors would surely phone it in, thinking a boy was being murdered in the road.

I knew from experience that it would be best to leave him to exhaust himself. Instead, I turned to Chelsea, who had followed me down the hill and stood gazing at her mother's body.

"She liked to come down here and get high," the girl murmured. "She said the sound of the water in the tunnel was like a river near where she grew up. She'd sit down here and sing and smoke and get lit, and after a while we'd come down and bring her back to the house so she could watch me put Paolo to bed. She liked to kiss him good night—and sing to him a little, if she wasn't too wasted."

My phone was losing power. I shut it off and stood in the gathering dusk, listening to Chelsea breathe as her brother's cries lessened.

From far away, I heard sirens approaching.

"One night, we came down to get her and she was...asleep. But I couldn't wake her up. Her bottle of pills was empty."

I could feel Chelsea's eyes more than see them.

"She took them *all*, Miss Aubrey! And a bottle of Old Crow, too."

The sirens were coming closer. I put an arm around Chelsea's shoulders.

"You did a good job," I told her. "I'm proud of you."

"The WIC card kept coming, so I could buy food for Paolo and me." Chelsea's voice was small, like a very little girl's. There was no toughness in it now. "But I couldn't pay the electric, and they shut it off. Otherwise, we woulda been fine."

Darkness had come, and pain was all around.

I took Chelsea's hand and led her up the hill as the first patrol car rolled to a stop.

THE ONLY LIVING BOY IN NEW YORK

Tom Mead

At the front desk, she checked in as M. March. "M for Margaret," she said, "but you can call me Peggy."

The clerk didn't bat an eye. Didn't even wonder what she might be carrying in her canvas bag. When she got to the room—a damp cube with dingy views of Washington Square Park—she tossed the bag on the bed and undid the clasps. She had gotten used to treating the bag as if it belonged to her. After all those hours of driving through relentless heat, the road wavering and rippling before her tired eyes, she could no longer bring herself to think of its contents as a living thing.

He was sleeping. She thought he must be sleeping: he wasn't moving, and his little eyes were closed. A miracle, really, that the kid could sleep through all this.

At first, he had cried. Terrible gut-wrenching shrieks from the back seat, muffled by the bag, but the crying had eventually tapered off. Peggy was grateful for that.

Less than two days had passed since the bag was handed to her in a gas station parking lot outside Topeka, Kansas, but it might have been a lifetime. She had driven nearly two thousand miles since then, swapping out cars from time to time to avoid any danger of a looky-loo latching onto a license plate. She was zigzagging her way across the United States, taking no chances. And everywhere she went, she was Miss Peggy March with her canvas bag.

She thought about the weirdness of it: a living thing, a tiny human being, in a bag. It was an interesting Schrödinger type of conundrum, the sort of scenario she might have debated back when she was a philosophy major. But that was years ago. The intellectual she once wanted to be was long dead.

She looked at the kid's pasty face. He had inherited Shapstein's sullen, slack jaw. That was enough right there to keep Peggy's hatred bubbling. If he were any ordinary baby, wrenched from his mother's arms and carried across the continent in a canvas bag, she might have felt something. But the shape of that sleeping face was a perpetual reminder of Judge Nathan Shapstein, a wax effigy in the great man's image.

"Margaret March" was an alias cribbed from *Little Women*. In her daily life, Peggy was a librarian in Lincoln, Nebraska, and had a different name. She was young and pretty—like a homecoming queen—but retiring, even shy. Unassuming in her big spectacles, with her hair pinned back, careful never to let the mask slip. Though she had come pretty close on the day she first heard about the Shreveport Six.

Six men—though some were only eighteen—prosecuted in the aftermath of the mass protests, riots, and destruction of property that had been brewing since the "Days of Rage" debacle. The voice of a nation, brutally silenced. And these six men were the martyrs, like the Chicago Seven had been before them. When she saw their photographs on the cover of the *New York Times*, she excused herself from the library's front desk and retreated to the bathroom, where she sobbed for a full five minutes. Then she went back to work, as though nothing had happened.

Judge Shapstein was a ballbreaker, everyone knew that, and he'd been *waiting* for a chance to stick it to the no-good beatniks. Only three days into the trial, he'd already held the defense team in contempt more than once.

Meanwhile, peaceful protests outside the courthouse were stamped out with unprecedented violence. Broken bones, bloodied noses. Three dead. Every day brought a fresh atrocity, and the six defendants could only sit in their cells and pray. Two of them went on hunger strikes and were growing weaker with each passing hour.

Shapstein was the protesters' obvious target. But the era of hitting the obvious target was over. The nail-bomb incident in Greenwich Village the year before had necessitated a change of approach, and the Organization had been forced to adapt its methods to suit the changing times. The frontal assault was getting them nowhere—had if anything forced them back into the shadows.

As much as it pained Peggy, she had to concede that Shapstein himself was untouchable. He was living in the penthouse suite of the St. Louis Hilton, surrounded day and night by armed guards. Uniformed police patrolled the foyer. He was like a sacrificial goat, tethered in the wilderness to lure a tiger. But the tiger was no fool, so Shapstein himself would live to die another day.

The judge had a daughter, though. This was not common knowledge—Shapstein had done plenty to keep it a secret. Her name was Alma, and she was a college dropout in a dead-end marriage to a car salesman, a source of constant disappointment to the beacon of truth and justice that was Judge Shapstein. Three months ago, Alma had become a mother at the age of nineteen.

Shapstein had not said a word publicly about any of this. In fact, he rarely acknowledged Alma's existence, not even in private. Despite the rift between them, though, she was and always would be his little girl.

The Organization had found out about her by digging into the judge's financial outgoings. He was sending her an allowance. For the baby, no doubt. His only grandchild.

With this nugget of information in hand, all it took was a little more spadework to unearth the whole story. Alma Shapstein had dropped out of college and run away from home to marry a fifty-year-old car salesman named Mel Kassner. Mel was bad at his job, a drunk, and in hock, but he must have had *something* going for him, since—whatever else she might be—Alma Shapstein was no fool. Maybe she'd just married him to piss off the judge. Peggy could respect that: it was the sort of thing *she* might have done.

For what it was worth, the judge *was* deeply pissed off. But Alma was a mother now, and that changed things considerably. Certain parties could do a lot with that information. A baby could be a bargaining chip.

These days, the Organization used all kinds of ingenious methods to disseminate information. Peggy got hers right there in the library, where the Dewey Decimal System had taken on a second, secret meaning, a language known only to her—and to the operatives who sauntered in from the street and used it to spell out their orders by moving books from one section to another. It was the sort of cipher you might find in a kids' adventure story—but to Peggy, this *was* an adventure. Since they'd recruited her two years ago—when she dropped out of college and said goodbye to her old life—she had been one of the Organization's sleepers, living like a coiled viper in perpetual readiness.

When the call finally came, Peggy was ready and willing to answer. There were hundreds—thousands—like her, all across the country, but the Organization had chosen *her*. It was a profound honor. She was a quiet soul, and you know what they say about quiet souls.

The baby—who had a name Peggy hadn't troubled to learn—had been snatched from Alma's home the previous week, but the story had been kept out of the papers, which perhaps explained Judge Shapstein's ongoing conduct in court. He was a stubborn old bastard, didn't like anyone telling him what to do.

Well, that was fine. The Organization was willing to do this the hard way.

Peggy had spotted the phone booth on her way into the hotel. It felt dangerous to make the call from right outside the building, but that was a risk she would have to take. In the morning, she would be gone, and no one would remember her. It would be as if she had never existed.

She descended the stairs slowly, passed by the untenanted front desk, headed out into the evening air via the revolving glass door. She glanced each way before crossing the street. There were a few cars, a few pedestrians. Nobody looked her way, except one old guy on a bench—and he had eyes for everyone.

She entered the phone booth and dialed the number she had burned into her memory by repeating it endlessly as she drove. She had sung it aloud like a lullaby, appropriating popular melodies to keep the digits in her head. She had used it to soothe the crying baby.

She was dialing it when she peeked through the booth's glass door and saw that the bench was now vacant. The old man, who had seemed rooted to his seat, was gone. She turned back to the phone, and there he was, right outside the booth. Must have crept up, stealthy and swift. He was staring at her, his nose almost touching the glass. Black hatred blazed in his eyes.

She looked down at the .38 in his hand. Delicately, she replaced the receiver.

"Out," he said. His voice had a smoky rasp to it; no doubt he was accustomed to people doing as he said.

She stepped out. *Stupid, stupid.* He'd been waiting for her the whole time. She looked him up and down: old and slack-shouldered, but stolid and squarely built. He was bald, but she could picture him with a buzz cut, back in the day. A retired soldier? That was fine—she was a soldier, too.

“There’s a car waiting,” he told her.

“Where?” She glanced around at the parked cars lining the street, but no obvious contender presented itself.

“Close by. This doesn’t have to be difficult.”

She clenched her jaw.

He motioned with the gun barrel, and she went with him. They strolled along the sidewalk at a ponderous pace, and Peggy’s eyes darted left and right as she assessed the situation.

They were on a public thoroughfare, and by rights somebody should have noticed the old man with the .38. But this was New York, after all. People went about as if they were the only ones on the face of the planet.

This guy and Shapstein had something in common: they couldn’t resist the opportunity to deliver a lecture.

“Haven’t you seen it on the TV?” he demanded. “Haven’t you seen that poor girl outside the courthouse, begging for you to bring him back?”

“I don’t watch the news,” Peggy told him.

“You’re more a weather report kind of gal, huh? Take me to him.”

The old soldier gripped the handle of the .38, keeping it trained for a gut shot. He wouldn’t kill Peggy. Not yet: he needed her alive, at least until he retrieved the baby.

“You’re working for that pig, aren’t you.” It wasn’t a question, the way she said it, and the man didn’t answer. But of course that was the only explanation. Ironic that Shapstein, that embodiment of the Establishment, should step outside the parameters of the law when it came to his own family. Peggy almost said something to this effect but held her tongue. No point trying to reason with these people.

“Think you’re real smart,” the old soldier said. What was he? A private detective? A bounty hunter? “Well, we know things about you. Where you live. Where you come from.”

She glanced at him over her shoulder and twitched an eyebrow inquisitively. He smiled. He knew he had her on the hook.

Maybe she was wrong about him. Maybe the judge hadn't hired him, after all. Maybe his employer was someone who knew her—someone with misguided notions about "bringing her home."

The old soldier was on a roll now. The smile was not just on his lips but in his voice. "I know all about your ma and pa you left behind. All the money they spent on you, and you ran off without a word. I know your real name—"

He stopped talking. His eyes were wide, his face a mask of sudden anguish. She had managed to slip the blade in without him noticing. It was a thin one, which she kept in a little spring-loaded leather strap on her wrist. This was a war, after all.

She twisted the knife clockwise, hearing the slither and tear of the old man's innards. He wheezed, but that was the only sound he could muster.

"I don't have a name," she told him as he died.

"You're late," said a voice at the other end of the line.

"I was held up," she answered.

"Don't be late again. You have the package?"

"Yes."

The voice gave her a series of instructions, which she committed to memory. At nine a.m. tomorrow, she would meet her contact at JFK. She would bring the package with her in his canvas bag. She would hand the bag over to the contact, and then her role in the operation would be complete. The Organization would take it from there.

Before ending the call, the voice on the line said, "You were held up?"

"Right."

"Is that something I should be worried about?"

"No," Peggy breathed into the receiver. "It's not."

***

"Miss me, Baby?" she said, reentering the hotel room.

Baby didn't answer. Didn't even twitch.

"You know, your mama misses *you*. She wants you back. But tonight, Baby, it's just you and me."

She peered at the child. It was looking less and less like a real baby, more like some kind of plastic doll.

That night, she didn't sleep. She sat by the window, listening to the sounds of the city beyond. She knew they would find the old soldier eventually. She had managed to get him off the street by clamping an arm around his sloping shoulders and half-dragging him into an alley, as if he were just another drunk. Then she'd heaved him up and into a dumpster. He was still wheezing, and she didn't wait around to hear the last of the life seep out of him. She just hoped he would remain hidden until after nine the next morning.

She watched the sun come up and went into the tiny en suite bathroom to shower. Baby was still there—still silent, still relentlessly unmoving—when she returned, dressed for the street. She clasped the canvas bag shut and hoisted it off the bed.

When she checked out of the hotel, there was a different clerk on the desk, and of course he would not remember her. What was there to remember? She thanked him politely, as her mother had always taught her, and headed out. A maid would come and clean her room, erasing any trace of her.

The car she settled on was a bottle-green VW Beetle. An ordinary vehicle, to match the ordinary woman and her ordinary canvas bag. It was her eye for such details that made her an asset to the Organization. Most of them looked like what they were: longhairs in ill-fitting clothes, stinking of pot. Idealists, dreamers. But Peggy did not look like what she was. She took care of her appearance, though it was ultimately little more than a mask.

It was early, but the sun was already blazing. Today would be a hot one, like yesterday and the day before. A clinging heat, when it feels as though the air itself is searing your lungs. Not a good day for driving.

She kept the windows down as she coasted out onto Grand Central Parkway. It would take an hour to drive the twenty-odd miles to the airport.

The canvas bag lay motionless on the back seat. Peggy was used to it by now.

She was herself only nineteen, the same age as Alma Shapstein, but she had no experience with little ones. The little Shapstein (she could not bring herself to think of it as the little Kassner) was the first baby she'd ever had dealings with. TV had taught her that babies were eating and shrieking machines, but this one had done neither for two days now. Was that normal?

The VW drew to a halt at a stoplight and Peggy let herself wonder for a moment. Not about the baby—she didn't care about the baby—but about the man she would be meeting. She was Margaret March, and he was Tom Sawyer. Another literary reference. Why had he chosen JFK for their meet? Was the Organization planning to move the baby out of the country? She had never met Tom Sawyer, but she'd received a detailed description of him: height, weight, the clothes he would be wearing. There would be no mistake.

Their conversation had been scripted in advance. To passersby, it would sound like normal repartee. But like the Dewey Decimal business, it would all be a code.

When she got to JFK, she found a parking space and unloaded the canvas bag. The baby was stinky by now, but she didn't have time to think about diapers. The drive had taken longer than anticipated, and after yesterday's hiccup, she couldn't afford to be late again.

She headed into the building and took a seat on a steel bench. With the canvas bag at her feet, she surreptitiously scanned the faces of the crowd. The terminal was filled with people of all shapes, sizes, colors, and creeds. So many bodies, so many lives. But the life in her canvas bag was more valuable than all of those others put together.

A man in a three-piece pinstriped suit with a watch chain draped across the front of his vest emerged from the horde, like an actor stepping out from behind a velvet curtain. He was almost handsome, with fashionably long blond hair parted to one side and a square, clean-shaven chin. It took her a moment or two to weigh him up, but there could be no question about it: this was the guy.

No doubt she had been described to him, too. When he got a good look at her, he sidled over. He might have been a traveling salesman or an executive of some sort, but for the casual glances he cast at the canvas bag lying at her feet.

"Forgive me," he began. "I can't help but notice you're looking a little under the weather."

"Jet lag," she answered.

So far, so good.

"You've come a long way, then?"

"About a million miles, seems like."

"I know what you mean. Do you ever feel as if your body is in one place but your mind is somewhere else?"

"Half the time I'm gone and I don't even know where."

"May I buy you a drink?"

"No, but you can carry my bag for me."

"Your wish is my command. Which way are we heading?"

"I need to buy some cigarettes."

He bent forward and picked up the bag. "You trust me with your possessions?"

"Why not? You have an honest face."

By rights, that should have been the end of their conversation. He had the bag. It had all gone exactly as planned. A perfect handover.

"Where are you taking him?" she asked, unable to stop herself from voicing the question.

Tom Sawyer glanced at her, doing his best to hide his discomfort at going off-script. "Mexico," he said. That was probably a lie—why would he tell her the truth? She was nothing to him, and he was nothing to her. All that mattered was the boy in the bag.

There was a moment of unpleasant silence as they studied each other.

"What's going to happen to him?" she said.

"Why do you want to know?"

"Just tell me."

He sighed, impatiently fumbling with his free hand for his wallet and passport. "There are people who will care for him until we get what we want. Then he'll be returned to his mother."

Peggy nodded. "He doesn't cry," she said, out of the blue.

"What?"

"He doesn't cry. Won't eat, neither." Her accent was slipping through. She had worked hard in recent years to lose it, but here it was, back again like a bad smell.

Tom Sawyer's nostrils twitched. He frowned and glanced down at the bag. The baby inside it was very still. But Tom didn't have time to stand here. He had a plane to catch. He walked away from her without another word, swinging the bag slightly with each step, looking every inch the business traveler.

It wasn't until she was out in the parking lot, her task complete, that Peggy began to wonder. Fact is, Tom Sawyer could have been anyone. He was just an ordinary guy, not handsome enough to be handsome, not ugly enough to be ugly.

She looked back through the terminal's plate-glass window and was unable to spot him in the crowd. Her heart lurched.

He was *not* Tom Sawyer. She was convinced of it. The realization hit her like an eighteen-wheeler. In a sudden panic, she doubled back, tried to catch up with him. But he was gone. And Baby was gone, too.

After everything she had been through, had she been played for a fool? How could it have happened? Was there someone inside the Organization, a turncoat intercepting messages?

She found a bank of phone booths but couldn't bring herself

to make the call. How could she be sure that the person at the other end of the line was—

Her shoulders hitching with frantic breaths, she headed back out into the daylight and the heat. A cab shrieked past, horn blaring.

Around her, she saw a man with a cigarette, a woman in sunglasses, a man with a briefcase, a woman pushing a stroller. She heard the roar of jet engines overhead and looked up at a cat's cradle of vapor trails. She heard cheerful and tearful goodbyes all around her.

She was heading dazedly across the parking lot toward the waiting VW when she caught the sound of clattering footsteps behind her. She whirled but saw no one. Whoever it was, they knew what they were doing. She broke into a run and dived into the driver's seat. Her hands shook as she twisted the key in the ignition.

Were these Shapstein's men? Or FBI? She could believe either. As she pulled out onto the freeway, a Lincoln Continental materialized in her rearview mirror. Standard-issue gray. Not exactly official looking, but not *not* official looking, either. Two men in front. It kept a couple of cars between them at all times—the kind of tail a trained professional can pull off in his sleep. Peggy picked up speed, knowing the VW was no match for the Lincoln's horsepower. But why hadn't they picked her up in the departure lounge? Why had they watched her hand over the baby and let her go?

The answer came immediately. They wanted her to lead them somewhere. They wanted to understand the nature of the Organization. They had tricked her into delivering the baby to one of their men, and now they were waiting for her to lead them into the belly of the beast. They wanted to see the heart of darkness.

Well, she was ready to show them.

The engine's throb became a kind of hollow whine as she picked up speed. She weaved between two slow-moving station wagons, then checked the mirror. Sure enough, the Lincoln was still in sight.

Peggy—who was not, who never *had* been, named Peggy—smiled to herself. She eased her foot to the floor and felt the VW straining like a wild animal on a leash. The steering wheel quivered slightly, but she was in perfect control. Her heart slowed. She felt an almost zen-like serenity. It was as if the car was not speeding—but the world around her had slowed to a crawl.

The sun was in her eyes, and she lost sight of the Lincoln. That wouldn't do—she wanted them to see, to know what she was capable of.

Yes, she might be young and foolish. Everyone thought she was. At the library, they believed her to be nothing more than a bespectacled little mouse. Quiet, smiling, scarcely saying a word. But what they didn't know was that she possessed a will of iron.

They were on a straight stretch of road now. The traffic was heavy, but it was flowing. There would never be a better time than this.

When the Lincoln reared up behind her again, she turned on the radio. Some mawkish nonsense, a pair of saccharine voices. She cranked the volume, as loud as it would go. She needed to dull her senses.

It didn't matter who was driving the Lincoln. It didn't matter about the guy she'd killed or the baby she'd handed over to God-knows-who. All that mattered was this moment. She closed her eyes and let the music flow through her.

Then she spun the wheel.

PART II

THE SOLO ALBUMS

The Paul Simon Songbook

Released August 1965

"I Am a Rock"
"Leaves That Are Green"
"A Church Is Burning"
"April Come She Will"
"The Sound of Silence"
"A Most Peculiar Man"
"He Was My Brother"
"Kathy's Song"
"The Side of a Hill"
"A Simple Desultory Philippic (or How I Was Robert McNamara'd into Submission)"
"Flowers Never Bend with the Rainfall"
"Patterns"

All songs by Paul Simon,
except "He Was My Brother" and "The Side of a Hill"
are credited to "Paul Kane,"
which is a pseudonym Simon used for these two compositions.

PATTERNS

Edwin Hill

December 1987

I was on the run again when I felt the stranger watching me from across the ferry's crowded deck. I should have been on guard. But anyone who mattered would be searching for me in Burgundy, not here on the Rhine. No one knew that I'd crossed the border from France into West Germany earlier that morning, that I'd had a *croissant aux amandes* for breakfast but planned to eat schnitzel for dinner.

My last correspondence had been a postcard to Julian, mailed outside the Dijon train station after I'd fled Clotilde's manor house. What I'd written to him was a string of lies: I was enjoying Burgundy, Clotilde was a generous host, I wished he had been able to make the trip with me. I signed my name—Henry Darling—with a flourish and a series of XOs. In a PS for anyone to read, I added, *Thank you for arranging everything!*

I was a master at beginnings and a failure at endings. Running away when things got tough was a pattern I'd followed with Julian and Clotilde and others before them, a pattern I could scarcely control. I'd expected to follow it again last night, with Sandrine in Strasbourg, but she'd been luckier than most. She'd surprised me by filling my ceramic cup with cider moments before disappearing into the night. She hadn't even said *adieu.*

It was easier to disappear in those days. There were almost no cell phones. No Facebook or Grindr. No data trails. No internet cafés. It was a world where we handwrote addresses and phone numbers in little black books and promised to stay in touch, where we were permitted to smoked indoors, where we didn't know what it meant to "disconnect."

Still, I wondered what I'd done wrong. Had I made Sandrine uneasy, or had she simply known that she'd be better off if she never saw me again?

I wondered if she'd sensed the darkness where I'd dwelled for so long.

As the ferry chugged up the choppy Rhine, I lifted my brand-new Ray-Bans and turned for a full view of the stranger, who was still watching me. He was in his mid-thirties, ten years older than I was, and rakishly handsome. He had a thatch of thick hair, a hook of a nose, and the kind of body that was made to show off fine clothes. A patterned scarf was draped around his neck, its ends tossed over his shoulders. A gray tweed coat hugged his waist and hung to just above his knees. At the beach, in the summer, I suspected he wore a Speedo.

I caught his eye. He met my gaze, exuding danger like a hunter tailing his quarry. I slid the Ray-Bans down again to ward off the December sun and waited for him to make the first move. The sunglasses had cost me two hundred dollars. Buying them and going on this trip had nearly depleted my savings, but it felt good to be frivolous, to spend money for the sake of spending. That, to put it simply, was what this trip was about: indulgence.

November 1987

"Live hard, play hard," Julian had said one night, at the bar

around the corner from his Soho apartment, and I'd decided right then that I'd fly across the Channel to join him in Paris.

December 1987

The ferry turned a bend in the river, and a village appeared, spilling down a steep embankment lined with grape vines and topped by a ruined castle. It was the fifth castle we'd seen today, and a voice on the loudspeaker told us about it as the ferry prepared to dock. Half the people on the boat laughed—the ones who spoke German. I laughed, too. I'd studied German for seven years and spent a semester getting drunk in Freiburg, and I wanted to appear as if I was in on the joke, though the only word I'd managed to isolate and understand was *Burg*, which meant castle—and I wondered if I'd have managed even *that* without the context clues.

Across the deck, the stranger didn't laugh at all.

But he continued to watch me.

The ferry docked, and the passengers began to disembark. I waited to see if I'd feel the stranger's hand brush against mine, if he'd come close enough for me to smell his cologne. I wondered if he'd speak German or go straight to English. Maybe he'd try French. Men still found each other surreptitiously back then, and perhaps this would be another of my masterful beginnings.

Below, in the town, crowds gathered around a giant Christmas tree, encircled small fires, sipped *glühwein*, and ate roasted chestnuts. St. Nicholas rang a bell, and children dashed amongst the stalls in a frenzy of excitement. The scent of gingerbread competed with the diesel fumes from the ferry.

The stranger didn't approach me, after all. He went down the gangway, his dark hair shining in the waning sunlight, one end of that patterned scarf tossed over a shoulder. I expected him to stop, to turn, to catch my eye and signal for me to follow, but he kept going till he disappeared behind a giant nativity scene, ending our encounter before it had even begun.

Maybe he was looking at the castles all along.

I paid a deutschmark to rent a glass and another to fill it with *glühwein*. I asked for the wine in German, but the woman behind the counter spoke to me in English: "Thank you, Mister."

"*Bitte*," I said.

I strolled past booths selling glass ornaments. I had a running list of people I would have bought presents for, had the circumstances been different: my parents, my boss, my sister and her kids. Julian, too. I finished the *glühwein*. A man in lederhosen danced by with a bottle of Riesling, pausing to fill my empty glass. I drank the wine in a single gulp, then someone grasped my hand and pulled me into a sort of conga line. My pack hit an old woman and nearly knocked her over. She said something I didn't understand, sounding angry, but maybe it was just the harshness of the German language, because she filled my glass from her own bottle of Riesling.

"*Prost!*" she said.

"*Prost*," I said.

I detached myself from the crowd. The early winter night had begun to set softly over the town. I dug out a guidebook and read it in the light from a streetlamp. It took a moment to orient myself. I followed the map up a steep street and into an alley where my hotel was supposed to be. I hoped my letter had arrived and a room would be waiting for me. The woman at the front desk called me *Herr Darling* and spoke slowly, in German. Was I was here for the *Christkindlmarkt*, she asked—or at least that's what I *think* she asked.

"*Ja*," I said.

She pointed at an illustration of St. Nicholas.

"*Ja*," I said.

I asked her where I might find a telephone, and she gave me directions, her voice becoming louder, her gestures grand.

"*Danke*," I said.

"*Bitte*," she said.

Up a narrow flight of stairs, I sat on the edge of the tiny single bed in my narrow little room and thought of the simple phrases I'd used downstairs. I realized how much I'd gotten wrong: I must have sounded like a child. The last rays of winter sun shone through the dirty window. The light reminded me of the stranger's scarf, of masterful beginnings and disastrous endings, of the patterns I couldn't seem to escape.

November 1987

I flew to Paris and trained from there to Dijon, where I stayed with Clotilde, an old family friend of Julian's, in a crumbling manor house. Clotilde was my mother's age. She was effortlessly fashionable, long and slender enough to snap in two. She'd appeared on French TV in the Seventies, had a supporting role in an art-house film that brought her to Cannes, and recorded a minor disco hit called "Ta Da! (Monte Carlo Magique)." Even though she hadn't worked in years, she didn't seem to want for much—like most of the people Julian knew.

At the train station, Clotilde eyed the heavy pack strapped to my back. It seemed a lot for what was supposed to be only a two-week stay.

"Where is Julian?" she asked me, craning her slender neck toward the departing train.

"Something came up," I said. "It's just me."

"Ah," she said, her meaning universal. Still, she kissed me on each cheek.

December 1987

Outside my hotel, a group of men in Santa hats sang "O Tannenbaum" so loudly that it was hard to hear myself talk, even inside the phone booth. Still, I added another deutschmark to keep the call going.

"I'm traveling," I said. "Seeing the world."

It was hard to admit to myself, but I really did wish Julian could have made the trip with me. I hadn't lied on my postcard, after all. I wanted to tell him everything, about the glorious night I'd spent in Strasbourg, about meeting Sandrine and squeezing into her Citroën and careening into the hills, about the *flammkuchen* and cider. I wanted to tell him about listening to a mix of French and German and English, and the table of old men who sat beside us and spoke Alsatian. I could have mentioned the stranger from the ferry—in case I turned up dead, later—but who knew who might be listening in on the call? I didn't want anyone to know where I was.

Perhaps I shouldn't have called.

November 1987

I remember the giddy excitement of showing up unannounced at Julian's Soho apartment on the night he was supposed to fly to Paris.

"Surprise," I said.

Since the moment I heard him mention that he was going to France, I'd secretly planned to join him.

He eyed the open doorway. Behind me, outside, a streetlight barely lit the early evening gloom.

"We're *not going to France," he said.*

December 1987

"I had a crepe yesterday," I said into the phone. "I bought it on the street."

Before I could mention that the crepe had been filled with Nutella, Julian's voice mail beeped to signal the end of the recording. I considered calling again, if only to hear his voice, if only to leave another message and, this time, acknowledge that I really did miss him. That would cost another deutschmark and my pockets were laden with coins, but I glanced though the phone booth's glass and saw, across the street, the stranger watching me.

Still rakish. Still dangerous.

Our eyes met, and he raised a bottle of Riesling in an invitation.

For the first time since I'd left Julian's apartment, I was truly glad to be on my own. If he were here, I'd have assumed the stranger was stalking *him*, not me. Julian was always the golden boy, the one others swarmed around, the one they wanted. All the light he reflected rendered me invisible.

I began with a simple "*Guten Abend.*"

The stranger responded in English, with a heavy French accent: "You are here alone?"

"With friends," I said.

"I see you on the boat." ("Ze boat.")

"I'm meeting them here. My friends."

Anyone could have seen that I was lying, that I was by myself, but we walked off together all the same. He opened his bottle with a Swiss Army knife and poured each of us a glass. He told me he was from Lyon, and I nodded.

"Do you know it?" he asked.

I didn't, but what I said was: "A beautiful city."

"I am a"—he searched for the word, then mimed a rolling pin—"a *boulanger.*"

"A baker? You should be fatter."

The words spilled out before I could catch them, and they sounded ugly and American, not what I wanted on this day.

But he turned and eyed me from head to foot, and without Julian there to distract him, I knew I could hold my own. In that moment, I was certain I could see the rest of the stranger that night, if I wanted to, in my dark room, on my narrow twin bed, and that anyone in the neighboring rooms would hear us through the thin walls.

Someone jostled me. The stranger put a hand to my arm to steady me and kept it there longer than he needed to. Our faces were close. He smelled of smoke and BO, but also of vanilla and cinnamon and chocolate. His arms were strong beneath his coat.

"I am Didier," he said.

He stepped in for a kiss, and I forgot for a moment that the French kiss everyone.

"Henry," I said.

"Henri," he said, and his replacing the *y* with an *i* made me feel like a different person.

By then, darkness had fallen on the village, but the Christmas market glowed with lights. Didier brushed his hand against mine and led me through the maze of booths and tents. We bought glass ornaments and candles and marzipan. I tried on a vintage hat and lederhosen. We ate pretzels and crouched to pet a schnauzer. It was like a montage from a holiday rom-com.

"Let's get blotto," I said.

"Blotto?"

"Drunk." Then I remembered a word from last night in Strasbourg. "*Bourré?*"

"*Oui, bourré,*" Didier said. "We get *bourré.*"

We bought more Riesling. We shared it with new friends. In a crowded restaurant, I ordered schnitzel with spaetzle, my German suddenly flawless. We smoked and moved closer, forgetting the crowd that surrounded us.

Didier loved Charlie Chaplin, the Smurfs, and Woody Allen. "Voody Ah-len," he said.

Under the table, my hand found his knee. I nearly told him that I'd once seen Woody on the street in New York, that I'd followed him for two blocks till he got into a station wagon and drove away, but Henri with an *i* was too sophisticated to stalk a celebrity the way I'd stalked Voody. Henri was a man who might well *know* Voody. Perhaps they'd met at the *Hannah and*

Her Sisters premiere, where Henri had sidled up to Mia Farrow and charmed her all night long.

I sat a bit straighter. Unlike Henry Darling, Henri had grown up wearing Ray-Bans and didn't worry about home or what waited for him there. He never looked back, certainly not to a street-level apartment in Soho, to the disappointment of being ignored. Or to a crumbling manor house in Burgundy, to a faded disco star whispering French into the phone, her voice quivering, her fear universal.

I felt worse about Clotilde than I had about the others, even Julian, because what I'd written about her on my postcard hadn't been a lie, either. She *had* been a generous host. In fact, she'd been nothing but kind. Still, I'd given in to the darkness where I'd dwelled for so long.

Her slender neck had snapped so easily.

All around the icy square, people danced—together, alone, in circles. Fairy lights cast shivering shadows through the branches on the many Christmas trees. The warm scent of simmering *glühwein* hung in the air. St. Nicholas tripped over a bench and lay face down on the cobblestones, laughing, while children leapt over his outstretched legs. A rat carrying a pretzel in its teeth scurried in and out of sight. The men in Santa hats sang "O Tannenbaum" and leaned into each other, too drunk to notice Didier sweep a lock of hair from my eyes.

"Do you know how handsome you are?" he asked.

We retreated into the shadows. Our bodies folded against each other's as I shut out the world, his hand on my waist, his breath on my neck. For a moment, I let go of the inevitable. I imagined seeing Didier off on the morning ferry, jotting his address in my little black book, promising to stay in touch.

I indulged myself—for just a moment—in the impossible dream that the patterns of my life would at last be controlled, and that Didier would survive the night.

Paul Simon

Released January 1972

"Mother and Child Reunion"
"Duncan"
"Everything Put Together Falls Apart"
"Run That Body Down"
"Armistice Day"
"Me and Julio Down by the Schoolyard"
"Peace Like a River"
"Papa Hobo"
"Hobo's Blues"
"Paranoia Blues"
"Congratulations"

All songs by Paul Simon,
except "Hobo's Blues" is cowritten by Stéphane Grappelli.

PARANOIA BLUES

Josh Pachter

"Whose side are you on?" I demanded.

"It's got nothing to do with *sides*," Edie said, rolling her eyes like I was an infant or an idiot—or both.

"It's got *everything* to do with sides," I countered stubbornly. "You're either with me, kiddo, or you're against me—and it sure as hell sounds like you're against me."

"Jonah," she said patiently, "honey, you *know* I'm with you. I'm *here*, aren't I? I mean, I *could've* stayed in New York. I could be in Chinatown right this second, at Lin's, sucking down a plate of *chow fun* like we used to, remember? It's just—"

I glanced at my wristwatch and saw that it was twenty to eight. "I can't talk about it now," I said. "I need to get over there."

Edie shook her head and breathed deeply, and—as I shrugged into my parka and wrapped a scarf around my neck—I could almost hear her counting to ten.

"If you're right," she said, and then she caught the *if* and backed up a step. "Let's say you're right," she tried again. "Then isn't going out the *last* thing you ought to be doing?"

"Fat Fish isn't negotiable," I said. "It's Wednesday. Robert likes seeing me there."

I kissed her cheek and went out into the cold.

* * *

It was Wednesday, November 3, 2004. Yesterday, George Dubya got even for the embarrassment of the Y2K election by slam-dunking that second-rate pair of Johns—senators Kerry and Edwards—into oblivion.

But the *date* isn't what was important. What was important was the day of the week, Wednesday, because Wednesday was Robert's day at Fat Fish, and I hurried down West 9th, shooting nervous glances up and down the streets and alleys of the Warehouse District, making sure no one was following me.

Paranoid, right? But don't forget what Joseph Heller wrote in *Catch-22*: "Just because you're paranoid doesn't mean they aren't after you."

They *were* after me, that was a given, so I kept swiveling my head left and right as I turned up Frankfort and scurried across Public Square, nodded respectfully at the Soldiers and Sailors Monument, and swung into the wind tunnel that is Ontario Street.

Maybe *I'd* better back up a step and explain a few things.

I'll start with Fat Fish. That's Fat Fish Blue, a busy bar and New Orleans-style restaurant on the corner of Ontario and Prospect in beautiful downtown Cleveland, Ohio, the heart of rock 'n' roll.

Robert is Robert "Junior" Lockwood. Born in Turkey Scratch, Arkansas—seriously, you can look it up!—in 1915, Robert was the common-law stepson of legendary bluesman Robert Johnson and the only person the King of the Delta Blues ever taught to play the guitar. In 2004, Robert was eighty-nine years old and living in the Land of Cleve, and every Wednesday night he showed up at Fat Fish Blue and sat on a folding chair on their little wooden stage and played and sang for a couple of hours. "Dust My Broom," "Selfish Ways," "Lockwood's Boogie," his stepdaddy's "Sweet Home Chicago"—those sessions were a master class in classic blues. Up until recently, Robert had been a solo act, but as the years passed and he got older and tireder, he'd added a drummer and then another guitarist and eventually a four-piece backup band, and by now they were doing most of the heavy lifting, with Robert playing a few licks and singing a song or two, then sitting there catching his breath as the band played on.

While I'm at it, I suppose I ought to tell you just a bit about me and Edie, too. For starters, my name's not Jonah, and Edie's isn't Edie. I was born Tico Triomfo, and Carrie Pescatrice and me have been what you call an item since we were kids on Mulberry Street in New York's Little Italy. Carrie got herself an education and made a decent living teaching third grade at PS 130, while I fell in with the goombas and wound up smuggling coke from Colombia into JFK, my heart going *boom boom boom* every time I rolled my wheelie bag past that customs man.

Things were going great for the both of us until I got busted with half a kilo of sneeze about eighteen months back. The DA offered to let me skate and put me in Witness Protection if I flipped on Berto Mambazzi, the *padrone*, and I was able to negotiate Carrie into the deal. The day the jury found Don Berto guilty on all seventeen counts, I was pacing outside the Manhattan Criminal Courthouse on Centre Street in nervous anticipation of their verdict. When one of the two burly bailiffs wrestling him down the stone steps to the van that would transport him back to Rikers Island to await sentencing spotted me and gave me a grin and a thumbs-up, I flipped the *padrone* a different finger. As they marched him past me, he looked back over his shoulder and shouted, "You're dead meat, Tico! You understand that, you *stronzo*? You're a dead man!"

So here we were in the WitPro section of Cleveland, living in a shithole third-floor walk-up in the Warehouse District and working shitty jobs that paid the rent and put food on the table, with not a lot left over at the end of the month. It wasn't the life either one of us had planned, but at least I wasn't in the joint and the two of us were together.

It didn't take me long to stumble across Fat Fish Blue, a ten-minute walk from the apartment, and as luck would have it,

I checked the place out on a Wednesday, Robert Lockwood's night. I'd never heard of the old guy before, but *man,* he could play. I started showing up every week, arriving early enough to snag a two-top right in front of the stage. I'd order a cup of coffee and nurse it through Robert's three sets, and after a couple of weeks, I guess he got used to seeing me there.

During his first break, he'd hang with his family, but for the second one he'd come and sit with me. My one weekly splurge was buying him a shot of Jack Daniel's Tennessee Honey, and he'd sip at it and tell me stories of the old days—when he played the clubs down South and in Chicago with Sonny Boy Williamson and Little Walter—until it was time for him to struggle to his feet and climb back onto the bandstand. It was *history*, man, and I lapped it up as eagerly as Robert lapped his sour mash.

Anyway, I'm rambling, sorry. I guess I'd better get to the point.

The point is, nobody back in the Big Apple had a fucking *clue* what had happened to me and Carrie—not until last Saturday, when I came home from my shift bussing tables at the Tower City Morton's to find her jabbering away on the landline.

Listen, I love my girl, but when she offered me the handset and told me to say hi to her sister Angie, I could've popped her right then and there. I grabbed the phone and practically screamed, "Don't tell *anybody* you talked with us, you hear me, Ang?" and slammed the receiver back down on the cradle.

"*Calmati*, baby," Edie tried to soothe me. "Angie's not gonna say a word. What *could* she say? I didn't tell her where we are."

"You think Don Berto's goons can't trace a phone call?"

"Tico, I—"

"Jonah! For Christ's sake, *Edie*, my name is *Jonah*. And your sister tells *a single soul* she talked to you and we are *dead*."

So we stayed in the apartment for four days, drinking water

from the tap and eating soup and beans and whatever out of cans, until Wednesday rolled around and I was about to bust with the claustrophobia and decided to head over to Fat Fish as usual.

Robert's band was breaking in a new bassist that night. He was a solid musician, but he wasn't in command of the repertoire yet, and that might have contributed to the sense I got that Robert was more tired than usual. Hell, though, the man was almost ninety years old! If *anyone* had a right to be tired, it was him.

He sat with me during his second break, same as always, and I bought him a shot of Jack and listened to him reminisce about the night in 1995 when then-First Lady Hillary Clinton presented him and a dozen other folks with the National Endowment for the Arts' National Heritage Fellowship. He still had the medal, he told me, wrapped in tissue paper and stashed in his underwear drawer, beneath his boxers.

Around eleven, right after an energetic take on "Every Day I Have the Blues" brought the third set to a close, I sidled up to the bandstand and shook Robert's hand and told him I'd see him next week.

I came out of Fat Fish into a chilly November night and paused to wind my scarf around my neck. The new bass player was leaning against the club's plate-glass front window, smoking a cigarette, and he nodded at me and said, "Looks like you and Junior are pretty tight."

"He's an amazing guy," I said. "I hope I've still got that much energy when *I'm* his age, if I make it that far. You did a fine job yourself in there. You taking over on bass?"

He shook his head. "Nah, Marcellus got another gig for tonight and asked me to fill in. It's just a one-time thing."

"Well, I enjoyed listening to you," I said. I peered up and down the street—paranoia strikes deep, you know?—and saw no threat in either direction.

"Hey, kid," he said, smiling right to my face, and I realized that not even the band's regulars knew a thing about me, not even my WitPro name. "Robert asked me to give you something. You mind if I walk with you a ways?"

I didn't mind at all. In fact, I was glad of the company—less chance Don Berto's enforcers would come after me if I wasn't alone.

So Mr. Bassman flicked his butt at the gutter and fell into step beside me. We talked about music in general and the blues in particular as we strolled through the night, and just before we got to the Inn of the Barristers on West 3rd he ducked into a darkened doorway to get out of the wind and light another smoke. I waited for him, and, when he got it going, he put his lighter back in his coat pocket.

"So what did Robert ask you to give me?" I said, the cold beginning to bite into my bones.

"Not Robert," he said, "Roberto."

His hand came out of his pocket, and I saw that he was holding some kind of a gun.

"This is for you, Tico," he said. "With Don Berto's compliments."

There Goes Rhymin' Simon

Released May 1973

"Kodachrome"
"Tenderness"
"Take Me to the Mardi Gras"
"Something So Right"
"One Man's Ceiling Is Another Man's Floor"
"American Tune"
"Was a Sunny Day"
"Learn How to Fall"
"St. Judy's Comet"
"Loves Me Like a Rock"

All songs by Paul Simon.

LOVES ME LIKE A ROCK

Cheryl A. Head

Katie Castle opened the drapes and looked out at Mrs. Garrick's pear tree. The fruit had fallen weeks ago, and the squirrels had collected the shriveled nubs for their winter's bounty.

She examined her graying reflection in the window. Winter was coming fast, bringing too many memories of those final days—a year ago—when Walter's chest had rattled with noxious fluids.

She made the bed, showered, checked the hamper for laundry, then mindlessly moved to the kitchen and turned on the radio. President Reagan was making one of his homey speeches. Walter couldn't abide the man: he was too anti-union.

She rummaged the freezer, put a roast in the sink, then—realizing the folly of her actions—slumped into a kitchen chair. She splayed her fingers on the Formica table and stared at her gold wedding band with its discreet diamond.

When the blare of video game music started upstairs, Katie checked her watch. Joey was running late for school. Her eldest, David, was married and living in Pittsburgh, and Valerie had recently gotten her own place across town. So now it was just Katie and Joey at home, and the last few months had been rocky between them.

She ascended the steps to his bedroom and knocked. They'd had arguments about his privacy, and she *tried* to honor her son's wishes about his space. (Walter would have never stood for it. "You'll have privacy when you have your own house," he told the kids. "In *this* house, doors get locked when *I* lock them.")

The music grew louder, and Katie tried the knob. When it didn't turn, her tentative rapping escalated to pounding.

"Joey!" she shouted.

The music stopped, but there was still no reply.

"Joseph Robin Castle, if I have to break through this door, *you'll* pay for a new one!"

Joey was in his skivvies and a T-shirt when he peered out—his hair disheveled, a smattering of hair on his chin, a joystick in his hand.

Joey had been their surprise baby. Ten years younger than his sister, he was handsome, with the broad shoulders and hazel eyes of her grandfather.

"What is it, Ma?" he asked, guarding the door's narrow breach.

"Aren't you late?"

"There's no school today."

"What do you mean, no school? I didn't know anything about that."

Joey shrugged.

"Well, if you're home today, you can help me change out the storm windows."

"I have to go out later."

"Out where?"

"Just out."

Katie used her ample hips to push past her son into his bedroom, which was in the same unkempt state as his hair.

"Joey, look at this room. Where are your school books?"

When he shrugged again and sat at the foot of his bed and resumed manipulating the joystick, Katie was fed up.

"Put down that damn game and pay attention. If you don't keep up your grades, you won't make it to State like your brother and sister."

"College is a waste of time. Dave can't even afford to buy a house, and he drives that dumb Ford. Valerie has to work most of her summer break just to save enough to go on vacation. Nope, college isn't for me. I'm going to be a businessman."

"A businessman?" Katie scanned the bedroom. She spotted a new TV, and sneakers she hadn't seen before. The *E.T.* movie poster had been replaced by one for *Scarface*. "Joey, what's this after-school job you're doing?"

"I told you. I work for a guy who details cars."

"What exactly *is* that?"

Joey rolled his eyes. "You wouldn't understand, Ma. Look, I gotta finish this game and get ready to go."

"I don't know what's gotten into you. You're always sullen. You never eat dinner at home anymore, and you haven't been to Mass in weeks."

"Church is for losers."

Katie's knees wobbled. "That's blasphemy," she shouted, fingering the gold cross at her neck. She wanted to strike her son. Instead, she planted herself in front of his TV, blocking his view of his game. "Who've you been listening to?"

"Somebody who knows only suckers waste their time on college and church and the mines."

Tears sprang to Katie's eyes. As a schoolgirl, she'd waited at the company gate to walk her father home—his face and arms covered in soot. Walter had been a miner, too. The job had taken a toll on his health, but it had also bought their house, helped them raise three kids, sent two to college. Now her youngest, once a dutiful choir boy, saw no value in church, or in the livelihood that had sustained them in Scranton for three generations.

"I gotta get dressed, Ma."

"Just promise me you'll keep up your studies. It's what your father would have wanted."

A half hour later, Joey left the house without a word. Katie was in the basement, examining the storm windows she stored there during the year's warmer months. Three of the windows needed repair. Walter had intended to replace the furnace this winter, and they were overdue for a new washer and dryer, but the household account had been depleted by funeral expenses.

The phone sounded, and she trudged up the stairs to the kitchen, catching it on the fourth ring. It was a pleasant surprise to hear the voice on the other end: Mitch Addison. The Addisons had lived down the street for many years, had moved away after the mine's first round of layoffs.

By the time Katie hung up, she was trembling.

She retrieved the key Walter kept in the metal box on their dresser. She didn't feel like a snoop as she searched Joey's room. She found another pair of sneakers in his closet—unworn, still in their box—and an expensive watch under the shirts in his top drawer. Stuffed in the back of his desk was a bundle of hundreds and twenties, bound tightly in thick rubber bands. Next to the cash was a chrome-plated pistol.

A wave of nausea roiled through her, and she got down on her knees to pray for her son.

Father Ryan had advised her to be patient with Joey. "He's lost his father. It's difficult for a teenage boy without a male role model. You must trust that the things you and Walter taught him as a boy will help him find his way as a man."

Katie hid the gun and the money in her bedroom. Distraught, she called Valerie. Her daughter was a competent, practical girl. A teacher. A helper.

"What's wrong, Mom?"

"Joey's in trouble."

"What kind of trouble?"

"You remember the Addisons? Their boy Mitch phoned. He says Joey stole money from him, and he's going to turn him over to the police. At first I thought *who does he think he's fooling*, but then I found the money hidden in Joey's room. He says Joey works for him."

Valerie had warned her brother not to get entangled with Mitch. She knew that the precocious little boy who'd been her childhood playmate was now a drug dealer, a pinch-faced, violent man, concerned only with building and controlling a gang that protected his money and territory. If Joey had been foolish enough to steal from Mitch, the police were the least of his worries.

When Valerie said nothing, Katie continued. "He's doing our family a favor, for old time's sake, but he'll call the police unless he gets his money back."

"You can't take what Mitch says at face value," Valerie cautioned. "What are you going to do?"

"I told him I have his money, and I'll meet him at the cemetery this evening."

"Even if you return it, Mom, he won't let Joey off the hook. Mitch isn't the person we used to know. He'll want to make an example of Joey."

"What do you mean?"

"Joey stole from him. He won't let him get away with it."

Katie was on the verge of tears, and her hand trembled as she held the receiver. Her son was in serious danger.

"Where's Joey now?" Valerie asked.

"I don't know. He didn't go to school, and he left the house hours ago."

"Mitch will never contact the police. He's a drug dealer, Mom. I don't want you to meet with him."

"What else can I do? I have to save my boy."

"Then let *me* go."

"No, no." Katie wiped her eyes with the sleeve of her sweater. "I'll talk it over with your father. But please come to the house tonight when you get off work."

Katie normally spent time at her husband's grave at Holy Cross Cemetery twice a month, but this visit would be November's third. She set the small bouquet she'd brought with her in the flower holder at Walter's marker and used her scarf to brush dried leaves from the nearby concrete bench. The bench and marker were embedded in fall wildflowers and encircled by decorative white boulders. Hummingbirds bounced from flower to flower.

For thirty minutes, Katie spoke to Walter about their son. The gun and money she'd found in his bedroom were clues to his wrongdoing, and the phone call from Mitch was proof.

Katie always gained peace and purpose from her time with Walter, but she had never actually heard his voice respond to her. Today she did, and he told her what to do. She would return to Holy Cross later tonight to confront Mitch Addison.

The cemetery's side gate was never locked, and Katie squeezed through it to minimize the squeal of its rusty hinges. She'd done the same thing years before, when she'd followed Valerie to a rendezvous with a boyfriend behind the large mausoleum. She'd never told Walter about that.

Katie was dressed for the cold in corduroys, boots, and a parka. With the full moon's aid, she traversed the graveyard's quarry, dodging tree stumps, grizzled roots, and massive mounds of quartz, marble, and granite. A bulldozer—locked in a raised position—hovered like a dinosaur against the chain-link boundary.

Katie followed the fence line until she reached the cemetery's main road, walked the paved path to the large oak tree and then the additional four yards over grass to Walter's headstone. She touched the stone, pulled her parka tight, and perched on the bench. She could feel the thick wad of bills in one pocket and the chrome pistol in the other. She'd brought the gun and the cash to return to Mitch—she didn't want them in her house. But Valerie had warned her: "Don't give him the money until you're sure Joey's safe."

The crunch of footsteps on dry leaves caused her to stand. The dark figure moving toward her wasn't in a hurry. A hooded jacket hid his face, but it was unmistakably Mitch, his hitched walk a result of the ankle he'd broken at age eleven, when he'd fallen from Mrs. Garrick's pear tree.

As Mitch approached the bench, the moon lit his face. Oh, how he had changed from the smiling boy she remembered! His eyes gleamed with the hardness of a feral cat. Tattoos covered one side of his face and neck. There was a flash of gold when his lips parted in a sneer.

"Been a long time, Mrs. C."

"Where's Joey?"

"How should I know? You bring my money?"

Katie sank her hands deep into her pockets and adjusted her stance. "I have it, but you won't get it until I know my son's unharmed."

Mitch's cackle startled Katie, and she was caught off guard when he leapt over the bench, piled into her like a Steelers linebacker, and knocked her flat among the wildflowers. He slapped her hard across the face and straddled her, spewing foul breath, clawing at her pockets. Katie tried to stand, her heels slipping as they dug into the soft soil, and she fought back, flailing her arms and screaming, until Mitch had had enough. He pulled a switchblade from his jeans. Its long point caught the moonlight.

"I'm not here to play, Mrs. C. Give me the money. I don't want to kill you, but I will."

"I buried it behind the cross," Katie lied.

Mitch rolled off her and used the knife's point to loosen the soil at the base of the cross.

Katie struggled to her feet and crept up behind him. She fingered the gun in her pocket but decided against it and bent over to pick up one of the white boulders. It was heavy. She held it aloft in both hands and hesitated for a moment, waiting to hear Walter's voice.

It came, and she slammed the rock against the side of Mitch's head.

And then again.

Oh, God!

"We found a body at your husband's gravesite," Detective Daniel O'Hara said. "I need to ask you a few questions."

Katie knew the O'Haras slightly. They'd never been close, but Walter had worked the morning shift at the mine with the detective's father. Now the son had commandeered her dining table's end chair for his brown wool coat and hat, and his notebook was open in front of him. He sat across from Katie. Joey perched on the chair beside his mother.

"We've identified the dead man as Mitchell Addison. He used to live on this block, didn't he?"

Valerie heard the question as she entered the room with coffee and a slice of pound cake for the detective. "Mitch is dead? That's awful! They lived right next door. That was what, Mom? Almost twenty years ago?"

Katie's throat was constricted. She nodded, and her gaze dipped to the heirloom linen tablecloth. Tears formed at the corners of her eyes. She was convinced that O'Hara was here to arrest her.

"We received an anonymous call that Addison would be at the cemetery. He was dead when we got there. Shot in the back at close range."

Katie gasped. She lifted shaking hands to wipe at her cheeks. "What? I don't understand. He was *shot*?"

"Don't waste your tears on him, ma'am. He was a drug peddler, as rotten as they come. We've had an undercover officer embedded in his organization for a couple of months. Operation Diablo, we called it. That means 'devil,' you know." O'Hara slurped coffee and glanced at Joey, then returned his gaze to Katie. "Any idea why he would have been at your husband's grave?"

It was Valerie who responded. "None, Detective. Was Daddy's grave disturbed?"

O'Hara shifted his large body to look at her. He'd graduated from Lackawanna High the year she'd started as a freshman. He'd always thought of her as a pretty girl from a good Irish-Catholic home, like his own.

"No. The grave itself wasn't damaged. The body was lying among some boulders. One was missing. We think someone used it to bash in his head, but that's not what killed him. We found the gun. It was wiped clean of fingerprints. There was also a knife and a sizable amount of money stuffed in Addison's jacket. To be honest, we're feeling lucky to be rid of the guy."

Apparently finished with his questions about the death of Mitch Addison, O'Hara pierced the buttery cake with his fork and turned to Joey. "What about you, son? Got plans for after graduation?"

Katie held her breath.

Joey straightened his posture. "My parents set up a college fund for me. I guess I'll be headed to State next year."

"Good man," O'Hara said, taking a final sip from his cup and closing his notebook.

"Will you let us know when you find out who killed him, Detective?" Valerie asked.

"I will. We old parish families have to stick together, don't we?"

Katie escorted the detective to the door. Her fingers trembled when they shook hands.

"I was sorry to hear of your husband's passing, Mrs. Castle," O'Hara said. "My father always spoke highly of him."

Katie returned to the dining room, still shaking and confused.

Joey voiced the bewilderment she felt: "You said you killed Mitch with a rock!"

"I thought I had."

"But he was *shot*. I don't understand."

"Neither do I. He wasn't moving, and there was so much

blood on his head." Katie squeezed her eyes tight at the memory. "I dropped the gun and put the money in Mitch's pocket. Then I left."

"So who shot him?"

"I did," Valerie said.

Katie and Joey stared at her. She'd remained in her chair, her hands clasped, her back straight. Her voice was calm, as if she was sitting at her desk in front of her class at the start of a school day.

"I killed Mitch," she said. "I followed you to the cemetery, Mom. There was no way I was going to let you face him alone."

"I didn't want you to get involved!" Katie sobbed. "I promised your father *I'd* take care of things."

"I was standing behind the oak tree when he knocked you down. I heard him threaten to kill you." Valerie rose and placed an arm around her mother's shoulders. "I saw you hit him with the rock. When you left, I checked on him, and he wasn't dead. He groaned and struggled to get up. I took the gun and pressed it against the back of his jacket and pulled the trigger."

"Jeez," Joey breathed, staring wide-eyed at his sister.

Katie saw the pride on his face and covered her eyes. She'd failed her children. She folded herself over the table and wept.

Valerie's arm tightened around her shoulder. "Don't you see, Mom? I had to do it. Mitch would have come after Joey *and* you."

"No. What I did—what we've all done—was wrong. Mortal sins," Katie said through tears.

Valerie stood and linked arms with her brother. "We're a family, and we protect our own," she stated with resolve.

"Pops used to say that all the time," Joey said.

Katie looked up at her son and daughter. "He said it again today," she said, wrapping the two of them in her arms.

Katie opened the drapes and stared out at the neighborhood.

Five decades of morning skies told her it would snow today.

She'd talked it over with Walter. Her home, her routines, no longer gave her comfort. When Joey graduated in the spring, she'd sell the house and go live with Dave and his wife in Pittsburgh. She'd give Valerie a third of the money from the sale of the house, and she'd add a third to Joey's college fund.

She started for the kitchen, then heard Joey moving around overhead.

"Come on in," his voice rang out when she knocked.

The chaos was unchanged: clothes covered the floor, a game console and more clothes were bunched on the bed. But Joey was dressed and stuffing papers into his backpack.

"You want an egg sandwich?" Katie asked.

"If I can take it with me."

She turned to leave.

"Ma, wait. I wanted to ask you. Why didn't you keep the money? You could have used it for things you need around the house."

"It wasn't ours to keep, Joey. Don't you understand the price we have to pay for what we did?"

The radio in the kitchen was tuned to a religious station. Katie fried three eggs, listening to an old hymn her Baptist grandmother used to sing. It soothed her some.

It would be a long time before she would feel worthy to visit consecrated ground again, but she knew Walter would understand.

She toasted bread, and began to hum along, praying the words of the hymn were true:

Let the water and the blood
From thy riven side which flowed
Oh, be of sin the double cure
Cleanse me from its guilt and power

Rock of Ages,
Cleft for me.
Let me hide myself in Thee…

Still Crazy After All These Years

Released October 1975

"Still Crazy After All These Years"
"My Little Town"
"I Do It for Your Love"
"50 Ways to Leave Your Lover"
"Night Game"
"Gone at Last"
"Some Folks' Lives Roll Easy"
"Have a Good Time"
"You're Kind"
"Silent Eyes"

All songs by Paul Simon.

STILL CRAZY AFTER ALL THESE YEARS

E.A. Aymar

We see the moment the woman realizes she's going to die. The fear behind her eyes comes forward and she bucks hard against the chair she's tied to in the living room. She desperately casts about, looking for something that might save her. For someone.

But the only people here are me and my sister Callie.

She starts to give us the answers we want, tells us who she is, who she works with. She tells us about her son, that she misses him. That hunting us was a mistake. She can't control her crying. Her face is a blur of tears.

Over the past year, my sister and I have seen a lot of people die.

None of them have gone with grace.

Callie pulls out her knife, and the begging turns to screaming.

Normally we'd gag her, but this cabin we found—nicely furnished, probably a rental property we were lucky to stumble on—is buried deep in one of Maryland's forests. The closest neighbor is miles away.

I leave her with Callie, head to the kitchen, pull a bottle of water from the fridge.

Drinking water calms me, like the way other people count to ten, or list items in a room, or tap their fingertips together, or pray.

The water fills my mouth. The plastic bottle crumples in my hand.

Callie washes her knife and hands and wrists in the bathroom sink.

"*Ella es simpatica*," she remarks, her back to me as I sit on the lip of the tub. She's been practicing her Spanish, getting ready for Panama.

"Yeah."

She flips off the water. "*Adios, señora* Aberdeen."

"Aberdeen?"

She switches to English. "Wasn't that her name?"

"We're *in* Aberdeen, dummy. Her name was Chloe."

"Really? I kept saying, 'Goodbye, Aberdeen.'" Callie snaps her fingers. "That must be why she looked so confused!"

"At least we know for sure she was working with the Daughters."

"They're never going to stop, huh?"

"No."

Ever since Callie murdered one of their members, the Daughters have been after us.

"Oh, well," Callie says, and she switches back to Spanish. "*¿Baltimore es mañana por la noche, si?*"

"Baltimore is tomorrow night," I confirm. "And the ship leaves Wednesday afternoon."

"*Estoy emocionada*," she says. "*Yo no visito Panama por años.*"

"You were a baby when mom took us."

She ignores me. "I wonder if we'll fit in. At least I sort of speak the language."

"Yeah, but you don't know anything about the country. Who's the president?"

"They don't have a king?"

"Cortizo. What's the capital?"

"The...Canal? I don't know, Vic. You can write the book report, but I'll do the talking. Deal?"

"To be fair," I say, to end the bickering, "neither of us really belongs there. Even though Mom was *from* there."

"I've always felt that way," Callie says. She peers into the mirror, touches the blood in her hair.

The fire starts before sunrise.

Four in the morning, and a long finger of smoke reaches down my throat. I roll out of bed, coughing, palms pressed into my eyes, elbows and knees on the floor.

Someone pulls me to my feet. Callie. Her shirt's lifted over her nose like a makeshift hospital mask, her backpack slung over her shoulder.

"The Daughters," she says.

I reach under the bed, grab my own bag. We stumble out of the bedroom, Callie first, me following with a hand on her shoulder. We hear the fire but don't see it, the cabin crackling as flames chew through wood. The world is smoky and blurry but visible.

We drop to our knees and crawl, breathe close to the floor. The cabin's front door is ahead of us. We see the orange light of fire in the living room. Heat wets our skin.

Callie reaches for the front door, unlocks it, turns the knob. And something occurs to me, something I should have realized sooner.

I pull her to the ground as gunshots explode over us. Slam the door as bullets rip through the house.

"We probably shouldn't go that way," Callie says.

"You think?"

We crawl back down the hall. I tap my sister on the side, motion her to follow me to the kitchen. We stay away from the smoke. I yank open the fridge, grab a bottle of water, twist it open, pour half over my face and into my mouth, give the rest to Callie.

She douses herself and tosses the empty bottle away. "What now?"

"They'll be at the back door, too."

She slips her bag off her shoulder. "Do we shoot our way out?"

"We won't make it off the porch."

"So, what then?"

"Hold on," I say. "I'm thinking."

But I'm not thinking of a way out.

I'm remembering what got us here.

The dead woman in the other room. All of Callie's murders. The ones I've accepted, the ones I've assisted. We've spent a lot of time close to death this past year, couldn't keep any of the Daughters we captured alive because they knew too much about us. We have reasons for the killings.

Those reasons used to be enough.

"Vic," Callie says. Her voice brings me back.

"The window," I tell her. "We'll go through the window."

She stares at me. "You remember we're on a hill, right? The drop is, like, two stories."

"There's no doors on this side of the house. They won't be watching."

"Shit." Callie scrambles to her feet, slides open the glass, pushes out the screen.

"I don't see anyone," she tells me.

Smoke curls into the room, like a hand reaching under the doorway. I feel it wrapping around my neck. Squeezing.

We climb onto the counter. My knees press hard against the granite. The fire has reached the kitchen, clawed through the wall separating this room from the living room. The dead woman's body is on the floor, her skin burning away.

Callie grabs my shoulder.

She's sitting on the windowsill like she's about to parachute out.

"Vic, come on."

She disappears into the darkness.

After a few seconds, I do the same.

Sunlight wakes me.

I grab my knee with both hands, pull it to my stomach. Squeeze with everything I've got until the pain shrinks to a small throbbing ball, stops hammering my heart, my blood, my brain.

"You're up."

Callie's voice. I turn from the sun. She's sitting on the ground, staring at me curiously.

We're in the woods.

"My leg," I explain.

"You landed funny," Callie says. "Well, not funny. Okay, kinda funny? Your leg just went out underneath you and you rolled down the hill. But you stopped when your head hit a tree."

"What?"

Callie nods. "Then I dragged you like a mile. I'm a hero."

"What?"

"Stop saying *what*," Callie says. "Can we talk about something else?"

Later, as the light fades, the pain gets worse.

"*¡Por favor, déjame ir!*"

I sit up, see a scared man tied to a tree.

"Who're you?" I ask.

"*¿Que?*"

"What?"

"Your Spanish *is* getting better!" Callie sings out. "Yay!"

I rub my eyes. "Who is this guy?"

He's older, short and chubby with curly black hair. His chin is shaking. Eyes impossibly wide.

"He was with you when I came back from the grocery store."

"Grocery store?"

"That's what you said the last time you woke up," Callie chides me. "When I gave you your medicine."

"You did?" Everything is fuzzy, sleepy.

But my leg doesn't hurt.

Not until I try to stand.

"I don't know what you did," Callie says, after I'm done rolling on the ground and yelling. "I don't think it's broken, but it's worse than a sprain. *Sproken*? Is that a medical term? Or *brain*? No, that's stupid. It's sproken."

The waves of pain recede. I lift my face from the ground. Spit blood.

"Who's he?" I ask.

"Someone we can't let go," Callie tells me.

As if he realizes we're talking about him, the man starts speaking again. "*Mi bolsillo.*"

"¡*Cállate*!" Callie tells him, and her voice is as sharp and sudden as a shovel striking dirt.

"*Mi bolsillo*," he says again, quieter.

Callie reaches into his pocket and pulls out a photo. She glances at it, tosses the picture on the ground.

I crawl over to the photo, my head and leg aching with each movement. See a picture of a boy, maybe six or seven years old.

"*Mi hijo.*"

Callie ignores him. "He was just standing here," she tells me. "I went to the store, and then I came back and saw him."

"*¡Por favor!*"

Clouds gather behind my eyes. "We should let him go." I stand and walk toward the man and try to untie his knots.

Or I think I do.

But I'm still sitting on the ground. I haven't moved.

"I don't think I'm well," I announce.

"*¡Por favor!*"

I lie down.

"I don't think you're supposed to sleep when you have a concussion," Callie tells me, right before my eyes close.

When I wake the next morning, she's ripping the guy's photograph to pieces.

I feel rested, recovered enough to realize I'm not going to pass out again. The pain in my leg has lessened. I stand slowly and walk, leaning on trees for support.

The dizziness has decreased.

I touch the back of my head, feel something soft. A bandage.

"He told me what to do," Callie says, when I ask her about it. "He told me to sit you up, lean you against a tree. Put a bandage on, so there wouldn't be any infection."

"I feel better," I tell her.

"There's another ship leaving for Panama tomorrow afternoon. I bought tickets with his credit card."

"Okay."

Callie hands me my backpack. I carefully sling it over my shoulders. I lean against her as we walk through the woods.

I don't look back at the body.

Baltimore is a thirty-dollar cab ride away. A taxi isn't exactly an inconspicuous way to travel, but we don't have much of a choice.

Callie chats with the driver the entire time. I stare out the window.

He drops us off outside a bar about a mile from the port. It's the first time I've been in Baltimore since I was a kid. Twenty-four years of life circling back on itself, a snake nibbling its own tail.

"Is it really sproken?" Callie asks, watching as I examine

my leg.

"Maybe it's a torn ACL? But I'm not sure what that means."

Callie is staring at my face. "You're sweating."

"I need something to drink."

We head into the bar, sit in a dark booth away from the windows. I drink myself a beer and then down Callie's. The cold air in the bar and the alcohol make me even more tired, as if riding in the cab and hobbling here are the end of a long, exhausting day.

"This meal will take the last of our cash," Callie says. "And I'm too nervous to use that dude's credit card again."

I wipe the sweat off my face with a napkin. Nod.

"Are you going to throw up? You look like you're going to throw up."

"Maybe."

A love song is playing quietly on the jukebox. I don't know it.

A waitress brings crab cakes for Callie and a hamburger for me. The burger is the best thing I've ever tasted.

Callie picks at her crab cake.

"What's going on?" I ask.

"Nothing."

"Doesn't feel like nothing."

"Honestly, I'm okay."

"You know you could tell me if you weren't."

"I know."

"But would you?"

"Nah."

"Great."

"I feel bad about Raúl," Callie says.

"Who?"

"The guy in the woods." Callie is picking at her food, pushing it around her plate. "I didn't have to kill him."

We're the only people in the restaurant, except for a bored hostess typing on her phone.

"These people are giving up their lives for us," Callie goes on. "Like the stories I've read about human sacrifices. The Aztecs or Incas or whatever, they didn't want to die. A king or a priest just killed them. And it didn't even matter in the end, because now *all* of them are long gone, even the kings. Everything fades."

"I don't get what you're saying."

"All those people dead, Vic, and none of it mattered. Maybe that's what we're doing. Following a fake god. We think we're doing what we need to do to stay safe, but it's been the same craziness since day one."

I try to think of the right thing to say. I've never heard Callie like this.

"I shouldn't have killed her," she says. Her eyes are crimson. "I loved her."

"You didn't have a choice."

"That night when I called you," she says, "and you came over, and you saw her body. Do you remember that night?"

I wipe my forehead with another napkin. Nod. "You told me she wanted you to join the Daughters," I say. "You said no. It turned into a fight."

"I didn't—I didn't want that to happen," Callie says. "I was happy, so was she. But they were such a part of her. That stupid militia. She went on and on about overthrowing the government and sovereignty, whatever that is. Like, all that wasn't just a *part* of her, Vic. It *was* her. She talked and talked and I told her she was crazy and she slapped me. And I laughed and she hit me again. I couldn't stop, even though it was everything I worried about, everything I was afraid of. But I kept laughing. I couldn't stop fucking laughing, even when she was choking me. I laughed until I had to fight back." She picks up her empty beer glass, gazes into it. "Maybe I was wrong."

Something in her voice reminds of that scared child I'll always remember, long ago, the little girl who desperately needed help. The child I stole away from our father's fists and lips.

"Was I wrong?"

"If they knew the truth," I tell her, speaking carefully,

"everything that happened, no one would blame us for any of this."

She just smiles.

We sleep with the other homeless in a park near the port, surrounded by tents and sleeping bags and blankets. The night isn't cold, and the grass is as comfortable as the forest was. Which isn't comfortable at all, but Callie and I are used to it.

The next morning, we cross the street to the port. The ship we're going to board is large, with a decorative whale fin arced in the back. A crowd of passengers wait to file up the gangway.

"We don't look like them," I observe.

"You think we'll stick out?" She still has that seriousness from the day before. Rain in her eyes.

"Yes."

She points to restroom doors on the side of the building. "Let's freshen up."

A guy is leaving the men's room as I walk in. There are two stalls and three urinals. A long mirror over a pair of sinks. I splash water on my face, look at my clothes. My rough appearance doesn't surprise me. The age in my face does. I don't look like me.

I clean up as best as I can, use wet paper towels to wipe dirt stains from my shirt and tamp down my hair.

I walk outside and lean against the wall next to the ladies' room.

It takes Callie a few minutes, but she finally emerges.

"Vic."

She drops to a knee, her hand over her stomach.

Her hand and stomach are red.

The next moments blur. I don't remember helping her back inside the restroom, rushing to the sink.

I've never seen this much blood.

I lock the restroom door.

Kneel next to my sister.

Callie's lying on her back. With every breath, blood is wrung from her stomach.

The dead woman on the tile floor has a neck cut so deep her head barely seems to be hanging on.

"I didn't see her follow you in."

"Yeah, I—" Pain contorts Callie's face and voice. "Me, neither."

"What do I do?" I ask, helplessly. I look down at my hands, gently covering the wound in my sister's stomach.

The bathroom doorknob shakes.

"It's broken!" I shout.

"I want to go to Panama," Callie whispers.

I see the fear in her face.

The same fear we've seen in so many others.

The moment the ship docks at the Canal, police speaking Spanish arrest me, hand me over to police speaking English. They drive me to an airport, lead me to a small plane on the runway.

As we walk from the car to the plane, I can feel the Panamanian air. That touch of wetness in the wind. Warm rain. Like a memory from a time I can't quite remember.

I must have had this same kind of moment years ago.

The law has me. They have me for the dozen or so women we killed, although no one refers to them as the Daughters. It's like the militia doesn't exist, never has. They even have me for the man in the woods.

The families of the dead are constantly on the news, weeping. I'm told by my guards that the country wants to kill me. I'm told pictures of me and Callie are everywhere, every news channel. Callie is pictured as my helpless younger sister, forced into killing by her malevolent older brother.

They blame me for all the deaths, even Callie's.

I don't fight it.

There's no hiding anymore. I'm alone in a cell. Around me, men talk. They talk to themselves or each other, they laugh, threaten, shout, scream. One of them prays, loudly and passionately and desperately to God, until the guards take him away and his voice is forever stopped.

Tonight another prisoner shouts to God, and I close my eyes and lie on my cot. My time is up. I spent weeks in a courtroom while a jury peered at me, sometimes with curiosity, often with hate. I knew they would convict me. And now they're going to fill my body with poison.

I don't know where you are, Callie.

I don't know if I'll see you again.

But I do have that one moment, that moment in the warm rain, that moment all these years later that connects me to you and takes me somewhere else.

Before we ran.

Before we killed.

Before the poison filled our bodies, all those years ago.

One-Trick Pony

Released August 1980

"Late in the Evening"
"That's Why God Made the Movies"
"One-Trick Pony"
"How the Heart Approaches What It Yearns"
"Oh, Marion"
"Ace in the Hole"
"Nobody"
"Jonah"
"God Bless the Absentee"
"Long, Long Day"

All songs by Paul Simon.

OH, MARION

Paul Charles

1

When we are younger, and I do mean much younger, we cry openly—maybe even bawl—when we are hurt. Babies cry themselves to sleep. Kids cry when they are hungry or when they want or need attention.

Eventually, we come to understand that pain is not really insufferable, if only because we see that we have survived it and lived to cry another day. We recognize that we *will* survive, so our pain becomes measured against benchmarks. *Okay, this sore head is painful, but it's not as bad as going to the dentist, which itself is not nearly as awful as having appendicitis.* Our knowledge helps us put hardship into perspective, put ordeal behind us.

But when we hit our teenage years, we find that our prior pain was nothing compared to the unbearable agony of unrequited love.

The first time your heart is broken, you hurt so badly you think the world is going to end—and even if it *does* end, the upside would be that you wouldn't have to deal with this massive hole in the pit of your stomach, this physical heartache, this sense of loss and loneliness, this never-ending feeling that something is eating away at your insides. You cry so much your eyes are bloodshot, your nose won't stop running, your face looks like a raw steak with two pinholes where your eyes used to be. But you don't really care, because your life is over and you don't give a fig who knows. You act out in front of your family and friends, shocked at your lack of embarrassment. You fight for each breath, seriously believing there won't be a next one.

The next stage is where your mum, who through all of this didn't crowd you, starts to sympathize with you and confesses some of her own tales of woe. You will still feel bad, though perhaps not quite as bad as before.

You finally start to accept that the loss will make you stronger, and as you get a little stronger you get a little wiser—and then you see your ex up the town, looking a million dollars, laughing and joking with her friends.

Aha, you think, *so I haven't gotten over her as much as I fooled myself into believing*. You fall off the cliff again, nudged over the edge by the notion that your ex never really cared about you in the first place.

If anything, this feeling is worse—but not as bad as the feeling you experience when you see her up the town again, this time with another boy, and imagine that he's doing the things with her that you used to do. If your mind is cruel, it will even lead you by your running red nose to imagine her new boyfriend doing things with her that she would never *let* you do.

This is good.

Really?

Yes, this is good, because this is where you hit rock bottom. You may still be suspended in midair, but at least your descent has stopped.

This is as devastating as anything in your life will ever be. But eventually, you will notice that you've survived it.

And, mostly, you have.

But, sadly, this is not the end of the story.

In *our* story, we have a couple: Tommy and Marion. They met at Royal Holloway College, London, twenty years ago, while both were studying music. They discovered that they shared the same birthday, and immediately felt closer to each other than they had ever felt to anyone else. They never subscribed to the theory that love is only easy when it's two other people playing the game. For them, being together was not a game. Purely and simply, to them it was life.

Until it wasn't.

2

On a cold March morning in 2022, a call came into North Bridge House, the home of Camden Town CID, to advise Desk Sergeant Timothy Flynn that a body had been discovered in 125 Parkway, literally across the road from the station. The Victorian building—whose checkered past had taken it from a shop to a piano factory to legal offices to a booking agency—was now the home of Frederic Records.

As Detective Inspector Christy Kennedy and Detective Sergeant Dot King crossed the heavy traffic at the Regents Park end of Parkway, little did they imagine how helpful the deceased would be in assisting them to solve the case.

The deceased, who quite literally looked like he was asleep, had been discovered by Jerry Landis, the managing director of Frederic Records, in a small bathroom on the fourth floor of the five-floor building. The room's floor, walls, and plumbing features—shower, toilet, sink—were all white. The only other colors in the room were a bottle of green mouthwash sitting on the sink's edge and a blue hand towel on the heated towel-rail.

According to Dr. Leonard Taylor, the dead man had passed away the previous evening, between the hours of ten and midnight. DI Kennedy took comfort from this information, as he had never known Dr. Taylor to be incorrect with his estimates. On the negative side, the good doctor did not have a clue as to how the deceased had died, not even if his passing had been due to a natural or malevolent cause.

"I'll have a better idea, I'm sure, when I get the remains back to the lab for the autopsy," he claimed, "but my first uncensored, maybe way-off guess would be that he drowned, perhaps even suffocated."

"But he seems...peaceful," Kennedy said.

"Not everyone who drowns ends their life kicking and screaming," Taylor said.

When Dr. Taylor concluded his preliminary examination, he passed the remains over to the scene-of-crime officers.

Kennedy started to empty the cadaver's pockets. "His clothes are bone dry," he announced, perhaps hinting that they could rule out drowning.

The deceased looked like he was in his mid-fifties. He had a clear complexion, an absence of facial growth, and a full bloom of copper-colored hair, cut in an old-fashioned short-back-and-sides style with a razor-sharp parting. He was a slim five-foot-eleven inches, dressed in a blue blazer with a glorious blood-red poppy in the lapel buttonhole, cream chinos, a blue Oxford button-down shirt, and a Queen's College CUNY blue-and-white tie meticulously presented in a Windsor knot.

The driver's license Kennedy discovered in the inside blazer pocket suggested the dead man was Tommy Graph, an American national. His wallet contained five ten-pound notes, two twenties, seven hundred-dollar bills, an American Express card, and a Mastercard. In the buttoned hip pocket of the chinos, Kennedy found a smartphone. There were no coins in any of his nine pockets, and the only other item about his person was a press cutting from the *Camden News Journal*. Kennedy was distracted by the fact that the article boasted the byline of ann rea, all in lowercase lettering, as was usual for her. He delayed reading his ex-paramour's article until he returned to North Bridge House.

First, he placed all of the above items in plastic evidence bags and turned the remains over to the SOCO team to complete their forensic examination.

3

"You found the body?" Kennedy said.

"Yes, as a matter of a fact, I did, man," Jerry Landis, the record company boss, replied. He was slightly overweight, unshaven, dressed in black tracksuit bottoms, a black logo-free T-shirt, and, according to DS King, "a pair of black Allbird Wool Runner Mizzles."

"Did you recognize the deceased?" King asked, her pen perched above her notebook like a nervous budgie.

"I've never been good around dead bodies," Landis admitted. "When I found it in my bathroom, I closed and locked the door and had my PA ring over to North Bridge House."

"Did you touch the body at all, sir?' King continued, scribbling in her notebook.

Kennedy, happy to leave the interview to her, stole a look around Landis's ultra-tidy office. The walls were covered with gold and platinum discs, mostly for an act called, coincidentally enough, Amy and the Kings.

"Definitely not. I got out of there and shut the door."

"What time did you get to your office this morning?" King continued.

"Eight o'clock."

"Do you always get in so early?" Kennedy asked, visibly surprised. When Landis replied only with a puzzled look, the Ulster-born detective added, "I mean, I was of the opinion the music business usually starts at the crack of lunchtime."

"I like to get in early so I can play my beats, man, check out the buzz on the biz on my Wu Tang LAN before the craziness around here starts, right?"

The interview went downhill from there and produced no additional useful information. Kennedy had, however, managed to glean at least one valuable nugget.

4

When Kennedy returned to his office in North Bridge House, he made himself a cup of tea, unfolded the *Camden News Journal* cutting, and read it.

The article was dated Friday, 26 November 2021. Its headline announced: *Holiday Inn Body Named*:

A Camden Town woman who was found dead in mysterious circumstances in a local hotel on 22 November has been identified by Camden Town CID.

The woman was pronounced dead at the scene. According to a hotel receptionist, her body was discovered when security officers were doing a routine check of the hotel.

Superintendent Geoffery Kramer from Camden Town CID said they are still waiting for the results of the post mortem. He appeals to members of the public who might have any relevant information to get in touch.

A Camden Town CID spokesperson said, "Police have identified the woman who was discovered dead at the Holiday Inn overlooking Camden Lock as Marion Graph, 44, of Chalk Farm."

Since news of the death broke, tributes have been flooding in for Mrs. Graph, who worked as the financial director at the Frederic Records office on the Regents Park end of Parkway.

Mr. Jerry Landis, the company's managing director, said, "Marion was the absolute rock Frederic Records was built on. I have lost a family member, not just a colleague. RIP, wonderful Marion."

Amy Lynn of Amy and the Kings, one of the recording company's most successful acts, said, "Marion was always in our corner, always watching out for us. She was a beautiful woman, inside and out. She always loved to stay in the background, though. Everyone thought she could be Sophie Marceau's twin sister, so we tried to get her to appear in the video for our biggest hit, 'Motorcycle,' but she made it clear that just wasn't going to happen. Jerry eventually booked Sophie Marceau herself for the shoot, but to this day everyone thinks it was Marion in the video. Rest in paradise, Marion, my dear sister. Love and support from all the Kings to her dear husband Tommy."

5

Kennedy immediately rang Superintendent Kramer, who, it turned out, was on leave in Los Angeles. But Harper Simpson, his DI, advised Kennedy that he and his super both believed Marion to have been the victim of an attempted rape. The pathologist had discovered flunitrazepam—aka roofies—in her blood, although there were no physical traces of rape.

Simpson and his gaffer assumed a predator had spiked the woman's drink and was attempting to rape her when he was disturbed, or else she went into trauma during the encounter, passed out, and died. Either way, the attacker scarpered, and security later discovered the body. Simpson reported that there were no further leads to follow, so the case had gone cold. The actual cause of death had never been spelled out, although the pathologist guessed it was heart failure.

Kennedy wasn't so sure.

6

Kennedy and King reviewed the slim pickings of evidence they had on the second member of the Graph family to die in mysterious circumstances.

"Why would anyone, particularly someone from another country, wear a poppy several months after Poppy Day?"

"Perhaps he was acknowledging his solidarity for his wife's country?" King suggested.

Kennedy put on a pair of gloves and removed the poppy from its evidence bag.

He felt there was something wrong with the artificial flower. Its petals were a more vibrant red than he had ever seen before. On closer inspection, the black button at the center—imitating the stamen in a real poppy—was bigger than it should have been.

DS King looked on, openly amused by Kennedy's preoccupation with the flower.

Examining the button more closely, Kennedy realized that it *wasn't* a button, after all.

It was a tiny camera.

"Hand me his smartphone, please," Kennedy said.

7

"If someone is watching this," a nervous American voice came from the phone's speaker, "it means I'm dead, right? And if I'm dead, I was murdered."

"Oh-kay," King whispered, "he's got my attention."

The face on the smartphone's screen clearly belonged to Tommy Graph.

"Until last year, November 22 has always reminded me of the assassination of President Kennedy. Now, it's also the date that my Marion—my dear wife, my soul mate, my best friend and spiritual partner—was murdered. Superintendent Kramer and his investigators couldn't find any incriminating evidence or suspects, though I told them who I suspected and why. They advised me that, in these litigious times, I should be very careful before making such allegations."

Kennedy noted that Graph's original nervousness had evaporated. He was using his hands to help get his points across. He looked like a gardener replanting flowers from pots into the earth.

"I will admit here that I don't know exactly *how* he did it, but I am convinced that I know *why*. My wife is—was, sorry—Marion *was* the financial director at Frederic Records, and she discovered that a senior officer of the company was a serial embezzler.

"She was concerned that the company's record sales were not reflected in their turnover and eventually discovered that, although the majority of the sales invoices were issued with payments due to Frederic Records, some were regularly made out to Fred & Rick Music, right? At first, she dismissed her suspicions, figuring that Fred & Rick Music must be a subsidiary of Frederic Records. But she remained troubled that the apparent income in no way reflected confirmed record sales.

"Marion was an honest and conscientious officer of the company, right? But she knew that, if there was something underhanded or illegal happening, she would be the obvious person to be blamed. She took to returning to the office late at night, after all the staff had left the building. She used this private time to plow through files, invoices, and relevant paperwork—and, about a week before her death, she uncovered a vital piece of information."

Tommy Graph's image paused on the smartphone screen. It was evident that he was aware of the laws of slander and was considering whether or not to name names.

"Fred & Rick Music turned out to have no official connection to Frederic Records. It is a non-limited company solely owned by Jerry Landis. And as far as Marion was able to ascertain, at least two hundred thousand pounds per annum was being diverted from Frederic Records to Fred & Rick Music.

"On the night she died, Marion had—against my express advice, I hasten to add—fixed up a meeting with Jerry Landis. She laughed off my protests, saying, 'He's not one of the Kray Twins mob, you know!'

"She explained to me that she was going to present Landis with the irregularities she'd uncovered and give him a chance to explain. Despite all the information she'd gathered, she thought there might be a reasonable explanation—and, more than anything, she wanted to avoid embarrassing herself. So she agreed to meet Jerry Landis at the office, right?"

Once again, Graph stopped talking. He took a deep breath and, in a much quieter voice, continued. "Landis says she never turned up for their meeting. I still can't figure out how she ended up in a conference room at the Holiday Inn."

Kennedy noted that DS King was taking notes throughout Graph's video statement. He would have expected nothing less, yet he was still pleased by her thoroughness. He wondered if she'd picked up on the fact that Tommy Graph frequently used the question "right?" to emphasize what he obviously felt were significant points.

"According to Superintendent Kramer," Graph continued, "Jerry Landis appeared distraught about Marion's death during his interview. He was waiting for Marion in his office, he claimed, and when she was uncharacteristically late, he rang her on her cell, but the call went straight to voice mail. Eventually, he took a date out for a meal and returned home late in the evening. Several fellow diners—people he knew—would vouch for their presence at the restaurant. His story checked out, according to Superintendent Kramer—the implication being that, at the time my wife was murdered, Landis had a very public alibi.

"I myself had no evidence of any embezzlement—Marion never told me what she'd done with it, and I was unable to find it. To be honest, the superintendent seemed to think I'd totally lost it due to my bereavement and fallen into Ga Ga Land. The fact that there were no marks, bruises or defense injuries about my wife's person led the police to believe that Marion died of natural causes.

"My two questions are: why was my wife at the Holiday Inn, right? And why did she 'conveniently' die of natural causes on the very night she planned to confront an embezzler?

"Marion and I enjoyed our life together. We ate well, drank a little, did not do drugs, exercised, practiced yoga daily, and had a full medical checkup twice a year. So I can tell you"—and here he paused to place his right hand on his heart—"Marion did *not* die from natural causes."

The talking head stopped talking, seemingly to take some time for reflection. After a few moments, Graph resumed.

"When someone close to you dies, your friends gather around and try to nudge you out of your grief. They say things like, 'You need to consider moving on. You'll meet someone special. That's what Marion would want.' Which only shows they don't realize how special the bond Marion and I shared was. It's not that I think I could never meet anyone else. I just don't *want* to. What I *do* want, and what I'm about to endeavor to do now, is to show you exactly how Jerry Landis murdered my wife.

"When I was younger and in pain," Tommy Graph continued, "experience taught me to believe the suffering would pass—and it always did, right? But that was then. This time, I know that—short of Marion rising from the dead—the pain will never ever go away. My life ended when Marion died."

Suddenly there were tears in Tommy's eyes. "Oh, Marion!" he cried. He took a moment to compose himself and went on. "In closing, I swear to you that I have never been in trouble with the law. I'm just a man who is desperate to bring justice for my dear wife."

The smartphone's screen dissolved to gray, then flicked back on again as the Spider X201 Mini HD camera connected by Bluetooth to the phone—disguised as the black button in the center of Tommy's poppy—focused in on a new character, who Kennedy recognized as Jerry Landis.

8

As Tommy Graph walked into Frederic Records, the motion sensor on the poppy camera paired with his phone clicked into action and revealed Jerry Landis waiting for him in the reception.

Landis hugged Graph and offered condolences, nearly blocking the camera's view for a moment.

"Come to my office," Landis said, leading Graph up a flight of stairs. "I have to tell you, man, Marion was our rock." He paused, apparently fighting to hold back tears, but hold them back he did. He offered Graph one of the easy chairs in his office and crossed the wooden floor to his drinks cabinet. "I'd like to propose a toast to Marion, man," he said, taking two already poured glasses of whisky and handing one to Graph.

They touched glasses and took a large swig of the whisky.

"I want to talk about what happened," Graph said, placing his glass on a low table. "I—ah—I—I mean *Marion* discovered..."

Graph sounded like he was struggling to find the words he needed.

Landis seemed content to ignore him and drank more of his whisky.

"Look...I know...you were em...em-bezz-ling..." Graph's words were slurred nearly beyond recognition, and he slumped down in his seat.

"Don't worry, man," Landis offered, coming back into the camera's field of vision. "Here, let me help you up."

"He spiked his drink!" DS King shouted at the smartphone in Kennedy's hand.

They watched Jerry Landis pull Tommy Graph to his feet, wrap an arm around Graph's back, and walk him out of the office, the way one might support a drunken friend.

Landis hauled Graph up a flight of stairs and into a bathroom, the same bathroom where Kennedy and King would later examine Graph's body.

Landis laid Graph on the floor, face up. He lifted Graph's right hand, then let it go and watched it fall like a log back to the white tile. The camera in the center of Graph's poppy was recording every detail and Bluetoothing the evidence to the smartphone.

When Landis took a blue towel from the rack and soaked it in the sink, Kennedy was confused at first, thinking the record company executive intended to try to revive the loving husband of the company's late financial director. But when Landis folded the towel twice and placed it over Graph's face, Kennedy realized exactly how Landis had murdered first Marion Graph and then her husband Tommy.

"Dr. Taylor was right," Kennedy offered, tapping the phone's screen. "The damp towel slowly suffocated Tommy, allowing Landis to scoot off for his alibi dinner while his victim died on the bathroom floor."

"And he used the same method with Marion," DS King whispered.

"He used the same method with Marion," Kennedy agreed. "Then, this morning, when Landis 'discovered' Tommy's body, he simply removed the towel from Graph's face and placed it on the hot towel rail to dry, neutralizing the evidence."

9

"I had a feeling," King began, after she and Kennedy had viewed Tommy Graph's video a second time. "I had a feeling you suspected foul play from our first interview with Jerry Landis."

"Well, not conclusively," Kennedy said, "but I think most people coming across a body lying on the floor would check for signs of life—yet Mr. Landis claimed he didn't touch the body. He told us he closed the door and had his PA ring the police, and that just didn't ring true."

DS King seemed happy that the case had been solved, but DI Kennedy took little solace from the fact that it had required Tommy's ultimate sacrifice to secure justice for the murder of his beloved Marion.

Hearts and Bones

Released November 1983

"Allergies"
"Hearts and Bones"
"When Numbers Get Serious"
"Think Too Much (b)"
"Song About the Moon"
"Think Too Much (a)"
"Train in the Distance"
"René and Georgette Magritte with Their Dog, After the War"
"Cars Are Cars"
"The Late Great Johnny Ace"

All songs by Paul Simon,
except the coda of "The Late Great Johnny Ace,"
which is by Philip Glass.

TRAIN IN THE DISTANCE

Rebecca K. Jones

Mack Wilson squinted into the rising sun. Even six a.m. wasn't early enough to escape the searing heat of Tucson in July, and under her blazer, her Oxford shirt was already soaked through.

"I ever tell you my mom wanted to be a hobo when she was a kid?" she asked.

"Huh?" Dave Barton straightened momentarily before resuming his casual lean against his undercover Tahoe.

The slim young prosecutor nodded and took a sip of her coffee, the ice rapidly melting. "Yeah. She was like four or five, I guess? A kid. She wanted to hop a freight train and ride the rails. She had a shitty childhood, and I guess she thought life would be better wherever a train might take her."

Dave ran a hand over his shaved head and looked at his palm, wiped the sweat on his jeans with a disgusted sigh. "She ever do it?"

"Nah. She escaped the modern way: planes and automobiles. Far as I know, she's never stopped running."

They stood quietly, listening to the whoosh of traffic and trying to enjoy the morning sky, washed clean and blue by the previous night's monsoon.

"Are you sure about this?" Mack asked.

"Yep. The Union Pacific from Yuma should be pulling in any minute."

Mack took her time gathering her blond hair into a ponytail—anything to get it off her neck. "And Joseph Smith is going to be on it?"

"Yes, Wilson," Dave said. "Like I told you, he's the locomotive engineer. This is his route. And in"—he checked his watch—"six minutes, we'll get him into custody."

"We'd better. Because in *seven* minutes, I'll be fully cooked."

Mack thought back to the moment, almost a year earlier, when she'd had to let Joseph Smith—who had just been indicted for the vicious beating of his ex-wife, the mother of his young son—out of custody.

Patrol officers had arrested and booked Smith on scene, when they'd responded to a neighbor's 911 call. Carrie Oates, the ex-wife—she'd returned to her maiden name after the divorce—said she'd invited him to dinner that night so their son Harper could see them together peacefully...and so she could renegotiate child support. But Joe had misunderstood, thought she wanted to discuss the possibility of a reconciliation, and that's when the trouble had started.

Harper was cowering under his bunk bed when police got there. The boy wasn't tall enough or brave enough to get between his dad and mom, wasn't strong enough to shove his dresser against the door.

Joseph Smith had refused to talk to the officers, but he'd written a letter to Carrie from the Pima County Jail almost as soon as he got there, promising her the moon. Mack didn't know exactly what he wrote, since Carrie had refused to show her the letter. She just knew that Carrie came to her office enthusiastic about Joe's change of heart, reminiscing about the way he used to make her laugh. Carrie apologized to Mack and Dave for the inconvenience, the waste of resources, the trouble, but she made clear her intention to avoid showing up for trial and testifying against her much older ex.

"If you make me testify," she'd said, nervously tapping her foot against Mack's desk, "I'll tell the jury I fell. That's what caused all this." She gestured to her still-purple face, her left arm snug against her side in a sling. "I fell, and Detective Barton bullied me into saying Joe hit me. But Joe loves me, in his way, and he *adores* Harper. He never would, I'll say. He never has, and he never will."

Mack and Dave stared at her, each performing their own calculations. There was no doubt Carrie Oates had been beautiful when she was younger, though it was hard to see a trace of that beauty now through the bruises and her jittery presentation. Ten years earlier, Joseph Smith had wooed her with love songs and promises of a better life. Once they were married and she was pregnant with Harper, the disagreements had begun. Nothing serious at first: a little yelling here, a smashed picture frame there. But then the arguments had become fights had become beatings. A trail of 911 calls littered the last years of their marriage and the first year after their divorce.

Neither Mack nor Dave was a stranger to recanting victims, and the gruesome photos taken on scene were on their side. Would a jury buy that Carrie's fractured orbital bone, dislocated shoulder, and petechial hemorrhages had been caused by a fall? Would a jury *care*, if Carrie so clearly didn't? Should Mack and Dave?

She considered the stack of files on her desk. Twenty more, just like Carrie's case, and those victims weren't trying to negotiate their way to a happy ending.

"Thank you," Carrie said, as Mack escorted her out of her office, still trying to decide what to do.

"For what?"

Carrie shrugged. "For hearing me out. I just really believe, if Joe and me get one more chance..."

Despite those hopeful words, she looked somehow disappointed, but Mack couldn't tell if she was disappointed in herself, in her ex-husband, or in love in general.

Dave agreed that even if they cared *about* her—and they did—they couldn't care *for* her, so they'd reluctantly dismissed the case, leaving Carrie and Joseph to their reunion.

Now, eight months later, Carrie was in the ICU, struggling to survive her latest beating at the hands of her smooth-talking, sociopathic ex. Her condition was listed as critical, and Dave was itching to make an arrest and put Joseph Smith right back where he belonged. It had been easy to find him online—surprisingly, there weren't that many Joseph Smiths in Tucson—and finding his schedule had required only a quick call to the railroad.

The sound of the train in the distance pulled Mack from her reverie. No use wasting time on the past.

The train pulled into the station and rumbled to a stop, a middle-aged white man hanging out the door of the engine.

"Joseph Smith?" Dave called.

The man nodded noncommittally. Mack saw his hand tense around the support bar he was holding.

Dave grinned. "Pleasure to meet you, sir. I'm Detective David Barton, Tucson Police, and you are under arrest."

Nine months later, almost nine months after Carrie Oates died in the ICU without regaining consciousness, Mack's ringtone—three bars from *Aretha Franklin Live at Fillmore West*—sounded in the otherwise silent office. Mack sighed and looked up from the motion she was drafting. Every fire she'd ever had to put out had started with a phone call—anything that couldn't be handled with an email was guaranteed to be bad news. She checked the time on her computer. It was almost four, and—although she'd already had a grueling ten-hour day of hearings, meetings, and trial prep—she was still on the clock.

"Wilson," she said, picking up the receiver. She took off her glasses and rubbed her sore left temple.

"Hey, Mackenzie. It's Dave."

She was happy to hear her friend's voice. The levelheaded and meticulous detective was one of her favorite people to work with, and she was looking forward to having him by her side through Joseph Smith's trial. "What's up?"

"Well, I've been reviewing the Smith case, and I think we've got a problem."

She sobered immediately. "One that's easy to fix, I hope. We start jury selection next Thursday. We owe it to Carrie's memory to make this stick."

Dave's long pause made Mack nervous.

"I was looking at the indictment," he said at last, "just making sure I knew which counts matched which offenses, and I happened to notice his date of birth."

"Yeah?"

"Well, it says he was born in April. But I know that's not right, because when I interviewed him back in July, he'd just turned fifty-four a few days earlier."

"Okay." Mack pulled the black rubber band out of her hair and let blond waves fall around her face. She ran her fingers through them, trying to work out the kinks.

"So I pulled his booking photos from the first arrest twenty months ago and the second arrest *nine* months ago—and, Mack, they're not the same guy."

She almost dropped the phone. "Excuse me?"

"That first time he beat her up, patrol got him, remember? He invoked, so I never interviewed him, just talked to Carrie and Harper at the ED. But then last July, when we hooked him at the rail yard, that was the first time I actually *saw* him."

"Wait, wait, wait." Mack's mind raced as she scanned the case's history. She hadn't seen Smith after the first arrest, either; before the first hearing, Carrie'd recanted and the case had been dropped. After the second arrest—after Carrie had succumbed to her injuries and the case had shifted from run-of-the-mill domestic violence to a homicide—the only evidentiary hearing had concerned the autopsy results, and the assistant medical examiner had been the only witness.

"Come on, Dave, shit like this doesn't happen in real life."

He coughed. "It doesn't happen *often*. But you know, Mack, when I took him into custody off the train, he *told* us he had no idea what we were talking about."

Mack recalled the half-dozen hearings she'd had in the case over the past year. Smith wasn't a small guy, but he was middle-aged and soft. He had shown up more than once with fresh shiners or other injuries, but that wasn't uncommon for domestic violence defendants in the jails—other inmates looked down on them for beating up on women and kids.

The first couple hearings, he hadn't said much, just looked scared and pale, but Mack read in the police reports that he was coming down off a pretty serious meth addiction. After a few weeks clean, he'd started to assert himself in court. Mack heard him talking to his attorney, and he participated actively in the evidentiary hearing. He even showed a flash of the nasty temper that had gotten him in trouble in the first place, snapping at a deputy who took his elbow to guide him out of the courtroom and jerking away. Sure, there'd been a settlement conference at which Smith had claimed that he'd been wrongfully arrested, but Mack had seen that happen a hundred times. Smith was a three-time loser, and he knew what to say, both to the cops and to the court. None of it *meant* anything.

Unless he was actually innocent.

"So you're telling me," she said finally, "that the guy I've had sitting in jail for the better part of a year, the guy I'm about to ask a jury to sentence to death, is the wrong guy?"

"I'm pretty sure, yeah," Dave said. "Turns out there are *two* Joseph Steven Smiths in Tucson, born about six months apart. The guy they arrested the first time for beating on Carrie—her ex-husband—is a high-school dropout, has a juvie history for theft and assault, and had three felony drug convictions by the time he was twenty-one. Then he puttered around doing odd jobs and a fair amount of meth into his fifties. But the guy sitting in lock-up now appears to be squeaky clean. He served a mission in Argentina, graduated from ASU, and has worked for UP for twenty years. Divorced, no family here in town. When I did the database search looking for our guy, I got the wrong Smith, and no one ever looked back."

Unfortunately for Mack, she was included in that "no one." She had blamed this Smith's behavior on his meth use, his criminal history, and his reputation for violence. But what if it was all the perfectly reasonable response of a man facing the criminal justice system for the first time from the wrong side of the bars?

She could hear Dave's uneven breathing as she switched him to speaker, grabbed the file out of her briefcase, and flipped through it. She found the indictment, the suspect information summary that Dave had written, the defendant's first and second booking photos. She had never looked at the pictures side by side; she'd never needed to.

The dates of birth were six months apart. The photos were different.

"Jesus," Mack said. "I'm not sure where to *start* to fix this. I'll call you back when I have a plan."

She hung up without waiting for a response and dialed Smith's defense attorney.

"Robert, Mack Wilson," she said. "Listen, I think we've got a serious problem in the Smith case. Have you actually *talked* much with your guy?"

"Of course I—I mean, what do you mean?"

Mack rolled her eyes. It was *impossible* to have a simple conversation with this bumbling defense attorney, who should have retired years earlier. He guarded his clients' lunch orders as if they were national secrets.

"I believe that the Joseph Smith currently sitting in jail is *not* the Joseph Smith who killed his ex-wife. I think we arrested the wrong guy, and the guy you've been working with for most of a year is actually, factually innocent. He never told you that?"

The defense attorney chuckled condescendingly. "Well, Ms. Wilson, as you know, any communication from my client would be privileged, so, even if he *did* tell me that, I certainly couldn't—"

"Robert," Mack cut him off, "I don't need a lecture on privileged communications right now. This guy's been wasting away in jail, and a murderer is still out on the streets. Can you cut the double-talk and help me fix the situation?"

"I don't know what you think needs to be done to, as you say, 'fix' the situation," the attorney said, "but my client and I intend to go to trial next week and prove that he is not the man who killed Carrie Oates."

"This is a *strategy* for you?" Mack asked, her voice strained. She gripped her coffee cup tighter and watched her knuckles turn white. "This is this dude's *life* we're talking about. He's been beat up, he's survived on horrible food for a year, and you and I both know jail never changes people for the better. I'm calling Judge Thibodeaux right now and asking for an emergency hearing in the morning."

"I'm busy with other hearings in the morning, Ms. Wilson, and I won't be able to reach my client before court tomorrow to see what he wants to do."

"Then we'll do it without you, Robert. I'm going to set this straight, whether you help me or not."

She hung up and hunted for the phone number for the judge's clerk. Luckily, Annie owed her a favor and was happy to put them on the calendar. The judge, she said, could fit them in first thing. Mack called Dave and let him know that he needed to be in court, in a tie, by eight.

It took her the rest of the afternoon to sort things out with her chain of command. Her boss was livid, his boss was worse, and she didn't even want to *think* what the district attorney would say when *he* heard about it. She could see the massive dollar signs from the civil suit that was almost certainly coming, but it wasn't the government's lost money digging the burning pit in Mack's stomach. She prided herself on her record—kept a binder full of minute entries documenting her trial wins—but she prided herself more on her well-earned reputation as an ethical prosecutor.

On her very first day at the Tucson District Attorney's Office, Mack had been handed three things: a badge, an ID, and a laminated note card with a quote from the Supreme Court case *Berger v. United States:* "[The prosecutor] is the representative not of an ordinary party to a controversy, but of a sovereignty whose obligation to govern impartially is as compelling as its obligation to govern at all; and whose interest, therefore, in a criminal prosecution is not that it shall win a case, but that justice shall be done...[W]hile he may strike hard blows, he is not at liberty to strike foul ones. It is as much his duty to refrain from improper methods calculated to produce a wrongful conviction as it is to use every legitimate means to bring about a just one."

She had carried that card in her wallet ever since, and she was proud to strike hard blows without striking foul ones.

It was almost seven o'clock by the time Mack left her office, all her ducks in a row for the next morning. She would dismiss the case against the wrong Joseph Smith with a sincere apology and the phone number of the city's risk-management department, then return with Dave to the grand jury that afternoon to indict the correct Joseph Smith. Dave's colleagues would find him, and he would hopefully be in custody by dinnertime.

Mack went straight from the office to the gym. It took an hour on the treadmill at an uncomfortably fast pace before she could quiet the voices asking why she hadn't caught this earlier, how she could have screwed things up so badly, and whether this one mistake would ruin everything she had worked so hard to build.

Walking into her empty living room shortly before nine, Mack threw her gym bag, briefcase, and keys onto the couch and slumped down after them. She sank into the gray upholstery and sighed. She hadn't eaten since breakfast and knew she needed something, but it seemed like too much effort to get up and cook. Her eyes drifted shut, only to shoot open as her phone rang. She checked the screen and saw that it was Dave Barton.

"What's up, Dave?"

"You watching the news?"

"No, I just got home."

"Turn it on," he said, and waited as she shuffled through the stacks of paper on her coffee table to find the remote. "Channel 4."

Mack navigated to the local NBC affiliate. A booking photo dominated the screen. Mack recognized it—she had examined it closely, earlier that day.

"—the inmate who is alleged to have committed this brutal stabbing," the newscaster said, "Joseph Smith, was already being held on capital murder charges and had a hearing set for tomorrow morning. Back to you, Allison."

Mack turned off the television. "What the fuck, Dave?"

He sighed. "I'll tell you what I know, which isn't much. I got a call from a buddy about twenty minutes ago. Something happened with a guard—it's not clear what, yet—and Smith snapped. He had a shiv made from a toothbrush and a piece of wire, and he stabbed the guard. Really terrible. The guy died."

"So the Joseph Smith in custody, the one who wasn't a murderer—"

"—is a murderer now. Look, Mack, I've gotta go. I'll circle back with you when I can, okay?"

Mack didn't respond. She started to cry, softly at first, then harder as she began to appreciate the magnitude of what had happened.

What had she *done*? Her reputation, her career, two men's lives...

From outside her living-room window, she heard a faint whistle in the distance as the late-night Union Pacific to El Paso went by.

Maybe her mom had the right idea, after all.

Graceland

Released August 1986

"The Boy in the Bubble"
"Graceland"
"I Know What I Know"
"Gumboots"
"Diamonds on the Soles of Her Shoes"
"You Can Call Me Al"
"Under African Skies"
"Homeless"
"Crazy Love, Vol. II"
"That Was Your Mother"
"All Around the World, or The Myth of Fingerprints"

All songs by Paul Simon,
with the collaboration of Forere Motloheloa on "The Boy in the Bubble,"
General MD Shirinda on "I Know What I Know,"
Lulu Masilela and Johnson Mkhalali on "Gumboots,"
and Joseph Shabalala on "Diamonds on the Soles of Her Shoes"
and "Homeless."

DIAMONDS ON THE SOLES OF HER SHOES

Anthony Lee Head

"Jackie Boy, that rich girl just might be outta your league." Desmond—a gaunt Rastafarian with graying dreadlocks—leaned over the bar and frowned, deepening the creases in his mahogany face. "She could end up making real trouble for you."

Jack Robbins took a sip of beer and smiled. He had stopped by the Buffalo Soldier Bar and Grill for a quick drink and to brag to his friend about his latest score, a beautiful and wealthy young woman from the States.

The bar was a whitewashed shack hidden among the twisted streets above the town of Charlotte Amalie on St. Thomas. Tourists rarely ventured that far up the hill, but the place was the old man's pride and joy. And it was a second home to Jack, who thought of Des like a father—though he did act like a fussy mother hen on occasion.

Jack was twenty-seven, with a head full of dark Creole curls and skin the color of *café au lait*. His looks and smooth style had earned him the nickname "Jackie Romeo" among his fellow con artists throughout the Virgin Islands.

"You worry too much, Des. Why don't you let me handle the ladies, and you stick to running this joint?"

Desmond shook a bony finger in Jack's face. "Damn right,

I'm worried. You keep saying how rich this Mandy girl is, how she got diamond earrings and a diamond necklace. Next you're gonna tell me she got diamonds on her shoes, too. If she's all that rich, she might be smart enough to see you're out to con her. She ain't no dumb college spring-breaker. Why not pass this one by?"

"Because I got empty pockets need filling, and scoring with a girl without a pot to piss in won't pay my bills. Besides, I've been playing her along for a couple of days, and I'm about to set the hook. I'll let her help me out with my problem, and then send her home feeling good about herself. Just like I always do with those Stateside girls."

"And what's your problem this time? What'cha gonna tell her?"

Jack shrugged. "I'm not sure yet. Maybe I need rent money. Or maybe my momma needs an operation." In truth, his prostitute mother drank herself to death while Jack was still a toddler. "Don't worry, Des. I know what I'm doing."

Desmond straightened up and sighed heavily. "I hope so," he said.

Later that evening, back in his rented room above a small grocery store, Jack decided he'd go with the sick mother. That might get Mandy to come up with a couple hundred bucks, maybe more.

He took his best shirt from the closet, brushing it with his hand. It was a black silk Tommy Bahama. He had lifted it from an open suitcase in a hotel room, right after making love to the wife of the shirt's previous owner.

Finally, he patted a few drops of Hugo Boss #6 on his face. Looking into the cracked mirror on the wall, he smiled at his reflection. A clean shirt, some nice aftershave, and confidence were all he ever needed to fool the vacation crowd. Especially the women.

Stepping out into the sticky tropical night, Jack headed downhill. It was the start of the Carnival season, and half the people who thronged the streets were wearing masks or costumes. He pushed past a devil in a red cape to jump on the bus that would take him around the bay to the Broadway Beach Club.

The Broadway was the fanciest place on the sand. Its cloth-covered tables were scattered about a roped-off section of beach beneath strings of pink and yellow lights. Waiters in bright guayabera shirts delivered umbrella drinks as jazzy samba music drifted from speakers wired to the tops of coconut palms.

The club's manager stood in his red jacket by a small wooden stand, welcoming arrivals and checking off reservations with a fake smile. As Jack passed him, neither looked at the other, and no one saw the folded bill Jack slipped into the man's hand.

Mandy was sitting alone at a table near the water, waving to him. *She looks like a sunrise*, he thought, taking in the waves of blond hair cascading over sunburned pink shoulders, bare but for the tiny straps of her cream-colored silk dress.

She was about Jack's age but somehow seemed younger. Every time he saw her, she took his breath away. The things he could do with a girl like that in his life.

He mentally shook off the moment of enchantment. *She's a mark*, he reminded himself. *Stay focused.*

As he neared the table, Mandy jumped up and covered her mouth with her hands. "Oh, Jack," she said, her eyes filled with tears.

He eased her back into her chair and sat.

"Sweetheart, tell me what's the matter."

She reached for a napkin folded like a fan and blotted her tears. "It's my uncle George."

Mandy had told him all about her uncle, who had let her tag along on vacation while he did some sort of banking business down here. Luckily, the guy seemed to spend most of his time flying between the islands, leaving his niece behind and giving Jack a chance to make his move.

"Did something happen to him?" Jack tried his best to sound concerned.

She shook her head and took a deep breath. "No. But he found out about us somehow, and he's furious because—you know—because you're..."

Jack nodded. He knew all too well what the rich tourists who came to the island thought about locals like him.

Mandy tearfully continued. "So now he says I have to go back home. Tomorrow!"

Jack's heart dropped. He hadn't anticipated this, needed more time to work his magic. While he scrambled to come up with a new plan, Mandy went on.

"But I have an idea how we can see each other again," she said, wiping away a tear. "What if I ask my uncle for some money? I'll tell him I need to go shopping—to buy presents for people back home. But instead, I'll sneak away and bring it to you tonight. That way you can buy a plane ticket to come visit me in a couple of weeks. I could meet you in Miami or somewhere. Any place you want. Would you do it?"

Jack could barely keep from bursting out laughing. Desmond had been worried she'd catch on to him, and here she was, practically running the con *for* him!

"Of course, baby," he lied. "Nothing would make me happier."

They agreed that she would get the money, then meet Jack later at his friend's bar.

"What's it called again?" she asked.

"The Buffalo Soldier," Jack said. "On Commandant Street, near Krystal. Any taxi driver will know it."

This could be my biggest score ever, he thought. *And the easiest.*

Still, as he watched her walk away, he felt a twinge of regret. She was so very sweet. So very trusting. It was almost too good to be true.

Out on the street, Mandy flagged down a taxi. She settled into the back seat and took a cigarette from the pack in her purse. She drew smoke deep into her lungs, let it out with a long sigh of relief.

That should keep him out of the way for the rest of the night, she thought. The last thing she needed was to run into him on her way out of town.

Mandy had pegged Jack as some sort of down-island gigolo from her first day on the beach. She worried at first that he might be seasoned enough to figure out her scam. But that hadn't happened. *He's cute, but thank God he's not too quick.* He'd bought her story—every bit of it. He even believed that George was her uncle.

Still, Mandy had to admit there was something about Jack she liked. The boy had style. Under different circumstances, they might have really connected. But not now.

He's just another mark, she reminded herself. And it was time for her to move on.

It had been almost a month since she'd cozied up to "Uncle" George in that Atlantic City casino, doing her standard "I just lost my job as a dancer in the show" routine. Poor George was a classic target for the short con: a boring middle-aged accountant with a wallet full of cash and no idea how dirty the world could be.

Mandy'd figured on a quick fling while spending his money and hopefully grabbing a credit card or two on her way out the door. But her plans had changed when nerdy George invited her "down to the islands" while he took care of some client's investments.

A free vacation, with all the gifts Georgy Porgy wanted to buy his sweet Mandy girl? That was a no-brainer. She'd even used her real name this time. If he checked up on her, most of her rap sheet was filled with aliases like Merry Wilson, Lily Cross, and—her personal favorite—Betsy Greenwood, a now-destitute former prom queen from Ladysmith, Virginia.

It had been fun at first, but lately George was more distracted by his business than by her bedroom acrobatics. When he hadn't invited her along on his latest flight over to St. Croix, she knew he was losing interest. She figured to make one final move on George's checking account before he dumped her. To pull off this last score, she needed to be seen in public with a local hustler, and Jack fit the bill perfectly.

Mandy told the taxi driver to slow down and take the long way to George's fancy rental house out near Smith's Bay. "I want to see the ocean."

What she really wanted was to give the goon spying on her a chance to get back and report. She had noticed him following her earlier in the day and felt certain he worked for Lawrence, George's ever-present "personal valet."

Lawrence didn't look like a valet to Mandy. He was tall, with a bodybuilder physique and his ebony head shaved clean. He came across more like a cage fighter than a personal assistant. Whatever he was, the guy gave her the creeps.

She was sure that Lawrence had sent the peeper to follow her. In fact, she'd encouraged it, making a big deal of going out and not saying where she was headed. The scene at the Broadway would give some real weight to the story she was about to drop on George.

The taxi let her out in front of the manicured lawn of the large house. Walking up the crushed-seashell driveway, she saw Lawrence blocking the open front door.

"Hi, Larry," she said brightly. She always called him Larry because she knew it irritated him.

The big man stared at her, his face expressionless. "George is back. He wants to see you." He stepped aside. "Right now."

"I heard you," Mandy said, breezing by.

George was sitting on a couch near the living room's open veranda doors, his suit coat and tie tossed over a nearby loveseat. His pale face was wet with perspiration, and the few remaining threads of gray hair were plastered against the pink bald spot on top of his head. He had a tumbler in his hand, half full of booze. He gave Mandy a weak smile as she entered the room.

"Hello, my dear," he said, patting the cushions next to him. "Come sit by me."

"Georgy, I'm so glad you're here," she said, settling onto the couch.

"Really? I'm surprised. Lawrence tells me you've been spending time with some local boy while I've been gone."

"That's right," grumbled Lawrence, easing into an overstuffed chair.

Mandy was prepared. "You already know!" She placed a hand on George's thigh. "Thank God. I knew I could count on you."

George raised his eyebrows in surprise. "And what is it you think I know, Mandy?"

"All of it. About those awful men threatening you and me and everything. I was so frightened." She took a deep breath. "But you're here now."

"Threatening *me*?" George shot a questioning glance in Lawrence's direction before returning his attention to the girl. "I did hear that someone made you cry tonight. Perhaps you should start at the beginning."

She had been right: she *had* been followed. Now she just had to bring it home for the win.

She began to weave her story. "It was my fault, I guess. I went to town to hear some music. I know you said not to go out alone, but I didn't think anything would happen, you know?" She gave George a wide-eyed, tearful look. "The club was almost empty. Just me and this one man at the bar. I never even spoke to anyone. I listened for a while, and then I left. I was going to get a taxi and come straight back here, but—"

She stopped to wipe a tear from her face.

"But what?" George asked quietly.

"—but a man grabbed me. I screamed and tried to break free, but he held on. He shoved a badge in my face and said he was a policeman. Then he marched me to the side of the building and made me pour everything in my purse right onto the street. It was humiliating. And when I tried to tell him I'd never seen that plastic bag of powder before, he wouldn't believe me. That's when the other guy showed up."

"The other guy?" George looked over at Lawrence, who shrugged.

"The guy from the bar. He started doing all the talking, so I kind of guessed *he* was a cop, too. He was just awful, saying I'd go to jail unless I paid them the fine."

George leaned forward. "How much did he want?"

She almost sobbed. "Five thousand dollars. He told me to bring cash to the Broadway tonight. But when I got there and said I didn't have it, he made all kinds of threats. He said he knew I had a rich friend—he was talking about you, Georgy—and he'd have you arrested as an accomplice or something unless I came up with the money."

George seemed strangely calm. "Five thousand dollars is a lot of money," he finally said.

"I know. I mean, I could call my family back in Virginia. I think my Uncle Josh has some savings bonds or something, and I could—"

George spoke in a reassuring voice. "Don't be silly. I'll take care of this. The only question I have is whether we can trust these men to leave us alone, once we pay."

Mandy knew she had him hooked. He would be too scared to think of anything but getting away. "He *said* you'd want a guarantee. He said you should give me the money and leave the island, but I have to stay here. After you're safely away, I'll go and pay them, and then I can leave, too. He said it was like a trade, me for the money. But he said it has to happen right away."

George smiled at her for a moment. "Well, that's very brave of you to be willing to protect me like that."

Mandy dropped her gaze, pretending to be embarrassed. "It's the least I can do, Georgy. I'm the one who got you into this mess. I wish I'd never gone to that bar."

"I'm sure you do, dear. Well, I guess we'd better do as you say. Why don't you go lie down and relax while Lawrence and I make the arrangements to leave."

Upstairs, Mandy replayed their conversation in her mind. Everything seemed to be going as planned. As soon as George gave her the money and took off, she would grab a puddle-jumper for a nearby island. Or maybe Belize.

From the bedroom, she heard a car start. Looking out the window, she saw Lawrence pulling away. *That's strange*, she thought.

She hurried downstairs. George was in the room he used as an office, standing at the desk and putting papers into a large briefcase. Behind him, the wall safe was open.

"Georgy?"

He answered without looking up. "What?"

"I just saw Lawrence drive away."

"Yes. He won't be long."

"Shouldn't he be helping you pack? Where did he go?" Lawrence's disappearance bothered her. This wasn't part of her plan.

George looked up, a sudden hardness in his face. "He's going to find that hustler of yours and have a little talk with him."

Mandy froze. Her mind raced, tying to think of what to say next. Before she could come up with another lie, George moved around the desk and stood in front of her. He took one of her hands and squeezed it, hard.

"Sweetheart, did you really think I'd be so thrilled to fuck you I wouldn't notice when you tried to steal from me?"

It was suddenly hard for Mandy to breathe.

"Maybe you thought I was some suburban bean counter who'd run home at the first sign of danger." George gave a snorting laugh. "The truth is, I work for some very powerful people. They pay me to come down here and hide their cash where nobody can find it. And while I truly don't care about you being on the hustle, I can't have my employers hear I was rousted by a punk kid and a two-bit slut. That would be bad for my reputation."

Mandy pulled her hand free, but George kept talking.

"So you're going to stay here while I get out of town. And Lawrence is going to babysit you, to make sure you don't pull any more tricks until I'm home in Jersey."

Mandy started to shake, fear overwhelming her.

"Don't be scared. Lawrence may be crude, but I gave him strict orders that you get to walk away when this is over. Try not to piss him off, though. He does have a temper." George's grin broadened. "You're lucky I like you, baby. Things could have gone a lot worse for you."

As he turned away, dismissing her, Mandy's fear turned to rage.

"You bastard!" she screamed. Seizing a small conch-shell lamp from the desk, she slammed it against the back of George's head. The shell shattered, and George dropped without a sound.

Mandy stared in horror at the blood. *Oh, fuck!* she thought. *I've killed him.*

Her strength gave way, and she fell to her knees. Her fingertips touched the body—and George's eyelids fluttered. He moaned, and she saw his chest rise and fall.

Thank God!

She stripped his Rolex from his wrist, grabbed the wallet and money from his jacket and more cash from the open safe.

Within minutes, she was hurrying down the road, her sparkly sandals clicking on the cobblestones. She knew she would find a taxi at the nearby Margaritaville resort, and it would take her straight to the airport.

Then she stopped, suddenly thinking of Jack. Lawrence would hurt him. Or worse. She tried to tell herself it wasn't her fault or problem.

He's a grifter. Those are the risks of the business, she thought, and resumed walking. She could see the resort up ahead.

Goddamn it!

It didn't take long for the taxi to reach the Buffalo Soldier. She paid the driver and ran inside. Sure enough, Jack was sitting at a corner table, waiting for her like a faithful puppy.

"Baby, what's wrong?" he said, spotting the worry in her face.

"We don't have time for this shit, Jack. We have to go. Right away. I'm heading for the airport, and you need to hide."

"What are you talking about? Did your uncle—?"

She slapped the top of the table. "He's not my uncle. He's a guy I was trying to con."

Jack looked confused.

"Damn it, Jack. I'm in the game, and I was using you to fool a mark. But now I'm burned."

She spilled it all out, her words coming in a rush: George's mob connections, the danger they were both now in.

Jack's mouth opened and closed, but nothing came out. "What the hell?" he finally said. "How did this happen? I thought—"

"It happened because she is one dumb bitch."

Jack and Mandy turned at the sound of Lawrence's voice.

As Jack started to stand, the big man opened his jacket, showing the butt of a pistol pushed into the waistband. "Don't be stupid."

Jack settled back, and Lawrence slid into an empty chair. "Calm down. You two won't be the first shit-for-brains idiots I've blown away." He looked at Mandy. "I never did trust you. I knew the boss was thinking with his dick when he invited you down here."

"How did you know where to find us?" she asked, failing to keep her voice from shaking.

"The boy I hired followed Jack straight here after you left the Broadway." Lawrence grinned, but his eyes remained cold. "So, this is how it's gonna be. I ain't gonna kill nobody tonight.

But Mr. G doesn't want no loose ends. He wants to make sure it's only you two bozos yanking his chain. So you come with me and tell me the whole scam. If nobody else is involved—no cops or anyone—then you can go on your merry, fucked-up way."

"And if we won't go with you?"

Lawrence reached inside his suit coat. "Then I fucking shoot you both and fly out of here on a private jet with a damn drink in my hand." He stood up. "What's it going to be?"

Jack and Mandy looked at each other—and then, without a word, got to their feet.

Lawrence smiled. "Good choice. Now let's go. Not too fast. Stay right in front of me."

As they moved toward the door, Desmond came around the bar, a worried look on the old man's face. Catching his eye, Jack shook his head slightly and kept walking.

Outside, the three of them moved slowly down the empty street, Jack and Mandy's shoulders touching. Lawrence stayed a few steps behind.

"He's gonna kill us anyway," Jack whispered.

Mandy nodded.

"Be quiet," growled Lawrence. "My car's up ahead a couple of blocks."

Suddenly a group of people rounded the corner, filling the narrow street and heading straight for them. In front, men banged wooden paddles on tin buckets. Behind them came people in masks, feathers, and brightly colored costumes. Some waved flags above their heads, others blew on battered trumpets. Everyone danced.

Lawrence grabbed Jack's shoulder. "What the hell is this?"

"It's a jump up," Jack said. "A Carnival party."

Lawrence pushed him forward. "Keep walking."

They were soon enveloped by the whirling crowd. A large woman dressed in what appeared to be no more than a handful of colorful scarves threw her arms around Jack's and Mandy's necks. With a broad grin, she planted a kiss on each of their cheeks, then pushed between them and reached for Lawrence.

"Come here, big boy," she shouted, grabbing him in a bear hug.

Jack saw their chance. "Run!" he yelled and propelled Mandy forward.

Lawrence shoved the scarf woman aside as his prisoners disappeared into the mass of dancers. He yanked his gun and tried to aim. "Stop!" he shouted, shooting wildly as the crowd slammed into him like a wave.

People screamed at the sound of the gunfire and ran in every direction. Lawrence struggled to keep his balance but tumbled to the street under the onslaught of panicked people. The gun fell from his hand and was lost in the stampede.

"This way!" Jack grabbed Mandy's hand and tugged her down the street and through an alleyway to a deserted dirt road lined by dilapidated wooden buildings. He suddenly stopped, bending at the waist and gasping for breath. "Hold on. I can't breathe." He stumbled into a shadowed doorway and collapsed.

Mandy stood over him, glancing back in the direction they had come. "We have to *go*, Jack. He might be right behind us."

Jack moaned. "Can't. He clipped me."

"What?"

"I'm hit. I don't think it's bad. Just ripped me up a little on the side. But I need to rest."

Dropping to her knees, Mandy pulled at his shirt. She couldn't see much in the dark, but her hands came back wet. "Oh, my God, you're bleeding. We've got to get you to a doctor."

Jack shook his head. "No. That bastard's going to be searching for us. We have to stay out of sight for a while."

Mandy ripped the lining from her dress and pushed it against his side. "Lie down."

Jack lowered his head to her lap, and they sat there in silence, alert to the island's night sounds.

"Why?" Jack whispered.

"Why what?"

"Why'd you come back for me? You could have gotten away."

She leaned back against the brick wall. It took her a while to answer. "I don't know. Why did you get between me and the gun when he was shooting?"

But Jack couldn't answer. He had passed out from the pain.

"Come on, son, let's get you outta here. Wake up now."

Jack opened one eye and saw Desmond kneeling in the sunlit doorway next to him, fussing with the cloth stuck to his side by dried blood.

"Hmmmm. This ain't too bad." He looked at Jack and smiled, showing a mouthful of yellow teeth. "I'll take you back to my place. The doc's waiting for us."

Jack looked around. "The girl..."

"She ain't here."

Leaning on Desmond, Jack slowly got to his feet. "How'd you know where to find me?"

"That Mandy came pounding on the bar door this morning, yelling like a crazy person. I was up already, 'cause I was worried about you. She tells me you've been shot and where to find you. Gives me a shitpile of cash money, saying I should get you a doctor. Then she left. Said she was gettin' off the island as fast as she could."

"What about that rich guy and his pit bull?"

"Gone. My cousin Shirley out at the airport says they skedaddled in that fancy plane of theirs late last night. The little guy had his head all bandaged up. I guess they figured best to leave before someone started asking questions about the shooting at the jump up." Desmond's weathered face split in a broad grin. "You home free, boy."

Later, in a room above the bar, Jack lay on the lumpy mattress of an unpainted iron-frame bed. The doctor had called his injury a flesh wound, stitched it closed, and left a bottle of pills.

Desmond stood beside the bed. "You look like you hurtin' bad."

Jack yawned, beginning to feel the effect of the painkillers. "Nah. I just can't believe she ran off and left me."

Desmond opened his dark brown eyes wide in surprise. "You talkin' about the woman you tried to scam? The one who was scammin' you? The one almost got you killed? You moonin' over *her*?"

"No, no, of course not. But for her to leave without saying anything..."

"Oh, she mighta said somethin'." Desmond's eyes twinkled. He pulled a folded piece of paper from his shirt and held it out. "I found this in one of your pants pockets."

Jack took the note and opened it.

We could make a good team. The Coconut Bar, Royal Bay Resort, Ambergris Caye in Belize. I will wait two weeks.

It was unsigned but for the imprint of a kiss in bright red lipstick.

Desmond leaned over to read the note. "Ooo-oo-oo," he said softly. "Now that there is some kind of woman." He grinned at Jack. "You best not let her get away. You know what I'm talkin' about."

Jack rested his head on the pillow and smiled. He knew exactly what the old man was talking about.

He knew he was going to Belize.

The Rhythm of the Saints

Released October 1990

"The Obvious Child"
"Can't Run But"
"The Coast"
"Proof"
"Further to Fly"
"She Moves On"
"Born at the Right Time"
"The Cool, Cool River"
"Spirit Voices"
"The Rhythm of the Saints"

All songs by Paul Simon,
with the collaboration of Vincent Nguini on "The Coast"
and Milton Nascimento on "Spirit Voices."

PROOF

Kristin Kisska

HIM

I've been killing my second wife for a year, and she doesn't know it.

My red Labrador retriever sits patiently wagging his tail as I pour a mug of coffee and add a dollop of vanilla creamer, just the way Lisa likes it.

"Don't worry, Rusty," I tell the dog, "we'll head out in a minute. Go get your leash."

Rusty goes, like the good hunting dog he's always been. He's accompanied me on every kill I've ever made, even this one...the slow kill.

Most of my prey ends up stuffed and mounted on the walls of my study. My prize trophy is the head of a fourteen-point buck. He spooked as I fired, so I missed the clean shot, but Rusty and I chased him until he collapsed.

As I do each morning, I deliver the steaming cup o' joe to Lisa's nightstand and open the shades to let sunlight into our bedroom. "How are you feeling today, my darling?"

She groans. Perfect. We're almost there. I can *feel* it.

Rusty's waiting for me at the front door, and we step out into a glorious Wisconsin spring morning.

***

Our home is on a large lot with pond views from the balcony. No one around for miles.

Privacy is underrated. My sons get it. Both of them moved away after college, got married, and established their own lives. We see them once or twice a year, tops.

My stepdaughters didn't get the memo, though. When Lisa and I married, nine years ago, they were still in high school, so I understood they'd be dependent runts for a little while. But Lisa can't seem to cut the fucking umbilical cord. One of the girls is always between apartments, between jobs, between boyfriends, and we wind up with a goddamned revolving door of squatters who eat my food, lounge on my couch, and get in my way. Man, that was not the deal we made, and my patience wore thin *years* ago. If I'd only known what I was in for, I'd have avoided the whole blended-family thing from the outset.

At the moment, however, we are empty-nesters, and I plan to keep it that way.

I trek down the gravel drive, Rusty trotting at my heels. We'd give anything to be forging new trails through the trees and checking my traps for small game. Instead, I wave at commuters and say good morning to everyone I pass.

I refuse to limp, so I perfected faking a normal gait years ago. Goddamn missing toes.

After a while, we turn around and head home. I'm running late for work.

HER

Steam rises from my mug. The warm scent of vanilla creamer fills the air, and I crave a sip, just a little one. But I don't dare. Instead, I wait for JT and Rusty to leave on their usual morning walk. Then I hop out of bed.

I've been feeling so *good* these past weeks. I didn't always live with debilitating pain, you know. In fact, the first years after JT and I got married were idyllic. This house was a safe haven from the hell the girls and I had survived.

But a year ago, the headaches started. The nausea. The tremors.

At first, Dr. Chenier ruled out the big worries—no cancer, blood clots, cardiac issues, or diabetes. There were so many scans, scopes, tests. I gave enough blood samples to feed a family of vampires. And JT stayed with me through thick and thin. He took off work and accompanied me to almost every medical appointment, a dedicated advocate on my behalf.

A few weeks ago, Dr. Chenier suggested I might be suffering from anxiety. At first, I was offended. How could all this physical pain stem from my mental state? I don't have the stress of a job. The girls are adulting. What did I have to be anxious about—other than my mysterious chronic pain?

But perhaps he was right. My health problems started soon after my mother's stroke. She survived, but she couldn't live on her own after that, so I relocated her from her Chicago condo to our spare bedroom here in Madison. We had three months together before her second stroke. That one was fatal, and my grief sent me into a tailspin.

When Dr. Chenier brought up the possibility of anxiety, I Googled strategies to minimize stress. I started practicing yoga and meditation, took Rusty on daily walks down to the pond, and went cold turkey on the coffee.

After weathering a wicked headache that I attributed to caffeine withdrawal, I've been feeling better and better, day by day. The pains have ebbed, my energy has returned to normal.

Of course, I don't want to hurt JT's feelings. He's such a creature of habit, and making my coffee is part of his morning routine, so I decided against telling him I would no longer be drinking it. But now, several weeks on, I'm ready to let him in on my secret.

The front door opens, and I hear Rusty dragging his leash

across the hardwood floor.

I slip into the bathroom to pinch my cheeks and smooth my tangled curls—and pour the coffee down the sink to prevent me from giving in to temptation later—then head downstairs.

"Good morning, darling," JT greets me. "You're looking well." He tilts his head, his smile softer than usual. "Are you feeling better?"

"I think I *am*." My statement couldn't be more of a mantra if a yoga master instructed me to repeat it with every stretch.

Outside the kitchen window, sunlight reflects off the surface of the pond like diamonds dancing.

"I've been feeling *much* more like myself lately," I say.

I kiss his cheek, and, as he heads up to dress for his workday, giddiness bubbles inside me. JT and I haven't been intimate in far too long. He's been so considerate of my aches and pains.

The seed of an idea germinates. I'll prepare him a lovely candlelight dinner tonight. Filet mignon, a rich cabernet. It's chilly at dusk, this time of year, but we can bundle up in blankets on the balcony and watch the setting sun.

It's not too late to rekindle our romance, is it?

HIM

Shit! Lisa ought to be getting worse, not better.

I double-check the Windsor knot on my power tie and button my suit jacket. Rusty follows me back down to the kitchen. I peck Lisa on the cheek and set off for my happy place—work.

It hasn't always been like this.

Eleven years ago, I was in my first term as treasurer for the state of Wisconsin, but campaigning for reelection was out of the question—I had far too many shady secrets in my past. Lisa's first husband, Scott, was working for me, and I was the whistleblower who started the dominoes falling. He was convicted of embezzlement and sentenced to ten years, and the day he donned that orange jumpsuit was the high point of my life.

I knew Lisa was innocent of any malfeasance, so I retained a lawyer to help first with her depositions and then her divorce. When the bank foreclosed on their house, I helped her find an apartment and a job. It was the least I could do.

But marrying her was never part of my plan.

Of course, neither was my first wife having an affair with a colleague and leaving me. At least our boys were both in college, so they didn't have to suffer the embarrassment of hearing their parents' divorce whispered about at every cocktail party this side of Lake Michigan. Meanwhile, the whore and her crooked lawyer bled me for every penny they could scrounge.

Lisa stepped in to console me, the knight in shining armor who'd saved her from her own devastation, and we married at Christmastime, three months after my divorce was finalized. She wore a dress trimmed in silver satin so shiny it looked like foil, and our reception was toasted as the social event of Madison's season.

I left politics and schmoozed my way into a managing director position at an investment bank downtown...a job that turned out to be tailor-made for me.

Everything was working out perfectly. Lisa's kids would soon be heading off to college, and she agreed to quit her job and stay home. I made that demand sound romantic, but the truth was I didn't want to risk another wife having a workplace affair.

Then Lisa's mother had that goddamn stroke, and Lisa insisted on moving her into our home. What a fucking burden. When my mother-in-law seemed to be on the road to recovery, I set things right the old-fashioned way: switching her meds caused a second stroke, and she didn't survive that one.

And then, one afternoon, I found Lisa snooping around in my home office. Well, screw that. I had too many skeletons hidden there.

I'm a hunter. I have guns. I could've ended it quickly and neatly. But they always suspect the spouse, so I decided to take it slow and began lacing her morning coffee with a sprinkle of pesticide. Brilliant plan. Since we live on the water, insect control is not only normal but expected.

The sicker she got, the more baffled the doctors became. I—the doting husband—insisted on escorting her to her appointments as often as I could, and I was able to steer the quacks away from testing her for poisons.

I *thought* I had her within a few months of a fatal collapse and have been relishing the prospect that, once she kicks the bucket, I'll be able to take her damn daughters off the payroll.

But now we seem to have backtracked. What the *hell* is going on?

As I pull into the bank's parking lot, I get a text:

Dinner on the balcony tonight, darling? Filet mignon?

HER

When JT leaves for work, I let Rusty out. The sky is flecked with signs of hope, and all I can think about is reviving our marriage.

Twelve years ago, my first husband and the girls and I relocated from Chicago to Madison for Scott's new job. Managing a scholarship program for the state of Wisconsin was too good an opportunity to pass up.

As exciting as the career change was for Scott, the girls and I felt like we were caught in a tornado: the chaos of moving to a new town, shopping for a house while selling our old one long-distance, enrolling Karen and Kim in school...not to mention managing my aging mother's care back in Chicago.

A year later, when we were finally beginning to feel settled into our new lives, Scott's arrest blindsided me. He was charged with embezzling from the scholarship fund, and the judge denied him bail. Our bank account was frozen. We lost the house. My perfectly crafted life shattered into smithereens.

The first time I took the girls upstate to visit Scott in prison, they sobbed the entire way home. My heart broke for them. How could I tell them why their father had become a thief, when I couldn't even explain it to myself?

The three of us would've been homeless and destitute had it not been for JT. He helped me find a job, an apartment, and a lawyer to defend me against a charge of complicity. The divorce was the frosting on the putrid cake my life had become.

Another year went by, I found my groove as a single mom—and then it was my turn to support my rescuer through his own scandalous divorce. That we fell in love was serendipity.

My new husband became my world. He asked me to quit working, and that was fine with me. I didn't mind staying home, like a half-moon hiding in the clouds.

At first, though, the demands of JT's position at the bank bothered me. While I spent evenings with my daughters, he was off wining and dining clients. On weekends, he'd be gone for hours on end with Rusty, hunting.

When the girls went off to college, I was left with nothing to keep me occupied. Who could blame me for letting them move back in when they need a place to stay, especially after all the trauma they'd survived?

When I started feeling so dreadfully ill, JT took over the grocery shopping and other household chores. I stopped attending my book-club meetings and turned into something of a hermit.

That's all about to change, though. I'm feeling *so* much better. It's time to reclaim my life.

Starting with my beloved husband.

My cell phone rings. My heart does a backflip when my screen shows that it's Dr. Chenier's office calling.

"The results from your hair and nail samples came back from the lab," a nurse tells me. "You have high levels of toxic heavy metals in your system, including arsenic."

***

HIM

Dammit, I was so close! How the *hell* could she be recovering?

Hoping my eyes have fooled me, I find my reading glasses and reread Lisa's text.

The last thing I want is a romantic dinner with her. I'll have to play this very carefully, keep up the appearance of the adoring husband.

Great, I type. *Should I pick up some tiramisu?*

What the fuck is going on? I guess I'll have to slip her a bigger dose of arsenic. Or, better yet, maybe there'll be an "accidental" misfiring when I clean one of my rifles. That happens around these parts, not every day but often enough.

The sooner the better, really. Maybe even tonight.

God help me if she's been snooping again. Under no circumstances can I let her learn the truth about what I've been up to, all these years.

An idiotic oversight on my part. For God's sake, I'm a *banker*. I should've hidden the documents someplace more secure, like a lockbox. First thing in the morning, I'll bring the file to the bank. Or just destroy its contents. It's not like I need that shit anymore.

Lisa has no fucking clue about the nightmare I endured as a kid. All I had to do to leave my ugly past in that loathsome little town behind me when I went off to college was substitute my initials for my given name. It was as simple as that.

And by tomorrow, my trail will be clean.

HER

"Rusty? Fetch your leash. We're going for a walk."

I stumble into my closet, searching for my sneakers. All I can find are my black lizard boots, but who the hell cares?

Arsenic?

So much for the doctor's anxiety theory.

My poisoning can't be of environmental origin because JT has remained healthy. The only difference in our diet is our coffee: he drinks his black, and I've always taken mine with creamer.

And that, of course, must be the explanation: my darling husband has been lacing my vanilla creamer with a deadly poison, has been murdering me for—is this even possible?—for an entire year.

But *why*?

Rusty is at the front door, his tail wagging, his leash dangling from his mouth.

As I reach for the knob, a memory surfaces of the one time JT ever yelled at me.

Is it possible that—?

I about-face and head upstairs to his study.

Shivers rush up my spine as I venture inside. JT's home office is off-limits, a private sanctuary I've rarely entered—usually only to surprise him with a cup of tea or alert him to a phone call. The mounted animal heads creep me out, especially the buck with its rack of antlers. Poor thing.

I step behind the desk, and Rusty—the only *living* creature in the room—waits on the threshold, wondering why we aren't heading outside. "Hang on, buddy. I'll be with you in a minute."

The mahogany desk's surface is pristine: calendar pad, green glass banker's lamp, pen-and-pencil set, each perfectly positioned. I open the top drawer, but all I find are pens and blank notepads.

As I slide the drawer closed, a glimmer catches my eye.

A small key. It couldn't possibly fit the locked credenza behind the desk, could it?

It does.

Inside the credenza hang a dozen file folders, each with an innocuous typed label—except for the last one, on which the word "TOES" has been handwritten in JT's distinctive capitals. I open it and find a yellowed newspaper clipping in a plastic sleeve.

The headline reads, *Football Player Fined While His Victim Recovers*. The photos that illustrate the article make my heart jolt: it's Scott and JT, their faces impossibly young. I scan the article and see that the journalist has used JT's given name—James.

So Scott's and JT's paths crossed when they were teenagers?

I read on, and my pulse quickens with each sentence. My two husbands apparently attended rival Chicago high schools, and, one early spring day at the beach, Scott bullied JT—who swam out into frigid Lake Michigan to escape the torment and ultimately lost two toes to frostbite.

Scott was found guilty of assault and fined two hundred dollars, an amount that seems trivial considering the harm he inflicted.

Why has neither of them ever told me *any* of this?

There are more documents inside the TOES folder: pages of journal entries and photos recording JT's revenge. The time he slashed Scott's tires and keyed his car. The anonymous complaints to Scott's previous boss. The internet trolling. Each action itemized, as if JT was adding notches to his ego's totem pole.

Then come page after page of the scholarship fund's bank statements, with certain payments highlighted, transfers to an account number I don't recognize—though I realize it *must* be an account JT established in Scott's name.

The enormity of it hits me like a sledgehammer: *JT framed Scott.*

A wave of dizziness washes over me. Fragments of conversation swirl in my head like miniature tornados. Missing toes, a job offer that was too good to be true—the pieces fit together like a jigsaw puzzle.

JT didn't marry me because he loved me. He was enacting an elaborate revenge against Scott, and the girls and I were just collateral damage.

And next I find the life-insurance policy Scott took out on me, with its exorbitant payoff in the event of my death. So *this* is why JT has been killing me? For *money*?

Ice pours through my veins. Just yesterday, my heart beat only for JT. How can I have fallen for his lies for all these years?

I turn away from the damning folder and find myself staring into the glassy eyes of the buck's head mounted on the wall above me.

At our romantic dinner tonight, it would be easy to lace JT's wine with a lethal dose of the same pesticide he's been giving me. But that would be too quick. Too merciful.

Instead, I fish my cell phone from my pocket and begin to take pictures. The authorities will be very interested in what I've discovered.

I return the documents to the TOES folder and lead Rusty downstairs and out to my car.

Until today, I didn't even have so much as a suspicion of JT's treachery.

But now I have *proof.*

Songs from The Capeman

Released November 1997

"*Adios Hermanos*"
"Born in Puerto Rico"
"Satin Summer Nights"
"Bernadette"
"The Vampires"
"Quality"
"Can I Forgive Him"
"Sunday Afternoon"
"Killer Wants to Go to College"
"Time Is an Ocean"
"Virgil"
"Killer Wants to Go to College II"
"Trailways Bus"

All songs by Paul Simon,
with lyrics cowritten by Derek Walcott.

THE VAMPIRES

Raquel V. Reyes

"'Buela, why did you get that tattoo?"

My grandmother put her hand over the faded red drops on her neck. "It's a birthmark," she said.

The Sunday evening talent show was on. 'Buela and her boyfriend—not my abuelo pero kinda my abuelo, they'd been dating for like all my life—hate-watched it like a religion.

"When are you going to tell me the truth?" I asked. "I'm nineteen y tengo tres. I know a tattoo when I see one." I flashed the Puerto Rican flag tattoo I had above my heart.

She stared at the Marc Anthony wannabe on the screen and commented: "Ese canta como si le estuvieran jalando los huevos." Even though I knew she was avoiding answering me, I laughed. The guy *did* sound like someone was squeezing his balls.

Sal—short for Salvador, like the country he'd escaped from—leaned toward me. "She got that tattoo because she killed un hombre malo."

"Callate la boca." 'Buela slapped Sal's bicep so hard his chain bounced on his chest.

Sal gave me a "my bad, drop it" look. I got a Presidente from the fridge and handed it to him. He rolled the cold beer over the handprint on his arm before twisting the cap off.

* * *

I signed in at the rec center, put on my name tag, and sat behind the registration desk. A whiff of chlorine wrinkled my nose, and a drop of water landed on my clipboard. The old lady at my window looked like a light bulb. The hair under her white swim cap was big and spongy.

"Where's Ricky? There's a mojón in the pool."

"Voy." I put the Be Right Back sign out. *Damn fifth graders and their stupid TikTok pranks.* I followed her to the pool. Ricky, the clean-shit-up guy, was usually taking a smoke break, aka hiding in the back alley with a wooden wedge keeping the door from locking him out. I didn't blame him. He didn't get paid enough for what he had to deal with. The afterschool kids were animals that left trails of litter, puke, and glitter glue in their wake.

I got the pole net and scooped out the offending floater.

"It's a Snickers. No te preocupes, you can keep swimming."

I heard cusses from the Ladies Laps women and laughter from behind the folding bleachers. The pole clanged on the tile when I dropped it.

I grabbed Yandel Vega by the collar and pulled him into the open. "Give it," I demanded.

"I didn't do nothing." Yandel, twelve years old, tried to slide his phone into his pocket.

"*Give* it." I put my hand out. "Unlock it."

"Come on, Xiomara. It's *funny*. Don't be like that."

"Like what? Show some respect, pendejo. You're not even suppose' to be in here. Women only from six to eight." I took the unlocked phone and deleted the video, but not before watching it. It *was* funny. A lady, not the light-bulb head, swam into the mini brown log. It hit her forehead, and she back-paddled herself to a bobbing stop like an Olympic water ballerina. The camera zoomed in on her disgusted face. She looked around, shouting expletives in Spanglish.

That's when I saw it. She had a tattoo just like my abuela's.

"Go apologize," I commanded.

"For what? I didn't do nothing." Yandel puffed out his chest like his asshole older brother, Carlos "Apache" Vega.

I pushed the kid over to the group and laid a hand on his right shoulder.

"Tell them," I said.

"Tell 'em what? I didn't do nothing."

I pinched Yandel's trapezius until he remembered his manners.

"I'm *sorry* my Snickers fell in the pool."

"Dude, don't play like that." I glared at him.

A woman from the back of the pack, the one from the video, advanced. She had a don't-fuck-with-me energy that radiated off her glistening still-fit-at-fifty body, which didn't sync with the cartoon coqui on her swim cap.

Yandel stepped on the toe of my kicks as he tried to escape. I held him in place and jutted my chin for him to apologize properly.

"I'm sorry I punked you," he said at last.

"And I won't do it again," I prompted, and he repeated.

I told the ladies he'd be helping Ricky clean bathrooms the rest of the week.

"Ah, don't be a b—"

He didn't get to finish his insult. The women attacked him with scolding words and warnings, their chorus of Puerto Rican, Dominican, and Cuban accents reverberating off the tiles.

"I'm gonna hold onto your phone until your moms gets here," I said.

"You don't need to tell my moms. Damn!" The kid was regretting his foolishness.

As the women got back in the water, I heard one of them say something like, *I hope he don't turn out like Apache.* Another added, *He's worse than his pops.*

Everybody knows everybody's business on the block. We all knew Yandel and Carlos shared a father but had different mothers. And that Carlos's mom wasn't around, but that's where he'd gotten his nickname: she'd left him a four-foot statue of a chief, who he told people was his grandpa. But we all knew it was fake as fuck. It was just like the ones you could get at the botanica.

Yandel's mom, still in her MTA uniform, dragged herself into the center around eight, asked him if he'd done his homework and kept out of trouble. She seemed like a good person, trying her best with no help from the other parent. Carlos and Yandel's dad was a sleaze who sat on the stoop all summer and called every girl who walked by in short shorts a mamacita. *As if!*

I felt bad for her. I didn't want to tell her that her son had behaved like a little shit.

"Hey, Mami, I need you to sign this incident report," I said.

"What he do this time?" She narrowed her eyes at Yandel. "What'd you do? Carlos better not have put you up to it. That's it. I'm done. I'm not sending you to your pop's no more. Qué clase de mierda. Y Carlos es igual. He turned out just like his father. I don't want that for you."

"It was a stupid little prank, but, um, he had a problem apologizing." I handed her the confiscated phone. "I've got him helping Ricky for the rest of the week."

"Make it a month," she said. Yandel kicked the wall but didn't back talk.

An ambulance wailed by as they exited. The sound bounced in the hallway as the double doors swung closed. It had faded down the street by the time an OG came through with a knee brace and a duffle bag. He was a regular at the pickup game that was just getting going in the gym.

"Rosa, Rosa, flora ma' linda," he said.

I followed his gaze. He was talking to the woman coming out of the shower room. The lady from the pool. The one with the tattoo like my abuela's.

"Where you been hiding?" he asked. "When you gonna let me take you to the club?"

I could tell they had history. She took his compliment about her beauty and strutted with it.

"I'm too much for you, viejito," she said.

"Who you calling old? I'm two weeks older than you."

"Yeah, but you're broke down, and I'm in my prime." She gave him a booty pop and a five-second twerk, and they both cackled.

"See you Saturday?" he asked.

"If you don't break anything. Watch yourself out there." She motioned to the ball court.

Her eyes were still on him as he walked away. She licked her lips and reached for the pen to sign out. "Mm-mm, Saturday. Sat-ur-day, come on and get here." She laughed.

"Hey, sorry about Yandel and the pool thing," I said.

"Pft. No hard feelings. He's still a kid."

"Can I ask you something?"

She signaled for me to go ahead and ask.

"Where'd you get that tattoo? My abuela has one like it."

I held my breath.

Rosa looked at my name tag and pronounced my name slowly. "Xiomara. You know that means warrior, right?"

I nodded.

"Who's your abuela?"

"Terri Ca—"

She cut me off: "Theresa Canals?"

I nodded.

She whistled and shook her hand, making her fingers and rings sound. "I bet she named you, one warrior to another. Like on Themyscira."

"Them-is-what?"

"The place where the Amazons live."

I shrugged.

She rolled her eyes. "Wonder Woman." She tsked. "Your abuela was like a superhero, like an Amazon warrior. She was so tough." She slapped her fingers again. "How's your moms? She still work at the hospital?"

"Yeah, she runs the breakfast crew in the cafeteria," I replied.

"You going to school?"

"Part-time, 'cause—you know." I rubbed my fingers together.

"What do you want to be?"

"Public health and urban planning."

Now it was her turn to look dumb, but I didn't roll my eyes at her. Most people have never heard of my major.

"It's like making the city better by making sure people's health and wellness needs are met," I explained. "So, affordable housing but also like services—access to behavioral health, addiction treatment. Even things like safe streets with better lighting, ya know."

"Oooo, girl, you got the right name for that. I like it. You're fighting for the community. Keep going to school. We need people like you. Mete mano." She put up her hand for a fist bump.

"¿Pa' donde vas?" my abuela asked.

"Out with Beba and Luz," I replied. I wiped the lipstick from my thumb where I'd fixed a smear.

"Tengan cuidado. Watch your drink."

"You worry too much, 'Buela. I'll be with my girls. We watch out for each other."

It was Saturday night, and there was a party somewhere. I mostly went for the music, but Beba went for the drinks and the boys—and Luz went for Beba. The girl had such a crush. Everybody could see it but those two.

The text Beba got sent us to a new place. It was still in the neighborhood, close to the river, but none of us had been to a party there before. It was a gentrification reno. We each gave a twenty to the guy at the door.

Inside the gutted row house, the staircase was gone. Against the wall, there was a stack of lumber covered with a clear tarp. Half a dozen people were sitting on it. Someone offered me a hit off their blunt, but I waved it away. The contact high was enough. I like to keep my head clear.

Orange extension cords crisscrossed the dusty floor to the DJ's station. Trap and drill were flowing from the speakers, and the three of us started swaying. Before long, Beba got thirsty and followed the red Solo cups to their source, with Luz puppy-dogging behind.

A couple of guys kept grinding up to me. The DJ noticed and dropped a hint by mixing in Bad Bunny's "Yo Perreo Sola." I gave him a head nod in appreciation. Luz joined me for the next song, and we danced.

"Where's Beba?" I asked into her ear.

"Talkin' to some guy," she replied.

I looked around to try and see who.

"Apache?" It didn't matter that the music drowned out my voice. Luz's disappointed face said she'd read my lips. I pulled her out to the cramped but quieter backyard. "What is she doing with him?"

"Pft. He has a bottle of Crown," Luz said. "I told her to be careful, but you know how she gets."

I side-hugged Luz. She bent her head onto my shoulder. I could smell she'd had a few beers. She sniffled and ran her finger under her nose.

"It's getting crowded," I said, "and somebody will probably call the cops soon. We should go. I'm going to get Beba. Yeah?"

Luz agreed.

I found Beba leaning against an exposed brick wall. Apache was pouring a glug of liquor into her cup.

"Chica, we're leaving," I said.

"She don't want to go," Apache said.

"Yeah, I don't wanna go," Beba said, with the beginnings of a slur.

They laughed. Apache slipped the bottle into his baggy jeans. He rested his forearms against the wall, caging in my friend. More laughter.

"Five more minutes," she said, poking her head out from

under his arm. "I got to finish my drink."

Apache looked at me and smirked. "You ain't her mom. Vete."

"We're leaving in five," I told her, then went to find Luz. "Come on. I'll walk you to El Chino, then come back for Beba."

We went through three hushed residential streets and then up a block of the boulevard. Chino's Cuchifritos was the only place other than the club that was open past midnight. It had two booths and a row of stools with a counter that looked out the big glass window.

"Get me some fries with the cilantro sauce," I said, leaving her to stand in line.

When I got back to the party, the vibe had changed. Everything felt darker. Even the music was more aggro. The place felt like it was about to pop off. Beba and Apache were not where I'd left them. At least I knew—with the stairs gone and no access to the other floors—he hadn't dragged her to a bedroom. I asked a couple of people if they'd seen them. The cannabis club on the lumber by the front door said they'd left a few minutes ago.

"Fuck," I said, and looked up and down the street. I hadn't passed them, so I took the chance they'd gone in the opposite direction. I jogged ahead and saw their shadows vanish around a corner. I ran and closed the distance.

"Beba," I called, when I got sight of them again. She was tripping over her feet a little and singing something. Apache took the bottle out of his pants and swished it in front of her. They stopped for a top-off.

My phone buzzed with a text from Luz: *Tired going home.*

I fired off a reply to wait: *Almost there.*

Luz was already typing: *See you tmrrw.*

"Fuck. Whatever."

When I looked up from my screen, Beba and Apache were gone. I checked the alley and half a dozen parked cars. "Where the fuck did they go?"

I called Beba's number, heard a faint ring, and followed it. It was coming from the park. I ran into the darkness.

"No! Get off me!" Beba's voice—slurred but strong.

"Bitch, you been asking for it all night."

I sprinted. I picked up the almost empty bottle of Crown beside them. With an upswing, I hit the back of Apache's head, and he rolled off her.

Beba scrambled away like a crab. Apache, stretched out on his back, moaned. I hit him again, swinging the bottle straight down, like an axe. This time, it smashed. With its jagged neck in my hand, I stepped back.

Apache was motionless. His pants were loose around his thighs, and one hip was out of his boxers.

"¡Ay!" I cried, when Beba grabbed my ankle. She wrapped her arms around my legs and sat there like a mermaid.

"Fuck, is he dead?" she asked.

"I don't know, but we need to get the fuck out of here." I looked at my friend. Her hair had leaves in it, and her makeup was smudged. I helped her to her feet. "Are you okay?"

"Yeah. Let's go."

We moved away from the tree. Dizzy from what had happened, it wasn't until we were on the sidewalk that I realized I was still holding the broken bottle.

"Xiomara?"

Beba and I turned toward my name and saw Rosa standing there.

"Xiomara, que paso?" she asked.

I blinked.

"Where's the rest of that bottle?" she asked.

I nodded over my shoulder. She went to see and came back quickly. She took off her short jacket and had me drop the neck into it. She wrapped it carefully and told us to follow her.

Her apartment was a block away. In the tiny walk-up, she put a pot of coffee on the stove and sent Beba to the bathroom to clean up.

"What happened?" Rosa asked.

I watched as she carefully scrubbed the jagged glass weapon with soap. "What do you think? Apache got my friend drunk and wouldn't stop when she said no."

"How far did he get?"

"Not far. I got there in time."

"Who saw you?"

"Nobody. The park was empty."

"Who saw you before that?" Rosa poured coffee into a mug of hot milk and mixed in a heap of sugar. She transferred half of it into another cup and put it in front of me. Beba came out of the bathroom and sat beside me. Rosa handed her the other mug. "Drink. Who saw you before the park?"

"Everybody at the party, I guess." I took a sip. "Beba left with Apache, and I went looking for her."

"So no one saw the three of you together?"

"No."

"What about you?" Rosa asked Beba.

"I don't remember," she answered. Her eyes were downcast, her voice small.

"Nobody saw them," I said. "There was nobody on the street, and I left the party alone."

"Good. Now listen. The two of you left the party together and came to my place"—Rosa looked at the clock—"at one. I made you coffee and walked you both home. Do you understand?"

We both shook our heads.

"What about—" I began to ask.

Rosa cut me off and said she'd handle it.

Two months passed, and nothing happened. There was no sign of Apache, dead or alive. It was like he'd vanished.

There was one rumor—somebody said they saw him with some Irish kid over in Woodlawn Heights—but that was all.

I saw Rosa every week at the rec center. She always asked me about college and my grades. It was like she'd adopted me or something. In my head, I started calling her Titi Rosa, like she was my tia. Mami didn't have any sisters, so it felt kinda nice to have an auntie. But then she'd ask me if anybody'd been talking about Dracula—that was her code name for Apache—and I'd remember what brought us together.

After six months, Rosa said the coast was clear and we could breathe. She invited me to her apartment on a Sunday. When I got there, I was surprised to see my abuela at the table, drinking a cerveza. Three other women were there, too. They were all about the same age, and they all had matching bitemark tattoos.

"Welcome to the Vampires," Rosa said.

"The what?"

"Siéntate, nena." 'Buela pulled out the chair beside her.

A woman in a muscle T with a fresh fade took the seat on my other side.

"We're the Vampires," Rosa said. "We stand for the neighborhood."

The woman with the fade took out a tattoo pen and a packet of single-use ink.

The ink was red.

You're the One

Released October 2000

"That's Where I Belong"
"Darling Lorraine"
"Old"
"You're the One"
"The Teacher"
"Look at That"
"*Señorita* With a Necklace of Tears"
"Love"
"Pigs, Sheep and Wolves"
"Hurricane Eye"
"Quiet"

All songs by Paul Simon.

LOOK AT THAT

Mark Bergin

"So to get into his Bitcoin account, we'd need his face?" I asked, nodding out the window at the beach house where our suspect was hiding.

"His actual face, Brooke," John Higgins, big-shot undercover DEA agent, mansplained. "Not a picture, but his *skin*. And it's not Bitcoin but a different cryptocurrency called Biizi. With two i's."

Actually three, I thought, *you pompous ass.*

"Cryptocurrency?" I said innocently, baiting him. I even batted my eyes.

"Cryptocurrency is electronically transferred fund sharing. It's intrinsically worthless, but it has the value that you give it. Like if I pay you in Mars bars, but you *like* Mars bars, then it's okay."

I could see him puff up and look right over little old me as he lectured.

He sipped at the beer he'd insisted on buying—as, he said, part of our cover here at this pier bar, a hundred yards across the surf from the rental cottage where Fernando "Fred" Aguila, the drug deal's moneyman, was holed up.

I was raised here in the Outer Banks and have been a Kitty Hawk cop for five years, so everyone within a radius of five miles except the tourists knows me—which made Higgins's attempt at a cover kind of pointless.

But it was his dime—his request for our department's assistance had got me picked to sit and watch him stare out a bar window grainy with salt spray from the waves below—so we were playing by his rules.

Actually, it was kind of like a date, only with guns.

I leaned into his field of view and said, "You *know* we could just watch the camera feed, right, John? The pier cam we set up, it's on the internet, shows the weather and fishermen and such. It also shows the houses on either side of the pier, including that one. It'll pick your man up if he comes out."

"*We* set up?"

"My family owns this pier—*and* the cottage we're watching. It's hard to make money in a seasonal tourist town, so we're into a lot of things." I started to turn and point to the cottage, but Higgins grabbed my arm and whispered, "We're on a surveillance, girl. Don't give it away."

I leaned back to pull my arm from his grasp.

"It's all family down here, right, Brooke?" Higgins said, spitting out *family* like it tasted bad. "Chief Stone is your dad, right? Maybe you should switch to ginger ale, or Daddy might find out you're drinking on duty."

"I already have, John. Mom's got me set up right." I nodded at the server in the U-shaped well behind the copper bar top.

Higgins raised his eyebrows. "Mom, huh? Your family owns this place, too? Kinda ramshackle, isn't it?"

"Things get beat up here on the coast. But we're thinking of expanding. Like I said, it can be tough to make a go of it out here, that's why we built those rental cottages. More income."

"So Mom's got the keys, right? That'll save us having to kick the door. One time I sprained my ankle going in fast."

You sure you didn't drop the ram on your foot, poor baby?

"*You* done any undercover?" Higgins asked, his knowing squint showing he assumed a negative response.

"Some, not much. Following known burglars and boosters, a

few stakeouts last year when we had some roofie cases—you know, tourists trying to get lucky."

"Ah, Rohypnol, the date-rape drug." He clacked my glass with his, as if welcoming me into the brotherhood of secret agents. "Takes away your will, your resistance, and your memory."

OMG, now he's mansplaining me on my own story. Can I squeeze your big agent arm, sir?

"So what about his face?" I said, getting back to business.

"His face unlocks the treasure," Higgins pontificated. "Seven million dollars, we think. See, the access system for the crypto is set to the imagery of the human face and is frequency-coded for the reflection of actual skin. Plus, Aguila has unique tattoos all over his forehead, looks like a Maori run over by a busload of graffiti artists." He smiled at his own cleverness. "Maoris are New Zealand natives, Brooke. They have tattoos on their—"

"So his face gets you into his system," I interrupted, sick of his self-important bullshit. "But what about his accounts?"

"Got the numbers right here." He tapped the breast pocket of the fishing shirt he'd selected to fit in with the coastal crowds—not noticing that *we* all wear hoodies over T-shirts and jeans. Mine was big at the waist to cover my gun and badge—and just the right amount of tight across my top, judging by the percentage of surveillance time he spent watching for action up there instead of over at the target's house.

"They're supposed to close the deal tomorrow. They rendezvous—that's 'meet up'—with an ocean-going cargo ship, using a chartered fishing boat that goes out from Manteo, which is just over the bridge from here."

"Yes, John, I know where Manteo is. My brother is an officer there."

Over his shoulder, I saw my mother's eyebrows go up. *Too much information*, her expression told me, and my lip curled to acknowledge her. I could have stuck out my tongue, for all the attention Special Agent Higgins was giving my face.

"Your brother's an LEO, too? Anyway, we have a team in Manteo set to go after the fishing boat, a raid team waiting a few miles inland, and two agents just down the road in case Aguila gets moving in that big fancy Jeep he's got. Nice ride, by the way. Awful lot of those down here, it's practically your state car. All jacked up with big tires and add-on parts—what's up with that?"

"They're fun, John, a way to show off. They can handle the sand, and we got a lot of that. I'd love to get one myself, but they're expensive. You take a Jeep, add a heavy-duty suspension, and change out the shocks and some transmission parts—hell, just the oversize tires and wheels can run two grand a set. Times five, that's another ten thousand right there."

"Five? Honey, cars take four."

Mom laughed silently at that but switched her expression to serious when he turned to order another beer. I popped exasperated eyes at her from behind him.

"Don't forget the spare, John."

With that, I closed him off from further consideration.

We sat, he drank, he watched the cottage.

And I planned.

After a quick run back to the station, I sat down at the bar again and ordered us a fresh set of drinks. When they came, Higgins left to offload some of the day's beer in the He Crabs, and I locked eyes with Mom down at the other end of the bar. She nodded and dropped a steel tray.

Everybody jumped and looked at her, and I leaned forward over Higgins's mug.

When he returned from the can, he took his seat and said, "What's that floating there?"

I about froze, then checked his eyes and saw he was looking not at his glass but at the cottage.

"There," he said, "that mist around the deck there."

"Hot tub, John. Sends up water vapor. Beach cottages all have one: the tourists demand them, so if you're setting up a vacation rental, you put one in." I turned and saw the tub's cover was up. Night was approaching, and a dim light inside the cottage backlit the steam rising off the heated water. "It's nothing."

"But what's the point? The ocean's right there," he said, waving a hand at the surf to emphasize.

"You expect *logic* from people who leave their own perfectly nice homes and pay good money to stay at somebody *else's*?" I drained my glass and motioned for him to do the same. "Well, their good money comes to us, so we give them what they want." I looked down at his empty mug. "What do *you* want, John? Another beer?"

He said yes, and we went on chitchatting for a while. Eventually, Special Agent Higgins snorted, lifted his chin off his chest, and decided maybe he wasn't feeling all that special anymore. When he asked if we have Ubers in our jackwater town, I said I'd drive him back to his hotel.

Late the next morning, Higgins got out of an Uber—yes, we do have them—and wove unsteadily toward the bar entrance, trying not to glance over at the rental cottage, where birds flew in and out of the mist over the back deck.

Not too slick, Secret Agent Man.

He stumbled getting onto his stool and countered Mom's offer of a beer with a muttered, "Coffee."

Mom suppressed a smile, and I could imagine Higgins wondering what had happened between him and me last night. *Did* something happen? Did the *big* something happen? Was it good for both of us?

Buddy, it sure would have been good for you, *if I'd stuck around instead of just dropping you off. And you'll never know just how good it was for* me *after I left you...*

"What are those?" he asked, nodding at the rental.

"So it's okay for me to look, this morning?" I glanced over my shoulder. "Turkey buzzards."

"You mean vultures? They eat dead things?"

"You're kinda city, aren't you, John? It's the circle of life."

"And they like hot tubs?"

I turned again, stared a moment at the cluster of heavy brown birds on the cottage's deck, then glanced at Mom. She looked stricken and walked back to the office, maybe to hide. Higgins rose unsteadily and moved to the window as a particularly large buzzard flapped up from the tub and wheeled toward our pier with something meal-sized clutched in its claws. It hovered for a moment, then landed on the boards outside the window, close enough for us to see that its meal was a stringy mess of tissue and bone, the size of a big sandwich or a small shoe.

Or a human hand.

Higgins raced out the door, heading back along the pier toward the dune and the cottage, his boots clomping on the wood. I caught up, and we climbed the stairs to the rental's oceanside deck.

The hot tub was set at the edge of the deck with a wooden roof cantilevered over it for shade, making a sort of cave now inhabited by a dozen cawing buzzards. They perched at the edges of the tub like diners at a table, and as I waved my arms to scatter them I couldn't avoid smelling the particular rotten-rubber odor all cops know and seeing the oily gray soup of muscle and sinew and chewed flannel and ripped denim that bubbled and churned in the water.

An eyeless, skinless skull bobbed in the center of the cauldron like a pool toy, batted back and forth by the pecking beaks of buzzards hungry for its insides but unable to break through the bone.

Two weeks later, Higgins came back to Kitty Hawk for follow up, and we met at the pier bar for a final drink. He was almost vibrating with fury but managed to hold himself in check until the first beer was downed. Then—

"Whaddya mean, it's not a homicide?" he shouted.

The other customers in the bar looked up, but soon went back to ignoring us.

"I just went to the medical examiner's office for a copy of the autopsy report on Aguila," Higgins went on more calmly. "It did not state cause of death and—with no apparent other person involved—did not declare the death a homicide. Or even suspicious!"

He waved the report like a checkered flag, then slapped it onto the bar atop his case file. "But you *know* he was murdered! Somebody messed with the hot-tub pump so it wouldn't cut off, and the damn thing *cooked* him. No soft tissue left, so no wounds to find, and no blood, so no possibility of a chemical analysis. What kinda town do you run here, Officer Stone?"

He banged his empty mug on the copper bar top, but Mom made no move to refill it.

"It's Sergeant Stone now, John." I lifted my hoodie hem and flashed the gold badge clipped to my belt. "And officially, Aguila's just an ordinary dead guy. According to that official report right there."

"No way. He was a dealer with seven million dollars—"

"Cryptodollars."

"Whatever dollars, they're gone now. We can't find the money or even *look* for it. His face is gone, so we can't crack into the system."

Higgins paused to wait for the carpenters outside to stop hammering on a new set of walls and planks extending the deck space around the bar out over the ocean. As their saws buzzed loudly and intermittently, I glanced through the autopsy report, pausing on the photos of the skull, glad Dad had warned me not to nick Aguila's jawbone and leave a possibly traceable mark when I cut his throat.

"The medical examiner's office is in Manteo," Higgins

rumbled. "Where your brother works. Did his guys on Manteo PD nail the shipment coming in?"

I got up and looked at him a moment, then shook my head and said, "Nope, it never *came* in."

Not officially, anyway.

"Drop it, John. It's over. I'm sorry it didn't work out for you."

I left the bar with Higgins close on my heels and walked down the pier toward my new lime-green Jeep Wrangler Rubicon with the modified taillights and the extra lift package, put a foot on the running board and climbed high into the driver's seat.

"This all worked out just fine for *you*, though, huh, Sarge?" he said, standing with his hands on his hips.

"Hey, hey," I said, "anything can happen here in the OBX. I've got to go, John. You take care now, hear?"

"Just a goddamn second," he growled. And then his voice turned plaintive and he practically whined, "What do *I* get out of this mess?"

I looked down at him, then reached into the glove box and tossed him a parting gift.

He caught it one-handed, read the label, and threw it away in disgust.

The Mars bar splashed in a puddle, ripples circling out around it.

"Well, look at that," I said, and drove away.

Surprise

Released May 2006

"How Can You Live in the Northeast?"
"Everything About It Is a Love Song"
"Outrageous"
"Sure Don't Feel Like Love"
"Wartime Prayers"
"Beautiful"
"I Don't Believe"
"Another Galaxy"
"Once Upon a Time There Was an Ocean"
"That's Me"
"Father and Daughter"

All songs by Paul Simon,
except "Outrageous," "Another Galaxy," and
"Once Upon a Time There Was an Ocean"
are by Paul Simon and Brian Eno.

ONCE UPON A TIME THERE WAS AN OCEAN

Andrew Welsh-Huggins

Once upon a time, Murray's job was a deal breaker.

Early on, he flat-out lied, typed in "financial services" as his occupation, which naturally garnered a lot of initial interest. Later, he just manufactured stories. He was in banking. He worked in investments. He did online trading.

Some women—the smart ones—gave up on him after exchanging a few messages, sensing a put-on, probably after failing to find him on LinkedIn. A few went so far as to meet for a drink or even dinner, but quickly saw through his vague responses and generalities and caught their own ride home afterward.

A very few, content with knowing they were being lied to, ended up back in his room, but one glance at the TV with actual rabbit ears and the hot plate on the counter where a stove should be, and they suddenly remembered a sick aunt or a dog that needed walking.

"So, no interest in being the love of my life?" he said to more than one woman's back as she retreated down the hall.

Eventually, Murray decided to just tell the truth. Figured it couldn't make things any worse, and maybe his honesty might count for something. "I'm a telemarketer for a collections agency," he explained, as soon as the question came up.

Okay, so the truth *could* be worse than a lie.

"How can you live with yourself?" was the most generous response he received. Two women told him they had relatives who'd killed themselves after being hounded by people like him and said they hoped he was proud of himself. He wasn't, but one thing was for sure: "I'm just doing my job" didn't appease that crowd.

Eventually, Murray gave up. Dishonesty, honesty, what did it matter when you ranked below even garbagemen and subway buskers in the eyes of the internet dating world?

Then he met Rochelle.

"You're from Rochester, aren't you?"

"I beg your pardon?"

A bleak, brown November day, nearly two years after he fled to the Big Apple with his tail between his legs.

The woman on the other end of the call repeated the question. When he didn't respond, she added, "I can tell from the way you said 'past-due balance.' Say 'I eat pasta at the plaza.'"

"What?"

"Just say it: 'I eat pasta at the plaza.'"

Reluctantly, Murray said it.

"Ow, my ears. Jesus, you sound just like my aunts. *Pass*-ta, like you're *pass*-ing a car. I can tell you upstate guys a mile away. Listen, I'm gonna be upfront with you. I don't have the money. I respect you have a job to do. I got no problem with that. But a fact's a fact."

"You do?"

"Do what?"

"You respect my job?"

"What I just said, isn't it?"

Murray hadn't seen himself as a cubicle guy when he hit

Manhattan, despite what had driven him there. He saw himself as more of a nightclub, pulsing-strobe-lights, tailored-suit-with-creases-as-sharp-as-carbon-fiber-blades kind of guy, the tough dude at the end of the rope line, passing judgment like a god— "You, *in.* You, *beat it.*"*—or the main man inside, meting out justice to the jerks, king of the bum's rush.*

Somehow, it hadn't worked out that way, surprise, surprise.

Turns out the clubs were serious when they said you had to be big to bounce, and no platform shoes in the world were going to push Murray much past five-ten. His way with words was not so impressive, either. "This is not a career path for Poindexters," the last doorman told him, right before throwing him out on his ass.

So he wound up spending eight hours a day on the thirty-first floor of a shiny new building near Navy Yard, placing call after call after call: This is in reference to your past-due balance...A payment plan is probably your best option at this point...Let's try to avoid taking this to the next level.

He was one of the lucky ones: by leaning back in his chair, he could just glimpse a window and, through it, a gray swath of the East River. On his lunch break, he grabbed a vending-machine egg salad or PB&J and retreated to the lounge, where he trolled the dating sites and licked his wounds.

How am I gonna get outta here? *he asked himself every day. Because slowly but surely, he was starting to heal, thinking about ways he might have done things differently that day at Ali Baba's. He even considered he might be ready to contact the Old Man and give things another chance.*

But every time, harkening back to how it had all played out, he decided to stay where he was. After all, nothing had really changed.

"Murray—you still there?"

"I'm here."

"OK, listen up. Hold on, is that your real name?"

"Uh, yeah?"

"You don't sound so sure. You guys have to use fake names or something?"

"No. That's my name."

"It's nice. Something to do with the ocean, right?"

"I'm not sure."

"I am. I'm into words and stuff. Anyway, I'm gonna assume based on your accent that you're at least somewhere *near* the city and not in, like, Bombay?"

"We're not permitted to divulge—"

"Because the thing is, I can *get* the money. I just need a little help in that department."

"Maybe a payment plan would be in your best interest."

"And maybe you didn't hear me, Murray. I said I need a little *help* getting the money."

"Right. And I said—"

"Listen, are you going to lend me a hand here, or what?"

"Lend you a hand how?"

"Help me get the *money*, like I said, some of which might also trickle down to you, if you take my meaning."

"I don't even know you."

"Ain't my name right there on your screen?"

He glanced at his monitor and saw to his surprise that she lived in Brooklyn. Not that far from him, actually. Rochelle Ransburgh, twenty-nine, single. Not the worst credit rating he'd ever seen, her current mess notwithstanding.

"I guess it is."

"So meet me at Bushwick and Pilling at six. Park Bodega. I'll explain it all then."

"Listen, Ms. Ransburgh—"

"Rochelle. They serve excellent Cubanos, even though the owner's Korean, so come hungry."

Before Murray could protest, she disconnected.

In the thirty seconds before the computer brought up his next call and automatically dialed the number, he stood, took a breath, and chastised himself for losing the contact so quickly. The lapse would show up on his status sheet, emailed each day at exactly 12:01 a.m., often the first message awaiting him when his shift began, oh joy. But he supposed there was nothing he could do about it, and he sat back down.

I respect you have a job to do. I got no problem with that.

What the heck. It was dinner out—of sorts—with a woman who knew exactly what he did and didn't appear to care. Maybe things were looking up, after all.

"The thing you gotta understand, Murray, is that Herman's a bad guy. I mean *bad* bad. You don't need to get your panties all bunched up about him conscience-wise, okay?"

"Bad in what way?"

"Bad like look what he done to my sister last week. Some fiancé. And this wasn't even the worst time."

As Murray took her phone to examine the proffered photo, he snuck another glance across the bodega's lone picnic table at Rochelle Ransburgh, twenty-nine, single, who was making good progress on her Cubano. A plus in Murray's book: he liked a woman who wasn't afraid of eating, not that he'd had much opportunity to test that theory recently. Maybe five foot, just holding her own in the battle between curvy and round, squeezed into a bright yellow dress and matching heels, with short red spiky hair that looked sharp to the touch and a brown face awash in freckles.

"Christ," Murray said, unable to help himself, staring down at the battered face of a woman who looked like a younger version of Rochelle if Rochelle had fallen out of a tree and hit seven branches on the way down and landed on a pile of bricks. "He did this?"

"With his own filthy hands."

"And she can't, you know, leave him?"

"Herman's not a guy you leave, you want to live to talk

about it after."

"I'm sorry to hear that. But what does it have to do with me?"

"Herman's got money, is what."

"Money?"

"A lot. Not *actual* money, mind you, but crypto money. Titcoin."

"Bitcoin?"

"*Tit*coin, Murray. Are you sure that's your real name?"

"I'm sure."

"If you say so. So, yeah, Murray, Titcoin is what Herman calls it."

"Why?"

"Because it's Bitcoin he gets in payment from guys who pay him for girls who nobody knows are here and who ain't going home anytime soon, if ever. He's a real charmer, Mr. Titcoin."

"It sounds bad."

"It is bad. Bad like what he done to my sister. But the good side is he has a lot of this currency. You know about it?"

"A little." More than a little, actually—they had a whole division that went after people whose debts were in crypto. Before Ali Baba's, he kept telling the Old Man they should look into it, to no avail.

"Good. Because if Herman goes away, we can get his Bitcoin and change it into *real* money. Then I can pay off what I owe and throw some your way—and, bonus, we can put a stop to the whole Titcoin thing."

"How does Herman go away?"

Rochelle stared at him, mouth full of sandwich, eyes as green as the first lilac leaves of spring. "You *make* him go away. Haven't I been clear here, Murray?"

"I do?"

"My sister may be beaten down, but she's not dumb. She knows all his passcodes. It's just they're worthless to us as long as Herman's around. But once he's gone: jackpot. So, yeah, you do. Whaddya say?"

Murray took another look at Rochelle, the first woman to share a meal with him in months who didn't look like she had ten other places she'd rather be, one of them cleaning her bathroom.

"I can't," he said slowly.

"Can't?" Rochelle said, indignantly. "Why not?"

"I just can't."

"You can't be fucking serious."

"Yeah," Murray said, swallowing.

"You mean, yeah, you can't?"

"I mean, yeah, I'm serious."

Twenty-five months ago. A dimly lit office in the rear of Ali Baba's. Running his first big errand for the Old Man. The job a simple one: send a message to that punk Ramsey, with his bleached-white designer hair and his tats and his piercings.

God, did the Old Man hate those piercings.

"Tell him to lay off the truck stops, pronto."

The Old Man had always had the truck stops, and his *old man before him, and they'd always kept things nice and tidy. Some packages fell off the back, some pills went south, some guns went north. No one any the wiser, and no muss, no fuss.*

Then, next thing you know, Ramsey makes a move on the truck stops, and there's trouble around the pumps from Day One, fistfights and hurt feelings and lots of shouting, and now the feds are showing interest and coming around the Old Man's house in Penfield asking what's what, and that's just not going to cut it.

"You tell that little ass-wipe bitch-made cock-gobbler to keep his hands off our real estate," the Old Man had rasped to his only son. "And you make no bones about it."

So Murray ended up here in the back of Ali Baba's—which hadn't been Ali Baba's Dining Hall and Banquet Center for twenty-five years but through unexplained circumstances had kept the name and the "For Lease" sign anyway—and told Ramsey to keep his hands off the Old Man's real estate.

Murray had come up with the idea of showing regard for Ramsey by going in unarmed. Except this turned into not such a good idea when the two muscle guys on either side of Ramsey's desk—a matching set of towering, clean-shaven Vikings with buzz cuts done with clipping shears—each produced a Desert Eagle and pointed it dead center at Murray.

"Nothing's ever different with you people, is it?" Ramsey said.

"Simple enough request," Murray said, giving it his best poker face, even as his testicles shriveled to the size of BBs.

"In that case, I got a counteroffer for the Old Man," Ramsey said.

"Okay."

"It's called 'The Day You Were Born.'"

"Okay," Murray said uncertainly, but feeling as if a counteroffer might have promise.

"Want to see how it goes?"

"Sure."

Ramsey nodded to Viking No. 1, who moved around the desk faster than you might expect for a guy his size. Murray didn't remember much after that. Except next thing he knew, he was stumbling down a street in the Old Man's neighborhood—which was not a stumbling-down-the-street kind of locale—bleeding here, there, and everywhere—and wearing nothing, not a single item of clothing.

"Naked as the day you were born, asshole," Viking No. 2 had told him, right before pushing him out of the rolling van.

Two days later, engulfed in shame, Murray was on a Greyhound to New York.

"That's why," Murray said.

"That's a nasty story," Rochelle said, polishing off the last of her Cubano. "You gonna eat that?"

Murray shook his head and pushed his half-eaten sandwich toward her.

"You're probably lucky to be alive, I'm guessing."

"Better off dead, you ask me."

"So you flubbed the job. I get it. I knew you a little better, I might suggest it was a big ask for your first time out and what happened is nothing to feel bad about. Also, bananas not to bring a gun. But I'm not seeing the whatchamacallit, the *nexus* between that and Herman. I mean, according to what you're telling me about your family background, just because you didn't carry that day don't mean you don't know how to handle a firearm. I got that right?"

"That's right."

"And you seem like you're doing okay now, right?"

He acknowledged that the time away from Rochester had given him an opportunity to reflect on how he might have done things differently.

"So life's about second chances, Murray. You don't always have to follow the map. You can go one way one day, another way the next. They ain't like mutually exclusive journeys."

"I suppose."

"So we got ourselves a deal?"

Turned out, they had themselves a deal. Murray couldn't put his finger on why he felt okay about it. But even after everything he'd been through, he still had some instincts left. The fact she hadn't resorted to a cliché like pushing a gun in a brown paper bag across the table at him, that was a good thing. That showed she respected him. And as odd as it seemed, he also liked the fact she hadn't promised to sleep with him in exchange for carrying off the job. That showed she respected herself.

He also appreciated that she didn't try to rush it. She told him Herman's address and routine and left it at that. So he took his time, acquiring a gun his own way and then familiarizing himself with the neighborhood. Where Herman parked his Montana-sized Ford Expedition. The routes people took, walking everything from Shih Tzus to Irish wolfhounds. What hour of the evening the most food-delivery guys whizzed up and down the street with their carryout Chinese and Mexican and Thai.

He also kept an eye on the weather, which is something you learned to do in the winter back in Rochester. And that's what cinched the deal in the end.

He executed on the night of the year's first big blizzard, three days after Christmas, snow falling two inches an hour—except it wasn't falling but streaking sideways in gale-force winds. Wrapped in a parka, face hidden beneath an itchy balaclava, he waited until Herman pulled up in his SUV and parked in front of his apartment in a space no idiot would ever dream of claiming.

"The fuck?" Herman said, when Murray materialized out of the swirling snow and showed him the gun.

"Yeah," Murray said, as the nerve he'd garnered from Rochelle's pep talk wavered.

"You have any idea who—" Herman said, thrusting his hand into his jacket, and Murray shot him between the eyes one exact second before it would have been too late. The storm swallowed the report of the gun like the sound of a leaf dropping onto an upstate lake. Murray knelt, found the casing, pocketed it, and plodded slowly up the snow-covered street and away.

The knock on his apartment door came a week later, as he sat on his sorry excuse for a bed and read the email one more time. His face burned as he reviewed the news it brought and the request his grandmother had made in that weird calligraphic font she preferred.

He pushed the laptop aside, opened the door, and looked down at Rochelle, rosy-cheeked from the cold, brushing snow off her coat.

"You gonna let me in, or I gotta stand here all night?" she said, but she was grinning.

Fact is, he was a little surprised to see her. A small part of him had wondered whether the whole thing was a setup, a way to take out an abusive future brother-in-law, with the cryptocurrency tale a side dish of hogwash. But no.

Inside, her coat drip-drying on the back of the door, he watched Rochelle set up her laptop, punch at the keys, and then swivel it around to him. A minute later, he stared in disbelief as a number with a lot of zeros behind it—a *lot* of zeroes—appeared on the screen of the account he'd opened at a bank situated near blue water and white sand and palm trees in preparation for this moment.

"I told you, didn't I?" she said, taking in his stunned expression. "Some for you, some for me, most for my sister, and no more Titcoin. You done good, Murray."

"Thanks."

"What's the matter? You look like you've seen a ghost—and I don't mean Casper."

"Nothing," he lied.

"You sure? I thought we were pals, here. You got something to say, say it."

"I'm sure."

"Well, then, listen up. I should be thanking *you*." She powered down her laptop, set it aside, and raised her arms over her head as if signaling a touchdown. "Help me with this, why don't you?"

"With what?"

"With taking off my sweater. My tea kettle's ready to whistle, Murray, in case you hadn't noticed."

Murray's bed creaked so much they gave up and dragged the mattress onto the floor and pulled all the blankets over them and added both their coats because the room was so cold and then humped like teenagers whose parents aren't due back until late.

"You sure you're okay?" Rochelle said, afterward.

Murray mumbled something inaudible.

"For a guy who just got done to him what we just did, you

seem a funny kind of blue. You don't like me?"

"I like you."

"Then what?"

Because he figured he had nothing to lose, and because of what just got done to him, he broke down and told her about the email. The news from home. The weird calligraphic font.

Ramsey hit the Old Man. That means you're *the Old Man now. It's time to come home.*

Only his grandmother would call her own son "the Old Man."

And now her grandson.

"This great aunt of mine does the same thing," Rochelle said.

"What?"

"With the font. Can't explain it. Like it reminds them of a handwritten letter or something. Listen, Murray, I'm sorry for your loss," Rochelle said, spooning into him.

"Thanks."

"You gonna answer? The email, I mean."

"You mean, like write back?"

"Sure, with a quill and inkpot and sheepskin. No, dumbass. Like answer in person. Go home. You can't take that shit lying down, present position notwithstanding."

"I'm not sure I can."

"You were sure about Herman."

"That was different."

"Different how?"

He had to admit he wasn't sure.

"You're not telling me this Ramsey guy is worse than Herman. You're not saying that."

"I'm not saying that, no."

"Listen, Murray. Hey—is that *really* your name?"

"I told you it was."

"I know you did. But you still sound just as not sure as over the phone that day."

"It's my name, okay? It's just not my *name* name."

"What the hell's that supposed to mean?"

"It's my middle name. It was my mother's father's name, and that's what she wanted to call me."

"So what's your first name?"

He hesitated. "Monte."

"Monte?"

"That's right."

"Whose name is that?"

"My old man's. But everybody called me Murray."

"Why?"

"Because my mom liked Murray better. And—"

"And what?" she said, flipping herself around to face him like a sunning seal changing places on a rock.

"And there can only be one Monte at a time."

"Monte," Rochelle said, touching her cold nose to his. "Like mountain. I like it. That's what I'm going to call you."

"Why?"

"Because that's who you are now. Ain't that what your grandmother said? You're Monte now, the Old Man. Monte the Mountain. You used to be an ocean, like Murray of the Sea. But now you're a mountain. Speaking of which"—she pressed herself close—"I think we have more work to do here, Monte."

"We do?"

"Yeah," Rochelle said, planting her lips hard on his.

"Come with me," he said, a few minutes later, catching his breath.

"I'm flattered, Monte. I really am. But I'm no Wonder Woman, despite what just got done to you again."

"No, I mean to Rochester. Come with me."

"Aw, Monte, that's sweet. But I can't."

"Why not?"

She put her hands on his face and drew him close. "I got my sister to watch out for," she whispered. "And I need to figure out how to spend all those zeros. This is where I belong. But maybe I can come visit sometimes. How about that?"

"That would be nice," Monte said, prizing how gently she'd worded the lie.

"You can't be fucking serious," Ramsey said.

Back in the back of Ali Baba's. He'd driven straight from the cemetery, the memory of the cold January sun filtering through the little stone chapel's stained-glass windows still fresh in his mind. His grandmother squeezing his hand as the priest said the things priests say. Except no one was listening, because all eyes were on Murray. On Monte.

"Pretty much," Monte replied.

He was more careful this time. He was armed, for one thing. And before he came in, he'd lured the muscle guys to the front by making a lot of racket with some old chinaware flung at the wall. He picked off Viking No. 1 first, then Viking No. 2. Taser to start with, then pepper spray for good measure, then expandable baton for the kneecaps, which cracked loudly in the echoing stillness of the old banquet hall. He left them alive, since guys that size could come in handy down the road, and like a couple of dumb steers, they probably didn't care who paid the tab for their feed.

"Listen, Murray. Maybe we can come to some kind of agreement," Ramsey said, standing up from his desk. Shifting from one foot to another. Surprisingly confident for a guy who had misplaced his two Desert Eagle lackeys.

"You mean like the agreement you made with my father?"

"Now, see, that was just a business thing."

"Business?"

"It was nothing personal, Murray," Ramsey said with a smirk. "I was trying to be reasonable, and he wouldn't listen. It's like nothing's ever different with you people."

"That's not exactly true."

"Meaning what?"

"Meaning everything's changed now," Monte said, doing

what he should have done the first time. Ramsey was quick, reaching for the gun in the back of his waistband like an old pro, but Monte was quicker.

The shots knocked Ramsey backwards and against the wall, and if you looked at the blood left behind as he slowly collapsed onto the floor, it brought to mind Rochelle's spiky red hair in an abstract-art kind of way.

"For one thing, it's Monte now," he said, and he turned and walked away.

So Beautiful or So What

Released April 2011

"Getting Ready for Christmas Day"
"The Afterlife"
"Dazzling Blue"
"Rewrite"
"Love and Hard Times"
"Love Is Eternal Sacred Light"
"Amulet"
"Questions for the Angels"
"Love and Blessings"
"So Beautiful or So What"

All songs by Paul Simon.

SO BEAUTIFUL OR SO WHAT

Debra H. Goldstein

"You holding out on us, Johnny?" The brawny redhead pointed the branch he'd been using to stir tonight's gumbo at me. "What you got in your pocket?"

Ignoring the men and women vying for a spot close to the garbage can fire, I focused on Red. The fact he had me by almost six inches and forty pounds—not to mention that branch, stripped of its bark and whittled to a sharp point—made me want to show him his suspicions were unfounded. The last thing I needed was trouble...and I didn't figure the tattooed words LOVE and MAMA on the backs of his fingers indicated a secretly sweet nature.

I dug a hand into the pocket of my camouflage jacket, drew out the can of okra, and held it so Red could see it. "I didn't realize it wasn't one of those flip-tops when I stole it, so I kept it when I dumped my corn and peas in the pot."

Red stuck out a beefy paw. "Give it here. Who's got a knife?"

There was silence until the new kid piped up: "I have a Swiss Army knife, Red. It's a doozy."

He grinned widely, freckles spread across his face, and held his knife up for everyone to admire, close enough to the fire that flames reflected from its shiny surface.

I groaned inwardly. Thanks to me, the kid would now be a target, soon as Red returned his prize possession. This was not a screw-up an undercover cop ought to have made.

What made it worse was that the kid's slight frame matched the body type of the three victims who'd been murdered under the bridge and in the nearby park over the past six months.

With elections coming up, the homeless and their encampments were once again in the news. The present mayor, the Queens borough president, and their respective challengers were all campaigning on platforms highlighting cleaning up the public areas that had been staked out by the homeless.

The difference between the candidates was in their management of the press after each of the murders. The incumbents dodged the headlines and touted their past accomplishments and future plans, while their opponents—noting that all three victims had been drug users—railed about crime in the streets and the incumbents' failures. The truth lay somewhere between those two positions.

After the second murder, with the uniforms and detectives stymied in their investigation, Paul Landis had been sent in undercover as "Pete Simon." After reconnecting with a former confidential informant, Paul reported making some headway, but the Powers That Be (and Those That Were Hoping to Be), playing on the transient nature of the homeless, thought it best after another month without an arrest to send in someone from a different station. The unspoken explanation was that Landis was what was called by some a SLAP, or "Stupid Lazy-Ass Policeman."

I'd just finished two years undercover on another case, and I was assigned to back up the SLAP. Paul and I had been working the same turf for three days, now, but aside from a nod in passing, we hadn't had any contact. Acting as if I were a bit of a loner, I'd picked a spot on the edge of the encampment to sit and observe its denizens.

Red was obviously the alpha male. Paul had his own group of followers to yuck it up with, including two guys who spent a lot of time shooting hoops in the park, a few who only left their spots under the bridge for the meals offered at nearby shelters, and Larry, who alternated running petty scams with ranting against the police and the establishment. The kid with the Swiss Army knife seemed to be on the fringe of Paul's group. There were also a small number of female members of the loose-knit community—Dishtowel Molly and a couple of others.

There'd been talk around the department about Paul being dirty, but he had a history of making solid arrests. On this case, though, I didn't see any evidence of him doing anything productive, and I seriously doubted any of his hangers-on were the CI he claimed to have.

Meanwhile, now that I'd put the kid in danger over his knife, I'd have to double down on protecting him.

There was something that drew me to the youngster. He just seemed too fresh and naïve to be on the street. Maybe he reminded me of myself at that age. Maybe I thought I could do a good deed and help him turn his life around.

I'd observed Larry using him more than once as the shill in a dice grift. Before the kid continued down that path, I hoped to gain his trust and convince him to go back home—or at least take refuge in a shelter. It's not that I'm some kind of do-gooder, but we *are* supposed to protect and serve.

With a couple of well-placed thrusts, Red opened the can. He handed the knife back to the kid, poured the okra into the pot, and resumed stirring with a theatrical flourish.

"Listen up, yooz guys," he said. "We're going to have a good dinner tonight, and your bellies'll be so full you'll probably sleep like babies, but yooz need to keep your guard up. The cops aren't doing a stinking thing about them three murders."

"Yeah," Larry yelled, waving his hands. "The politicians want us gone, and the pigs'll look the other way until we're all dead."

A frown crossed Red's face, and I figured either he didn't agree with Larry or he wasn't about to be distracted from the point he wanted to make. He waved his stirrer past the bridge. "The first two killings were in the park, but the third one was closer to home, right under our bridge. We got to stay vigilant, yooz hear me?"

Later, with our bellies full and the fire dying, we broke into smaller groups and staked out places to sleep. I deliberately edged near the kid, who was setting up beneath the center of the bridge.

"Supposed to be cold tonight," I said. "It's warmer near the grate on the far side."

"Thanks." He picked up his backpack and followed me to one of the wing walls. I positioned my bedding so I could lean against the bridge's brace, and the kid did the same.

"Want a smoke?" I offered.

"Not that kind." He pulled a joint from his backpack. "This'll relax me more than the stew." He lit up and took a long toke, then offered it to me. As I shrugged it off, Paul materialized, as if drawn by the sweet scent.

"Good timing," the kid said.

Paul smiled. He waved a hand, and Red and Larry joined us. Larry, Paul, and the kid passed the joint around. When it was gone, Paul and Larry got to their feet, but Red stayed on the ground, one of his hands resting on the kid's backpack.

"Be careful where you put your stuff tonight." Red's words were addressed to the kid, but his gaze was locked onto mine. "Most of us've got each other's backs, but you never know."

Looming above us, Paul nodded. "Yeah, we're not all saints. Come on, Larry."

The two of them wandered off. Eventually, Red pushed himself up and sauntered away in the same direction.

Things soon quieted down in the encampment. Lying on my bedroll, I was lulled into that peaceful fullness Red had warned us about. The sky was full of stars, and—even for the homeless—the night was beautiful, so beautiful.

A noise startled me. I propped myself up on an elbow and looked around, finally convincing myself it was nothing to worry about.

So beautiful, I thought, stretching out again, *but so what?*

There's loads *of beauty in the world, but I get stuck dealing with the ugly...*

I woke up a couple of times during the night and checked on the kid. Other than rhythmic snoring somewhere nearby, a few guys mumbling to themselves, and the patter of raindrops on the bridge, nothing much was happening—

—until just before dawn, when a woman's scream interrupted my dreams.

I jumped up and was second only to Red in reaching the spot where Dishtowel Molly rocked on her knees in front of a pile of rags, a stained towel clutched to her breast. I bent down to see if she was hurt, but she ignored my questions and went on screaming.

Red, I saw, was staring at the rags. When I followed his gaze, I realized that they were wearing shoes. Leaving Molly in the care of the others who'd by then joined us, I bent down to examine the dead man.

Careful not to disturb anything, I circled the body, memorizing as much as I could of the scene. Cell phone pictures would have been useful, but, since I was supposed to be homeless, I'd decided not to carry one. My memory would have to do.

When I saw that the victim was Paul, my poker face slipped for a moment. I glanced up to see if Red had noted my reaction, but he remained expressionless.

I continued my examination. There was no sign of a bullet hole—just a puncture wound in Paul's neck. I was pretty sure the techs would conclude that, like the first three victims, Paul had been stabbed icepick style and left to bleed out.

The detectives investigating the earlier murders had hypothesized that they were drug-related robberies gone bad. Seeing Paul's body, I disagreed. The cold-blooded preciseness of his murder suggested an intentional stabbing rather than a reactive killing. I searched for something to confirm that gut feeling.

When I took a closer look at Paul's shoes, I knew I'd found

it. Undercover work requires dressing to fit the situation, and Paul's tattered clothes were appropriate for a homeless man—but for some reason he'd opted to wear his own shoes, an unblemished pair of black leather loafers. A robber rolling him for drugs or other valuables would certainly have taken them to wear or sell.

I was also convinced that Paul must have known the person who killed him, since his expression was peaceful, not agitated.

Sirens announced the approach of the police, and Red yelled, "Yooz all need to make yourselves scarce!"

Most of my fellow under-the-bridgers grabbed what they could and scattered. Dishtowel Molly stayed where she was. She'd stopped screaming and sat beside Paul, rocking back and forth, singing in a voice just above a whisper. Her hands still held her towel, which I now saw was stained with blood.

I squatted next to her, close enough to hear that her song was a hymn: "Savior, Pass Me Not."

Red grabbed my arm and jerked me to my feet. "Johnny, we got to get out of here."

I hesitated. "What about her?"

"She'll be okay. If she did this, she'll end up someplace warm. They'll feed her three meals a day and give her a bed with clean sheets. More likely, they'll try to take her to a shelter. She'll refuse to go and end up back here. Come on!"

With a mock salute and an "Aye-aye, sir," I made a beeline for my bedding. It wasn't much—a couple of sheets and a towel that did double duty as a pillow—but it was mine.

As I bent down to collect my goods, the kid stepped in front of me, holding his backpack.

"My knife is missing," he said.

I didn't react—until I saw the tip of a plastic baggie peeking out from between my two sheets.

Either someone was trying to set me up, or my bedding had just happened to be the most convenient place to stash whatever it was that someone didn't want the cops to find. Didn't matter: at that moment, a deluge of blue uniforms blocked any means of escape.

Once the officers separated us as best they could, I had no choice but to huddle under the bridge with the rest of the stragglers, where they wouldn't even let us talk amongst ourselves.

I wound up in the back of a paneled truck with several people—Red, the kid, and Larry—for the journey to the station house for questioning.

Larry again began to rant, and Red tried to calm him down. I backed away from them and found myself next to the kid.

"What am I going to do?" he whispered, clearly terrified. "What if it was *my* knife that killed Paul? Everyone knows I had it. They'll think I did it."

"Did you?"

"No!"

"Then," I said, cupping my hand on his shoulder, "all you have to do is tell the truth."

I knew that my being embedded with this group of homeless men and women would result in my receiving different treatment in the private parts of the station, but that knowledge didn't make the way I was manhandled in and out of the van any easier to take. As we walked into the station, I smelled my own sweat, as pungent as if I'd peed in my pants. No matter how many assurances were made that this was a custodial non-arrest situation, and we were simply being questioned as material witnesses to a homicide, the sugarcoating didn't change the reality that we weren't free to leave.

I kept my face averted from those we passed as we were guided to the elevator bank used to take detained "guests" to the second-floor interrogation and conference rooms.

One flight up, I was the first one out of the elevator. A detective held the automatic doors open for us, and a clerical I'd worked with in the past gave me a big "Hey" as she strolled by. It didn't take a clairvoyant to interpret her realization of her mistake.

Her face said it all.

I ignored her and stayed in character, praying Red and company were still far enough behind me to have missed the exchange.

We were brought to separate interrogation rooms for questioning, and the detective assigned to my room—once he'd confirmed my identity—brought me a decent cup of coffee. He debriefed me, then ushered me back to an unsecured area where others waited to be returned to the encampment.

Red sat on one of the benches.

"Can I join you?" I took his grunt as acquiescence. "How'd it go?"

"Probably about the same as it went for you."

"There wasn't much I could tell them," I said. "I was sound asleep. When I woke up enough to realize Dishtowel Molly was really screaming and it wasn't just a bad dream I was having, you and I were the first to react. I stopped to check on Molly, and you checked out the pile of rags and found Pete."

"Well, at least our stories matched."

"They should. That's what happened."

"On the surface, anyway."

"What are you getting at? If you've got something to say, say it."

"Getting touchy, Johnny?"

"No more than you." I braced myself in case Red got physical.

He did, but not in any way I would have expected. He threw his head back and laughed.

It took a while before he got himself under control. He leaned closer to me and lowered his voice. "Do you know why Pete died?"

I shook my head.

"Because it was his time."

The hairs on the back of my neck prickled. "And you decided that?"

"Not me, Johnny boy." He pointed toward the ceiling.

"Somebody up there called Pete home."

"You believe that?"

He nodded his large head. "We're only given so much time on Earth, and we make of it what we will."

I shrugged. "I don't know if I buy into that."

"I believe existence is a miracle," Red said. "And once I accept that premise, I have to assume that everything happens as planned—or at least within the limits of the choices we can make. Pete made some bad choices."

I dropped my gaze to the floor. Where was this philosophical stuff coming from? And why was Red opening up in the middle of the station house? Was something on his conscience from last night?

I asked him outright, and he laughed again.

"Nah. Never even thought of it that way. Johnny, do you know why I stay on the street?"

"Because it's your home?"

"Not just my *home*." He looked at his hands. "Being out there every day is my *calling*. My mission. Years ago, addiction cost me everything, until a Southern Black gentleman years older than me took me under his wing. He was fired up by the speeches of Martin Luther King, he told me, but it was that picture on the balcony, the one where King's friends are pointing out where the kill shot came from, that led him to realize the power he had. From the moment he saw that picture, he knew he could either live in the past, or he could live the words Dr. King had preached."

Red stared at me. "I was a broken man, but he awakened something in me. I've been clean and sober ever since—and, like him, I took an oath to stay on the street, helping others to find their paths, making sure bellies are full, a bed in a shelter or a treatment program is found, sometimes simply lending a non-judgmental ear. That's how I interpret redemption."

I didn't know what to say. Either Red truly *had* found redemption, or he was for some reason feeding me the biggest cock-

and-bull story I'd ever heard. But why? Had *he* been Paul's CI? That would make sense: he was always out there, observing. But wouldn't ratting people out to a SLAP like Paul be anything *but* redemptive?

My thoughts were interrupted by an announcement that we were being bussed to a nearby shelter for dinner. Nothing was said about what would happen after the meal.

The kid caught up to me while the bus was being loaded. "Thanks," he said. "I took your advice and was honest about going to sleep with my knife but finding it missing when I woke up. Gotta get me another one." He winked at me and strode away from those of us lined up for the bus. Something bothered me about his leaving, but, rather than go after him, I chose to follow the others to dinner.

The meal flew by, with everyone relishing the fried chicken and mashed potatoes, and most of us chattering about Pete's murder and our questioning by the men in blue. After vanilla ice cream and coffee, a good many of us took advantage of the shelter's offer of a shower and a night out of the cold, but some—including Red, Larry, and me—walked back to the bridge.

By the time we got there, I was beat. It would soon be dark, so I headed off to stake out my warm spot by the grate. The kid was already there, with his backpack and some other junk. Before I could get mad, he slid his things to the side, making room.

My bedding was gone. As I tried to figure out how I was going to stay warm, the kid reached into what I'd thought was a pile of trash and handed me a rolled yoga mat. "I always like a little padding," he said, "so I skipped dinner and did some shopping." He patted a second mat. "I figured these would make us both a bit more comfortable tonight."

I didn't have to ask what else he'd picked up while "shopping," because he opened his backpack and pulled out two packaged camp-sheet sets, the store tags still attached. He gave me one. "Sorry, though, no pillows."

I smiled. "I think I can make do without a pillow."

Larry appeared, and he and the kid shared another joint. I stretched out on my new bedding and was asleep almost immediately.

Scuffling and a woman's voice shouting "Not this time!" woke me to the sight of the kid, knife in hand, crouched over me. Dishtowel Molly was straddling his back, riding him like a bucking bronco and pounding him with her tiny fists.

He twisted and turned, trying to throw her off, and finally swatted her, hard, with his free hand.

My body broke her fall, but her weight pinned me in place. As the kid came in for the kill, Red jumped onto him from behind. They crashed to the ground, the kid coming out on top.

As I lifted Molly off me, the kid raised his knife.

"Red," I screamed, "look out!"

Red rolled the kid over with an old-fashioned wrestling move and dropped onto him with his full weight. The kid went limp.

Releasing his hold, Red backed away. Blood gushed from where the knife—a new one, bigger than the Swiss Army knife, probably stolen from the same store where he'd lifted the yoga mats and sheets—had penetrated the kid's stomach.

I snatched up a sheet to staunch the flow, but Red grabbed my arm. "Forget it, Johnny. He's gone."

"He was going to do it again," Molly gasped. "He didn't like cops like Paul and you."

I stared at her, realizing that she'd used Paul's real name. "*You* were the CI," I said.

She smiled. "The kid was dealing."

Sirens sounded in the distance.

"Marijuana?"

"That and more. Paul was sure the other three victims were customers who got on the kid's wrong side, so he made examples of them. Then Paul tried to muscle in on the action, but the kid had him figured for a cop."

The shoes.

"Paul thought he'd scared the kid into taking him on as a partner, but the kid didn't want a partner and killed him. When I saw him make a move on *you* just now, I couldn't let it happen again."

"You knew *I* was a cop, too?"

"We all did," Red said, "as of this afternoon. You were made getting out of the elevator at the station." He held out his beefy hands, fists clenched. "Your brethren will be here in a minute. I'd prefer to have *you* take me in."

I looked for Molly, but she was gone, blended into the crowd of onlookers.

"I don't see why," I said. "Way I read it, he fell on his own knife. Must have been a drug deal gone bad—I understand the officers found another knife and a stash right around this spot last night."

Red's hands dropped to his sides, and he gazed at me with a respect I hadn't gotten from him before.

"So," I said, "you making your beautiful gumbo again tomorrow night, or what?"

Stranger to Stranger

Released June 2016

"The Werewolf"
"Wristband"
"The Clock"
"Street Angel"
"Stranger to Stranger"
"In a Parade"
"Proof of Love"
"In the Garden of Edie"
"The Riverbank"
"Cool Papa Bell"
"Insomniac's Lullaby"

All songs by Paul Simon.

COOL PAPA BELL

Eve Fisher

I heard a while back that someone's printed up a little handbook called *So You're Going to Prison!* I'd like to read it, see if there's any truth in it. Of course, times change, so unless they're rewriting it every year, there's no telling how out of date it is.

I think the most important thing to know about prison is that you've got to find a way to make a living. Some people come in, figure, *Hey, I'm gonna get fed, clothed, housed—why the hell should I work?* Then you find out how crappy the basic hygiene unit is. How little food gets put on your tray. So you realize you *gotta* make a living.

If you've got skills—welding, carpentry, that kind of stuff—or if you're smart enough to learn, you can make a damn *good* living. I mean, good for prison wages.

But there's all kinds of ways to make money in prison. You can set up a store and sell soups and other goods—just mark 'em up a little more than the commissary does. If you have your sources, you can also sell contraband: chew, hooch, drugs.

I tried that for a while, but it wasn't me. I'm a thief by trade, not a drug dealer, and stealing stuff in prison will get you killed. Don't get me wrong, I like my high, but I had a come-to-Jesus night after I got sentenced to life for murder. I'd gotten high and not only botched the robbery but tweaked out in the middle of it and shot up the store. Five people hit, two dead. I feel real bad about it now.

I gave up drugs entirely when I turned sixty and finally decided that lying in a bunk flying high on meth is *not* exactly the road to happiness. Just the opposite. Plus it's bad for my heart.

Anyway, if you can do tattoos or give haircuts, you can make some serious cash. And then there's the bullshit shop: sovereign-citizen cards, Moorish Science Temple cards, fake IDs, green cards, every damn thing else that's no good whatsoever in the joint, but the poor schmucks that buy 'em don't figure it out until they're back on the street. All kinds of bullshit. Gives 'em hope—which is what every con man's been selling since the dawn of time, amiright?

I've done some of that, too, in my day.

But now I work in the infirmary, pushing wheelchairs, emptying slops, sitting with guys who are old and senile and sick.

I get asked, *Don't that depress the living shit out of you?*

Nope. I'm grateful to do it. I'm getting up there in the decades myself, and I'll sure want someone to sit with *me* while I try and figure out where my fly is.

My best friend, Doc Welbon, is another lifer. He's not really a doctor, but everyone calls him Doc 'cause of his remarkable skills in pharmaceutical manufacture. He's also not bad at distillery. The two of us coach the softball teams. Welbon's a gifted amateur, but I used to play minor league baseball down in Florida, when I was young and still had a future. Ted Bell of the Dunedin Blue Jays. People said I was *damn* fast, like Cool Papa Bell, so that's my nickname here in the joint, Cool Papa. No relation—I'm white, he was black—but you never know *where* your daddy's been, do you? Anyway, I *was* damn fast. Made me good at baseball—and stealing. I just chose the wrong one of those two to focus on. Wish I could've done my time in Florida, but they sent me up here to New York after a while. Been freezing every winter since.

Doc and I met many years ago at a minimum-security prison upstate. That was sweet. Had plenty of privileges, plenty of yard. We managed to field four softball teams, so there was some good competition. One team was nothing but the Brand—the Aryan Brethren, that is, or AB for short—which worried me some. But it turned out they didn't wanna turn the game into a gang war. They just wanted to prove their racial superiority and all that. Actually showed up for practice. That was something—taking time away from working out on the weights to play softball. They ran a lot of laps, too. I mean a *lot* of laps, which made me start to wonder. But it was when they got to fighting to play outfield that I knew something funny was going on.

"What's wrong?" Doc asked.

"I don't know, but it smells fishy. When Drake wants to play centerfield, I know there's more out there than fly balls."

See, there was nothing out in the field but lawn grass and a fence, behind which was a row of red oaks, set way back, that looked cool and green in summer and almost vibrated red in winter. But they were too far away to provide cover—and besides, to get to the fence and over, you had to pass two watchtowers. No good for escape.

So what the hell was going on?

Well, Doc and I took turns coaching and watching the outfield. And one day, early morning, everyone was running around the field...

"What's that lyin' on the ground out there?" Doc asks, just as Drake reaches down and snatches it up.

"I don't know, but you watch, it'll be up his ass in a minute."

But Drake is in no hurry to stuff it down his pants.

So when he comes back around, I ask, "Hey, Drake. What'd you find out there?"

"Dead catbird," Drake says, showing it to us. "I was thinking I could use the tail feathers in a dream catcher."

Doc and I look at each other, then at Drake.

"Nice," Doc says.

***

From then on, we paid more attention, and sure enough, almost every morning there was a bunch of dead birds and squirrels just lying out there in the yard.

"You want to go pick one of them up?" I asked.

"You're Cool Papa Bell," Doc said. "The fastest man alive. You jog out and get it."

"You lazy fat fuck," I grumbled, but I went. I brought back a large dead robin and handed it to him. "Take a look at the underbelly," I said, trying not to sound out of breath.

"Definitely not a natural demise," Doc said. "It's been sewn up with fishing-lure thread."

"I reckon we better see what's inside."

Doc pulled a blade from his waistband and cut the stitches. Out came a mess of stink and a little plastic bag full of white powder.

"Well, well, well," Doc said, admiringly. "What a clever idea. I wonder how they lobbed it over the fence?"

"Potato gun?" I suggested.

"Only you would think of that," Doc said. "Let's stroll back out and leave it where you found it."

We put the dead bird back where it was, then went and washed our hands—"You never know *what* that thing might be carrying," Doc said—and returned to our usual place behind home plate.

We didn't tell anybody about it, and we didn't hint we knew anything about anything. We did warn our friends that we'd heard there were some bad drugs going around, so be careful. As Doc said to me, "How healthy can doing drugs from a dead bird's gut *be*?"

Well, the answer was, the stuff was fucking toxic. Practically the whole unit got sicker than a dog. At least five ended up in the hospital. One guy in the throes of narcotic hell poured out the whole story, and there was a huge crackdown. Even though we had nothing to do with it, Doc and I were sent off to separate prisons, just because we'd coached the team. Before we left, they even cut down all the red oaks.

That's prison for you: one guy fucks up, everybody pays. And pays. And pays.

A few years later, I was taking a break at the infirmary, and who comes in with a bunch of new guys but Doc! I'd heard from a mutual friend that he'd been transferred, and I was so glad to see him. I'd really missed him. But we played it cool and rebuilt our friendship slowly. Kept the administration guessing.

"Here's the setup," I explained to him over a game of chess. "Lot of gangs here, but the one in our unit is the Brand."

Doc's eyes rolled.

"Yeah. Can't get away from them. Connie Mack and Portland are the PR guys. They shoot their mouths off twenty-four seven, but that's about it. AK's the enforcer for this tier. Bowie's the shot caller. With any luck, you'll never run into him."

Doc nodded.

"But they're getting some rivals. Jackass name of Bergen's decided the Brand's too warm and fuzzy and has set up his own bunch of neo-Nazis."

"Oh, great," Doc said. "I just love walking into the middle of a gang war."

"Maybe. Maybe not," I said. "Administration's playing it pretty close. But I can't believe they don't know what's going on. Nothing's happened yet, so you know what I say: Don't worry—"

"—don't think," Doc finished my old motto. "What about jobs? I've been working in a library the last five years."

"Library here's on lockdown. Appointment only to visit. But we can check out books and magazines on our tablets. They got two orderlies who handle all that, and they're not going anywhere: it's quiet, they got coffee and some internet access." I moved my pawn. "I advise you to join me at the infirmary. We always need someone—most inmates don't want to get their hands dirty. It's not that noisy, and *we* got a coffee pot, too."

"You sold me," Doc said. "Why is the library on lockdown?"

"There was a riot, couple years ago—nothin' major, not like Rikers. But enough to scare the crap out of the administration. The rioters occupied the library for a while, so they shut it down and never reopened it."

"My cellie told me the rioters stashed contraband in there."

"Urban legend has it a gun and a cell phone got left behind."

Doc whistled.

"Yeah. But believe me, that damn place has been searched so often even the hardcover books are limp. They found chew and some paper laced with drugs, but that's it."

"Even so. Think about it: that's the kind of legend that will never die, like the Sword in the Stone," Doc said. "The Gun in the Library—hell, if I were younger, I'd spend *my* time looking, too. Talk about dreams of wealth and power. That search will never end."

"Until some watery bint with a scimitar shows up," I said.

And we both laughed ourselves silly.

So Doc and I settled in to our new life, almost the same as our old life, only we were older and fatter. Well, *he* was.

The infirmary was always busy. We had a doctor during the week, a nurse practitioner on weekends, a couple of LPNs, and me and Doc for orderlies. And Forrest, who did all the literally shit jobs. Forrest wasn't his real name, he just got called that after the movie, only our Forrest wasn't nearly as smart as Tom Hanks's. But he was hard working and willing and laughed most of the time.

Which helped, considering what we had to deal with. Besides the flu, bronchitis, and pneumonia patients, the guys who were just too damn old to stay in the cell hall, the dying, and the guys who didn't even know who they were anymore, there were the heart attacks, overdoses, diabetic crashes, mental breakdowns, strokes, men recovering from everything from a ruptured appendix to getting shanked in the shower, and someone was always getting beat up.

Like Hatchet, who should've been called Potato Head.

Here's an example of the kind of stuff Hatchet would pull.

Colman Carlson, a newbie, arrives. In his sixties, first time in prison, facing twenty years for manslaughter and looking like a dead man walking: dazed, confused, apprehensive. Everything you'd expect, right?

So of course Hatchet goes right up to him and says, "Hey, you! Old man! I'm Hatchet, this is my fuckin' tier, and you owe me fuckin' rent. I'll be by later to pick it up."

"What rent? I don't have *nothing," Carlson mumbles.*

"You better fuckin' well get *something then. Or you gonna be one sorry ass motherfucker."*

So I go up to Hatchet and tap him on his shoulder. He whirls around all tough and says, "What do you—oh, you."

"Yeah, me," I say. "This here's my new friend."

"So what?"

"So you got permission to do this?"

"I don't need any fuckin' permission—"

And while he goes on a profane tirade, I spot AK coming up the tier, looking mean as a snake. I walk on over and say, "AK, I'm—"

"I know who you are, Cool Papa. What's going on?"

I point at Hatchet. "This lame-ass punk is trying to hit up Mr. Carlson here for rent. Mr. Carlson is new. He is also an honorable man. You may have seen his case on the news. He killed the chomo who kidnapped and raped his grandchild, which has earned my *respect, at least. So I stopped this punk, and asked if he had permission—I mean, is this* his *tier and no one told me?"*

AK looks at Hatchet like he's a small turd, which is what I'm willing to bet is what his underwear is full of by this time. "Get the fuck out of here," he says. "Now."

"I—I—I—" Hatchet stammers, and then he turns and takes off.

AK turns to Carlson. "I saw your case in the news. You got screwed. I give you my word, that won't never happen again."

AK and I nod to each other, and AK goes on about his business. And that night Hatchet gets the shit beat out of him in the shower.

Now I'm not saying that Carlson's life was all roses and cream, or that it wouldn't have been different if he'd turned out to be an asshole. But he wasn't. He was a gentleman, with a pretty good sense of humor and a high tolerance for his new life. He was like me and Doc: he didn't worry, didn't think, just did his time, day by day. Everyone liked him, and agreed he'd been screwed and should've got a medal for what he did. Probably would get a commutation, if he behaved himself, which he did. Became a church orderly and spent most of his time with the religious crowd. Doc, who also likes a good church, saw more of him than I did, but Carlson came and watched the softball games, too.

"I'm too old for weightlifting or basketball," Carlson said, as Forrest dragged out the equipment for us. Doc and I had made Forrest our batboy, because he was always around anyhow. "But I can sit in the bleachers and dream of hot dogs."

"I'm with you there," I told him. "Hot dog and a cold beer, and life would be pretty damn near heaven."

Survival in prison is mostly about manners. Money and connections help, but they only go so far. Unless you want to fight all the time, you behave. Don't cut in line. Don't talk about your case too much. Don't brag. *Ask* before you sit down at chow. Keep your eyes to yourself, no matter what's going down—and especially when your cellie or your neighbor's using the john, in the showers, that kind of thing. Don't stare at anyone, unless you want trouble. Don't steal. Always pay your debts. If your section goes to bed early, you do, too, and don't make a lot of noise. If your section's all night owls...well, get used to it.

Oh, and you gotta stay clean. Good hygiene is mandatory. You don't wash regular and brush your teeth, sooner or later a pack's gonna hustle you into the shower and do it for you. You'll come out clean—and bruised up but good. So just do it yourself. It's not that damn hard.

But aren't I gonna get beat up, you might wonder, *just 'cause I'm old or weak or whatever?*

No. Witness Carlson. Or me and Doc.

'Course, we work in the infirmary, and everybody already knows we're not gonna steal drugs out of there, 'cause otherwise we'll lose our job, so they don't bother us about that. And we take damn good care of people—and folks remember that.

We took care of Old Dakota when he was dying. He was a Native American guy transferred to the New York State prison system to get him away from some gang or something. The few NAs we had, they acted like he was some kind of shaman, and maybe he was. But he was old and worn out when he got here, and then he had a series of TIAs. Mini-strokes. Got more and more incontinent and incoherent. We kept him clean and fed and as entertained as we could. We made sure he had more visitors than the rules allowed. When he died, the NAs held a huge sweat in his honor, and we were their guests. I still have a dream catcher Wildcat gifted me. Some of them still thank us when they run into us at rec.

Sometimes, though, the assholes do seem to take over.

As I said, Doc likes a good church service, and, being an ecumenical kind of guy, he hits more than one: St. Dysmas (which is Lutheran) on Thursday, Baptist on Sunday, Buddhist meditation on Monday morning.

A while back, a new church started services on Friday nights, and he checked into it.

"Well?" I asked, as we watched the game the next day.

"Hard core. 'Repent, ye sinners. There is no easy path.' They've got a contract you got to sign if you want to join them. No drugs, no alcohol—"

"Ha!" I snorted. "I'll believe that when I see it."

"—and you can't go to any other church or service of any kind. Theirs is the only path."

"How do they feel about softball?'

"Probably against it," Doc said. "They seem to be against most things. And everyone else is going to hell but them."

"Haven't they heard?" I said. "God is love and all that. Even the ugly sinners get a shot."

"So you say, but apparently half the attraction of heaven to these guys is looking down on all the folks that didn't make it."

"That's why I don't go," I said.

"Oh, and did I mention they're all white?" Doc asked.

"You did not. Hell, Asatru's all white, nothing wrong with them." I paused. "Don't tell me. This new bunch is Bergen and his boys?"

Doc nodded.

"Oh, great. Just fucking great."

"I thought about goin' last night," Forrest said. "But I didn't. But I shoulda, right?"

"Why?" Doc asked.

"'Cause I wanna go to heaven," he said earnestly. "And I dunno if I will."

"What if there is no heaven?" I offered. "Just softball?"

Forrest laughed his head off. "Of *course* there's a heaven, Cool Papa! Everybody knows that!"

I just nodded. Far be it from me to shake the kid's faith. It was about all he had.

Meanwhile, I didn't like the idea of Bergen having his own little cult shop. Seemed to increase the possibility of a gang war, not to mention general violence. Doc and I would do our best to stay out of the whole thing, because minding your own business is the best way to do time.

But what about Forrest?

By rights, Forrest and Bergen should never have crossed paths, except that apparently even neo-Nazis like softball. One day, Bergen's gang showed up to root for the Odin's Warriors, a team made up of members of the Asatru church, which is *very* Nordic, but apparently not Nordic enough. They were playing the Toochie Tucks, a ragtag bunch of young meth heads. The Tucks were good, better than the Warriors, and when one of them—black guy, friend of Forrest's—scored the winning run, Forrest leaped up, laughing, ran over, and hugged him, then ran around the bases himself, cheering.

Forrest showed up to the infirmary next morning with two black eyes, a split lip, two cracked ribs, a bruised kidney, and swollen nuts.

"I'm fine!" he gasped. "I just fell down the stairs."

"Bullshit," Doc said. "Nobody ever got kicked in the balls by a set of stairs."

Forrest just cried, while Nurse Practitioner Lydia mopped him up and strapped his ribs.

"Can he stay here a couple of days?" Doc asked.

Lydia nodded.

"I'm gonna find out who-what-where," I told Doc. "Then we can figure out what to do about it."

Well, I know a lot of guys, and I found out what I already pretty well knew. The Odin's Warriors didn't give a filthy rat's ass about Forrest's happy dance, because most of them lived in the real world of prison, where everyone is stuck together and, when it comes to things like games and drugs, hey, pass it on, let's all have some wall-to-wall fun.

But Bergen and his stormtroopers wanted to be the hard core, and they had decided the best way to achieve that goal was to punch down on poor little Forrest and anyone else who would hug a black man instead of fight him. There's always assholes who think punching down will somehow make them better, stronger, mightier.

Won't get them any time off—in fact, it'll just pile more on—but the assholes never quite get that.

"So, Cool Papa, what do we do?" Doc asked over chess that night.

"Well, I was thinking back to the old days upstate. The one thing everyone agrees on in this place is the desirability of drugs."

"I am not looking for dead birds to stuff."

I shook my head. "I was thinking more of soaked paper. Soaked in something suitably toxic that you mix up."

"How toxic?"

I shrugged. "You can *kill* 'em for all of me. But it would probably be better if some of them survived."

"And how do we get the paper into the right hands?" Doc asked.

"There's some guys who'd love to get in with Bergen, and how better than to give his gang some free drugs? Hatchet, for one. Granted, he'll do some of 'em himself, which is also fine with me."

"And to get the stuff to Hatchet and whoever else?"

"Weight room, janitor's station, chapel. I've got quite a few people I can call in favors. Couple of janitors, some others, they'll be happy to help with the distribution. Might be a small fee, but—"

"How much?"

"I'll cover it. I don't have anything else to spend my money on, other than your cheap hooch."

"I'll chip in," Doc said.

***

A couple of weeks later, a flurry of K2-soaked paper showed up around the prison. Seriously *bad* stuff. The infirmary wound up full, mostly with guys from the Brand and Bergin's neo-Nazis.

So much for their "no drugs, no alcohol" rule.

Bergen himself was so bad the doctor finally got admin's permission to send him to the hospital, but by then it was too late.

The Brand said the neo-Nazis had tried to poison them, and Bergen's gang said it was the other way around. Tensions ran high, and when the survivors finally got their strength back, the yard exploded into one of the worst gang battles I'd seen in years. But with Bergen dead, his bunch didn't really have a chance. Most everybody had a grudge against them, and payback is a bitch.

By spring, everything was pretty much back to normal. Bergen's gang was either dead or transferred to other prisons. Doc and I were still working at the infirmary, getting ready to coach a new season of softball with Forrest as our batboy. We had eight teams: the Toochie Tucks, Odin's Warriors, the Wind Walkers, the Yard Wolves, the Soup Skippies, the 5150s, the CTQs, and the Spider Monkeys.

Softball.

Every year I'm grateful, 'cause that's one thing that's never gonna stop.

In the Blue Light

Released September 2018

"One Man's Ceiling Is Another Man's Floor"
"Love"
"Can't Run But"
"How the Heart Approaches What It Yearns"
"Pigs, Sheep and Wolves"
"René and Georgette Magritte with Their Dog After the War"
"The Teacher"
"Darling Lorraine"
"Some Folks' Lives Roll Easy"
"Questions for the Angels"

All songs by Paul Simon.

DARLING LORRAINE

Martin Edwards

The first time I saw him, I couldn't be sure.

Who or what was he looking for, that big man with the backpack slung over his shoulder? Someone or something in particular? As I watched from the bedroom window, he consulted a foldout map. Probably the one they sold at the post office in the village. The Mill—where Joe and I live—is the starting point for half a dozen walks.

The man strode back to the bridge and scanned the gorge. This uncertainty wasn't typical of him, I guessed. The way he moved—everything about him, really—struck me as confident and decisive. This was a chap who would make up his mind what he wanted and then do his damnedest to get it.

Not like Joe, I thought.

My husband was in his music room, supposedly writing a jingle for a radio commercial. It wasn't going well. He was doing what he always did when inspiration fled, humming that wretched old song, his one big hit—and even that a cover of another composer's original. Its melody clung to him like a comfort blanket. Or a cloying smell. Even all these years later, someone occasionally recognizes Joe when the two of us are out together and insists on crooning the chorus.

"Oh, my darling Lorraine..."

All I can do is simper like a backing singer while he signs an autograph and accepts condolences on the long-ago tragedy. With a melancholy smile, he puts his arm around me and says I helped him make it through, he's truly the luckiest guy in the world. But there'll be a catch in his voice, and no one ever quite believes him.

It's obvious to all and sundry that I could never take the place of darling Lorraine. How could any woman made of flesh and blood compete with a ghost, untouchable in her wooden perfection?

People look down their noses at me, always have done, ever since the days when I was in care. I can read their thoughts. They look at my hair and my clothes and my makeup, and they find the case proved. Open and shut: I'm a gold digger.

Funny thing is, when I first met Joe, I was the one who was loaded. Yep, I was the one who owned the Mill, this classy home in a beautiful spot on Cheshire's east edge, where Macclesfield's streets give way to open country and the steep inclines are a warm-up act for the Derbyshire peaks. Joe was just a tall, handsome American with sorrowful eyes who played the piano in Mancunian bars.

I took another look out the window. The man with the map was about Joe's age, but taller and better looking. He was staring up at the gargoyle—no, the *grotesque*—above the door. I dodged out of his line of sight and trotted downstairs.

"I'm going for a walk," I said, leaning into the music room.

Joe stopped humming. "Give me five minutes, honey, and I'll come with you. I could do with some fresh air, get those creative juices flowing."

You'll need more than a breath of air for that, I thought.

"No, finish what you started. I won't be long."

With a shrug of defeat, he turned back to his piano. As I squeezed into my boots, I heard him humming that awful dirge again.

***

An April shower had washed the landscape overnight, and the afternoon was bright and mild. From my vantage point on the top step, I watched the man with the map stare moodily at the brook. When he turned his head and caught my eye, I felt a rush of adrenaline and looked away. It was like being sixteen again. A bit of fun. A distraction. There was no harm in it.

I went into the cobbled yard that separates the Mill from the main path. Between the wars, the Mill was a tumbledown wreck, its ground floor converted to a scruffy café with a space for customers to sit outside. Now there's a log store joined onto a garage, at right angles to the main building. Arthur—my first husband—designed it: an underground car port with grass steps on the far side, plus a ramp for mowers leading to the steeply sloping lawn laid on top of a roof made of corrugated iron sheets. It looks good and ensures privacy, so I can take my top off and relax in the sun by the millpond—and the walkers chattering fifty yards away are none the wiser, as invisible to me as I am to them.

A clever man, Arthur. For all his faults, he was a bloody good architect, a success in his chosen field. Nothing like Joe, a loser who only ever had one lucky break in his life. Two, if you count meeting me.

The man with the map came toward me. "Excuse me, ma'am."

An American accent, similar to Joe's. Well, well.

"Can I help you?" I used my haughtiest tone, very English. I'm not a pushover.

"Do you happen to know where I can find Frank Garr?"

I looked into his pale blue eyes. They were worth looking into. "Frank Garr?" I was taken aback. When was the last time I'd heard anyone say that name?

"Sorry," he said, smiling in a way that made me wonder what was going through his mind. "I meant to say Joe Sherman." He put his hands in his pockets. "You know him?"

"I should do," I said. "He's my husband."

***

For a few moments, I felt as if this stranger and I were the only people in the world. Silly, really, but there was something about the man. As if he was a knight on a quest. Out to rescue a damsel in distress?

Was that what I was looking for? Not exactly, but I found myself wanting to linger in his presence.

He put out his hand. "Name's Woodley, Mitch Woodley. Pleased to meet you...Mrs. Sherman."

"It's Kathy." We shook. "I was just going for a walk. If you're a friend of Joe's, why don't you tag along?"

He considered me. "Is he around?"

I jerked a thumb toward the Mill. "Busy working."

"Then I'd be glad of your company...Kathy."

"I was heading for the woods." I indicated the path that led past the Mill and a scattering of small cottages. "Eventually, the route forks. The right-hand track brings you to the gorge. Follow the brook, and you come out back at the bridge."

"Lived here long?"

"Ten years. My first husband was senior partner in a firm of architects. He converted the Mill. It was his pet project."

He raised his eyebrows. "I hate to sound corny, but you must have been a child bride."

I tried not to look flattered. "Not quite." I paused. "Arthur died twelve months after our wedding. The day before we were officially due to move in."

"I'm sorry."

I breathed in the smell of the damp earth. "It seems like a lifetime ago. Shall we get on?"

For about five minutes, neither of us spoke as we made our way up the incline. Mitch Woodley's stride was brisk, but I kept pace as we passed the ruins of the old stone chapel.

"Seems like you're pretty much cut off from the rest of the world."

"We have our own train station," I retorted. "In England, nowhere is really remote. A hundred years ago, this was a hive of industry. The locals cut trees and peat for fuel. When the railway came, they started quarrying." I waved toward the birches in the distance. "Looks lovely now, but before those trees were planted, the landscape was horribly scarred. Things aren't always what they seem."

"Mining area, huh?" He smiled. "And you're a mine of information."

"My late husband's to blame," I said. "Arthur was obsessed with history. When we came here looking for a place to live, we fell in love with the Mill. They made flour there; later it was a sawmill, then a refreshment room. When that failed, it stood derelict for years, but Arthur dreamed of giving it new life. I couldn't have kids, and he used to say the Mill would be our pride and joy, our baby."

He glanced at me. "Not quite the same thing, is it?"

"No."

I didn't tell him that I'd never actually *wanted* a child. It was Arthur who felt that we needed something more. To be "a complete family," he called it.

"Looks like he did a good job. What's with the gargoyle?"

"Arthur rescued it from the chapel. At first, he fixed it over our main window, facing the millpond. I begged him to move it, said it should look out on the world, not our back garden. If only..." I hung my head. "He used to correct me when I called it a gargoyle. He said it's a *grotesque*, because it's just for show and not a working waterspout."

"It looks sort of like a dragon. Creepy."

"In olden days, everything rotten in the world was supposed to be kept outside the chapel. Arthur said the same about the Mill. It was our safe place, our sanctuary." I changed the subject. "So what brings you here, Mitch?"

He grinned. "Back in the day, I was a folk-rock fan, same as Frank. Sorry, Joe. So when I found myself in England, I decided to look for the place where that Simon and Garfunkel song, 'Homeward Bound,' was written. Sort of a pilgrimage, I guess."

"Did you find it?"

"I thought so. Widnes Station, right?"

"Don't ask me."

"Then someone told me it was *Ditton* Station. Or maybe Wigan. Or Warrington Central. Everyone I asked had a different answer." He shook his head. "This country…"

It was time to change the subject again. "You and Joe go back a long way?" I asked.

"Uh-huh."

"I don't think he's ever mentioned you. Of course, he doesn't like to talk about the old days. Not after what happened to—"

"—to darling Lorraine?"

I nodded.

"Yeah, well, I sure do understand." He shaded his eyes from the sun.

I took a breath. "So when will *you* be homeward bound?"

"Oh, I don't know. I have no ties. No reason to go anywhere real soon."

"Where are you staying?"

"I'll find someplace." He indicated his backpack. "I travel light. Best way."

As we walked through the trees, I considered inviting him to stop the night with us. If Joe didn't like it, I could play innocent and say I'd thought I was doing him a kindness. Old friends, getting together after years apart, what could be nicer? But for the moment, I held my tongue.

"When did *you* meet Frank?" he asked.

"Joe," I said. "He's always gone by Joe, as long as I've known him, five years. Of course, I know his full name: Francis Joseph Sherman Garr. He says that's too much of a mouthful."

"Five years, huh?"

"After Arthur died, I kept myself to myself. I like my own company, and I couldn't bear to leave the Mill. I felt I owed it to Arthur to stay in the home he'd made for us, but it was more than that. I love this place more than anywhere else in the world."

"And Joe?"

"A chance encounter. I went shopping in Manchester and stopped for a drink in a big hotel. Joe was there, playing...well, you can guess."

"'Darling Lorraine'?"

"Not my sort of music. I'd never heard of the group that recorded the original."

"The Knockouts. Way back, late Fifties."

"Joe's cover version was the one I knew. For a while, it got a lot of airtime on local radio. Almost like a novelty song. A throwback. Some DJ heard a rumor that Joe was inspired to sing it by a real-life tragedy. His wife Lorraine had died, of a brain tumor or something. One thing led to another, and Joe wound up with a hit and fifteen minutes of fame."

"Only fifteen minutes?"

"More like five, to be honest. He followed it with a song of his own, but that one went nowhere—and he was no good at the business side of things. Not that any of that mattered to me."

"A whirlwind romance, huh?"

"He proposed on our second date, and I accepted. Spur of the moment."

We joined a path taking us into the narrow, wooded ravine. The gorge had scarcely changed in a thousand years. There was nobody about, nothing to hear but birdsong and the rush of water.

"Watch your feet," I said. "Easy to trip on the roots."

"I like it here," he said abruptly, as if surprising himself.

"Very different from the States."

"I might just get the urge to hang around."

I shrugged. "I wouldn't complain."

We moved on, and I said, "Did you know Lorraine?"

"Sure did." A note of curiosity entered his voice. "What's Frank told you about her?"

"Joe," I sighed. "She was a paragon. Saint Lorraine of New

Jersey. Hard to live up to someone like that."

"You shouldn't worry," he said. "Lorraine is dead and gone."

The note of satisfaction in his voice caught my attention.

"You didn't like her?"

"I hate to speak ill of the dead, Kathy, but take it from me, Lorraine was a pain in the ass. I mean, great to look at. Really *hot*. And yet so cool, too. Why she ever settled for Frank...I gotta be honest, that never made sense to me."

I knew what he meant. There was an innocence about Joe, a naive and boyish nature I'd mistaken for charm.

The path brought us under branches that overhung the brook. We stopped to watch the waterfall tumbling over the jumble of rocks.

"Anyway, every Friday night he played piano in a bar to earn some extra dough. And one evening, who shimmies in but Lorraine? Frank's fate was sealed the moment she asked him to play her favorite song.'

"'Darling Lorraine.'"

"What else? She went crazy about the fact he knew it. I'd never even heard it, but you know Frank, mad about that doo-wop stuff."

"This was in New York?"

"No, he lived there, but he worked in New Jersey, Hasbrouck Heights. Next thing I knew, the two of them were hitched."

"But you stayed friends?"

His wolfish grin somehow confirmed my suspicions. *This man's not to be trusted*. Yet my skin prickled with an excitement I'd not felt in years. "You could say that."

He strode off, and I ran to catch him up. "You...were seeing Lorraine?"

He sniggered. "When Frank had to travel for work. She told me she got lonely when he was away. Truth is, she got lonely very easily."

"Did he know?"

"We never talked about it. I don't like to rub a man's face in the dirt unless I have to. For all I know, she threw it at him when they went at it."

"I didn't know they fought."

"Strikes me, Kathy, there's a lot you don't know about Frank." There was an edge to his voice.

I didn't speak again until we reached the bend in the stream. Then: "The Mill isn't far away. See the slates of the roof through the trees?"

He peered through the curtain of leaves. "That land on the other side of the water? That's all yours?"

"Yes. When we first came, it was a wilderness. The pond was silted up. You could barely see it. Arthur cleared the millrace and the pond. These days, with all the ducks and dragonflies, it seems like our own little nature reserve."

"Private paradise, huh?"

I giggled. "And now there's a stranger in paradise."

After zigzagging through the trees, the path finally brought us out by the bridge. Hardly any people around now, fewer cars parked on the lane. I ran up the front steps and unlocked the door of the Mill.

Joe came out of the music room, rubbing sleep from his eyes. There was a couch in there, and he liked to lie on it, saying it helped clear his mind. I was sure he'd not written a note all day. He didn't care about earning money. He was content to drift along in life. But who am I to talk?

"Joe," I said, "I've got a surprise for you. I met an old friend of yours."

He blinked. It was probably on the tip of his tongue to say that he didn't have any friends, but not even he was sad enough to admit that out loud. Instead, he wore a look of bewilderment.

I stepped aside, and Mitch strode past me, arms outstretched.

"Hey, Frank, how are you, old buddy?"

There was no mistaking the look on Joe's face. He was *afraid* of Mitch.

"Mitch? What...what are you doing here?"

"I thought I'd pay you a visit. Wanted to see how my pal is doing, now that he's settled down and made his fortune."

"Fortune? What are you talking about?"

Mitch waved a shovel-like hand. Arthur had transformed the shell of the old Mill into an elegant home. Behind Joe rose a wide open-tread staircase, to his left was the vast living room, with a double-height window overlooking the millpond. Even ten years ago, even with all Arthur's contacts in the building trade, the renovation had cost a mint, had bitten such a large hole in his partnership profits that, if not for his life insurance, I'd have needed to sell up when he died.

Mitch touched my arm. "Kathy just took me for a walk in the woods."

"You two must have a lot to talk about," I said. I was thinking hard. "I'll get some beers and wine from the cellar and order a pizza. We can sit out till it gets too chilly."

Joe stared at Mitch. "Won't you be heading back to wherever you're staying?"

"I said he could spend the night with us," I lied. "I'll make up the spare bedroom, throw an extra blanket on the bed."

Mitch smiled at me. "That's very hospitable of you, Kathy. I truly appreciate it."

"Lovely for you two to have the chance to talk," I said. "Reminisce about the good old days. I'll make a stack of my famous pancakes in the—"

"Sweet of you, Kathy," Mitch cut in. "But I gotta be honest. I haven't tried to *forget* those days, but I sure haven't fought too hard to remember them. Same for you, I guess, Frank?"

"Joe." He sounded mulish.

"Sorry, chum. Old habits die hard." A smirk. "Joe, then."

***

I left them to their reunion and went downstairs for the booze. The Mill doesn't have an ordinary cellar, just the old wheelhouse. One wall is lined with wine racks, another is stacked with crates of beer. The men took their bottles outside and sat on the paved area between the millpond and the lawn.

I ordered the pizza and busied myself in the log shed. By the time I joined them, they'd had plenty to drink. But they weren't talking.

Mitch poured me a glass of Merlot.

"Beautiful." He let the word hang in the air, teasing and ambiguous. Was he talking about me or the scenery? Nobody spoke until he added, "How much land do you have?"

"Three acres," I said. "I know that's nothing in the States. In England, it's a lot. We're very lucky."

"People make their own luck." A few pints, and men become philosophers. Mitch leaned back in his chair and took another swig. "So, Kathy, I know plenty about Frank—sorry, *Joe*. Tell me about you."

"Not much to tell," I said. "I never knew my dad, and my mum died young. I grew up in a sort of orphanage. Ran away a few times and finished up in care—what you'd call a foster home. Later on, I worked in retail. Finally, I had a spell as a croupier in a casino."

"Hey, I like to gamble. How about you?"

"Not with my own money," I said. "And at the time, I had none to spare. But that's where I met Arthur. He liked the high life. Expense-account lunches, a flutter at the tables. He came in one night, and I suppose I caught his eye."

Mitch gave my cleavage a measuring stare. I'd changed into shorts and my most revealing top. The temperature wasn't ideal for something so skimpy, but I was in a reckless mood.

"I bet you did."

"Marrying me was a gamble, same as converting the Mill, but he liked taking risks. That's what killed him. He climbed up a ladder to shift the gargoyle. I begged him to get the builders to do it, but he was a proud man, that was his trouble. The gargoyle was loose, and, when it came away in his hand, he fell."

Mitch made a face. "Messy."

I cast a glance at the thick slabs of York stone. "Superstitious of me, but after he died, I had the gargoyle moved."

Joe grunted and opened another beer.

Mitch said, "You're a lucky guy, Joe. Your second wife is even more beautiful than the first."

"Mitch was telling me about Lorraine," I said.

Joe cast a fierce glance in my direction. "I never knew you were interested."

"You've always told me she was an angel."

Mitch laughed. "Is that right? Well, let me tell you one or two things about her, God rest her soul."

"Don't," Joe said.

"No need to be grouchy, pal. I knew her really well, remember?"

A blatant provocation, but Joe refused to rise to the bait. Saying he needed a piss, he went back into the Mill. Joe could be peevish, but he was slow to anger. Maybe he'd have been happier if he didn't always hunch himself up so tightly, keep a lid on whatever went on in his head and his heart.

He reappeared just as the pizzas arrived. Our conversation meandered along as we drank and ate. Joe chewed his food even more loudly than usual. If I lived to be a hundred, I'd never get used to his harsh munching.

"Mitch," I said dreamily, "you were going to tell me about Lorraine."

"She wasn't the easiest of women. She'd get bored, or depressed. If you ask me, she never really knew what she wanted. Not like you, Kathy."

That, I thought, *is the drink talking.*

"Go on," I said.

"After she and Frank got married, she gave up her job." He gave Joe a mocking smile. "Suited you, didn't it, pal, to be the man of the house, the breadwinner? It's a pity that old American Dream never quite worked out. The usual marriage stuff, Lorraine never found that much fun. She wasn't romantic, and she was no homemaker. She'd whine about headaches, get upset over nothing."

"Perhaps that was the illness," I said. "An early sign, before she was diagnosed."

"Diagnosed?" Mitch winked at me. "Ah, right, I've heard about her 'illness.' So touching. How her tragic death inspired Frank to follow his dreams and become a wanderer, cross the ocean to earn a crust playing piano in Britain. Poignant, ain't that the word? There's an interview online, fifty thousand people have seen it. I've watched it twenty times myself. My old pal's a modest guy, you and I know that, Kathy. Doesn't like to boast, doesn't give many interviews. But you can't have a hit song, you can't even creep in at the tail end of the charts, without finding you have a presence online."

Joe shrugged as if he was hardly listening.

Mitch took no notice. "I was interested, pal, in what you had to say about Lorraine. Truly fascinated, 'cause it didn't square with the woman I knew. She was no pale angel, fading away in the arms of her man. Lorraine was a feisty girl, who gave as good as she got."

I was puzzled. "Are you saying she didn't die of cancer?"

Joe sprang suddenly to life. "I never said she did!" he exploded, leaning forward and jabbing the air with his finger. "People put words in my mouth. All I said was she died in tragic circumstances, and I dedicated the song to her memory. But journalists make stuff up, embroider things, twist your words. Happens all the time."

"It made the song a success," Mitch said. "You took advantage of a tragedy."

"I meant to honor her," Joe snapped.

"What *did* happen to Lorraine?" I asked.

"I only heard this secondhand," Mitch said carelessly. "I

pieced the story together years later."

"You weren't there," Joe said. "This is all bullshit, Kathy. Don't listen to him."

"So tell her yourself how Lorraine died," Mitch said.

Joe turned to me. "You want to know *why* he wasn't there, Kathy? Because he was in prison, that's why, for killing a guy in a brawl. How many years did you serve, Woodley? Not enough, that's for sure."

A glassy look came into Mitch's eyes, and a strange thrill of excitement made my spine tingle.

"Who did you kill?" I asked.

"Some kid in a dive. I'd never met him before. We'd both been drinking. He came on to me, and I didn't care for it. One punch was all it took. Just caught him on the temple"—he snapped his fingers—"and the guy went out like a light."

"And what about Lorraine?"

"The way I heard it, she got wasted one night. She flew at Joe, and he fended her off. She lost her footing and hit her head on the stone floor. Joe persuaded everyone it was an accident."

"Of course it was!"

When was the last time I'd heard Joe raise his voice like that?

"I never provoked her. She was out of her mind."

"Yeah, sure."

"It's the truth, I tell you!" Joe was shouting. "I barely touched her, and it was self-defense!"

Mitch turned to me. "The way I see it, Kathy, what Frank and I did was pretty much the same thing. Except I spent some of the best years of my life inside, while Frank changed his name and came over here and wound up lord of the fucking manor. He killed his wife, but everyone felt sorry for him 'cause of 'Darling Lorraine.'"

Joe got to his feet, not too steadily. "Get out of here!"

"Or else what?" Mitch laughed. "You know what, Frank, I reckon I'm gonna stick around. Kathy needs a real man. Trust me, I can sniff it out. Same as I did with Lorraine."

Joe shot me a frightened glance. I tried to look blank.

"I ain't in no hurry to move on," Mitch said. "Kathy's made my bed, and we're both gonna lie in it."

Joe reached for him, but Mitch was up in an instant. He clamped Joe's shoulder with one of those huge, rough hands, and Joe spat in his face.

Mitch gasped. He'd not expected defiance.

He's not stupid, I thought, *but he's not the brightest, either.* I swallowed hard as the two men glared at each other.

Then Mitch reached down for his beer bottle and smashed it on the metal table. With one swing of his hand, he drove the broken glass into Joe's throat. Blood sprayed, and I cried out in shock as Joe collapsed, his head crashing against a moss-covered slab of paving.

For a few moments, there was an eerie silence. I couldn't help shivering.

Was anyone still out on the lane at this hour? Would someone come running to see what was going on?

Nothing happened.

Blood pooled around Joe's head. Mitch kicked him, but there was no sign of life.

Be careful, I told myself. *He's unstable. You'll be next, if you don't watch out.*

"It was an accident," I said. "I'll swear to it." I was thinking fast. "But we'd better not take any chances."

"What do we do?"

I stared at the pale reflection of the moon in the water. "The millpond is deep, but we'll need to wrap him up, tie a weight to his feet. We don't want him bobbing to the surface."

Mitch shook his head. "You're a cool one."

"Self-preservation, that's all." I let out a breath. "Here's what we'll do. There's blood on the stones, but we can hose them clean. You need to drag Joe off the paving and onto that strip of lawn, okay? I'll find some blankets to swaddle around him and a couple of bricks, one for each leg."

Mitch gave me a bleary stare. "You really are something else. Did you *mean* for this to happen?"

I managed a hoarse laugh. "You think I *knew* a stranger was going to turn up on my doorstep, a killer who knew Joe's secrets? A helpful gent who would kindly get him out of my life forever?"

He laughed, too. "Put it that way, and I see your point. Okay, Kathy, you win."

I pointed at the body. "Grab hold of his feet and pull him onto the grass."

"You're the boss."

He bent down and seized Joe by the ankles, looked up and grinned at me.

He took a step back. Two steps. Three. Four. Five...

...and screamed as the turf gave way beneath his feet.

Beneath the thin layer of grass on the surface was nothing but air. Arthur had designed the log-store roof to support the lawn, but a week ago I'd cut out a section of that roof. Before our pizza arrived, I'd removed the last supports.

And Mitch dropped onto the jagged teeth of the sawing machine positioned below.

Everyone was very kind. Even the police, though I'm sure they scoured my phone records and Mitch's to see if we'd ever been in touch before that afternoon. Thankfully, half a dozen people in the States confirmed that, during his years in jail, he'd become obsessed with jealousy about Joe's good fortune.

I was glad I'd held back from killing Joe myself. My original idea was too much of a gamble: if Joe was repairing the roof of the log store, why would he step onto the lawn above, *knowing* that would plunge him to a messy death? I hadn't yet solved that puzzle when Mitch came along.

My indolence—no, let's call it my avoidance of the sin of impatience—had worked to my advantage, and the dice had rolled in my favor, just as they had when I'd provoked Arthur into shifting the gargoyle—no, *grotesque*—by himself.

Everyone expected me to leave the Mill. *How could she stay there*, they wondered, *after all that had happened?*

But I saw it the opposite way: how could I possibly leave this home I loved?

Especially now that I'd exorcized the ghost of darling Lorraine.

ACKNOWLEDGMENTS

My thanks to the authors who enthusiastically contributed stories, to Eric Campbell and Lance Wright at Down & Out Books for green-lighting my fifth "inspired by" anthology, to my wife Laurie Pachter and daughter Rebecca Jones as always and for always...and, most of all, to Paul Simon, whose words and music have kept me company, kept me enthralled, and kept me still crazy about him after all these years.

ABOUT THE CONTRIBUTORS

E.A. AYMAR is the author of the widely praised novels *The Unrepentant* and *They're Gone*. He has a monthly column in the *Washington Independent Review of Books*, is a former member of the national board of the International Thriller Writers and was for years the managing editor of *The Thrill Begins*, an online resource for debut and aspiring writers. He is an active member of Crime Writers of Color, the Mystery Writers of America, and Sisters in Crime. He also runs the Washington, DC Noir at the Bar series and speaks at crime fiction, writing, and publishing events nationwide. *eaymarwrites.com*

MARK BERGIN spent four years as a newspaper reporter, winning the Virginia Press Association Award for general news reporting, before joining the Alexandria (Virginia) Police Department in 1986. Twice named Police Officer of the Year for narcotics and robbery investigations, he served in most of the posts described in his 2019 debut novel *Apprehension*, a finalist for the 2020 Silver Falchion Award from Killer Nashville. He and his wife divide their time between Alexandria and Kitty Hawk (North Carolina). *markberginwriter.com*

PAUL CHARLES, born and raised in the Northern Irish countryside, is the author of eleven books in the Detective Inspector Christy Kennedy series, most recently *Departing Shadows*. Charles may be unique in that, not only was he *around* in the

1960s, but he also *remembers* the decade vividly, as seen in his latest publication, *The Essential Beatles Book*. He is currently working on *The Return of the James Gang*, a new DI Kennedy mystery. *paulcharlesbooks.com*

ROBERT EDWARD ECKELS submitted a short story to *Ellery Queen's Mystery Magazine* in 1946, when he was fifteen years old. That first effort was rejected—but a second story, submitted twenty years later, was accepted. It was followed by fifty-three more, two of which were included in the 1972 and 1973 editions of *Best Detective Stories of the Year*. He stopped writing in 1982, but after the publication of *Never Trust a Partner*, a collection of his con man stories, by Crippen & Landru in 2021, he agreed to come out of his forty-year "retirement" to write a new story for *Paranoia Blues*. He died, aged ninety-one, on May 16, 2022—but in the months before his passing he wrote more new stories, several of which are forthcoming in EQMM and *Black Cat Mystery Magazine*. *roberteckels.com*

MARTIN EDWARDS is the author of twenty-one crime novels, including the Harry Devlin, Lake District, and Rachel Savernake series. He has written many short stories for EQMM and anthologies. His nonfiction books include *The Golden Age of Murder* and *The Life of Crime: Detecting the History of Mysteries and Their Creators*, a history of the genre. He is a former chair of the Crime Writers' Association, consultant to the British Library's Crime Classics, and current president of the Detection Club. He has received the CWA Diamond Dagger, Short Story Dagger, and Dagger in the Library awards, plus other honors including an Edgar, an Agatha, and two Macavitys. *martinedwardsbooks.com*

EVE FISHER's stories have appeared in *Alfred Hitchcock's Mystery Magazine*, BCMM, *Mystery Weekly*, *Crimeucopia*, and elsewhere, while her historical articles have landed her on the BBC and in a textbook on economics. Her volunteer work with the Lifers Group and the Alternatives to Violence Project provides great satisfaction—as well as tips on prison tattoos and etiquette. A regular contributor to the SleuthSayers blog, she lives in South Dakota with her husband and five thousand books.

DEBRA H. GOLDSTEIN is the author of the Sarah Blair mystery series (Kensington Publishing). She has been a finalist for the Agatha, Anthony, and Derringer awards for her short fiction, which has appeared in AHMM, BCMM, *Mystery Weekly*, and anthologies including *Mystery Most Edible* and *Jukes & Tonks*. Prior to turning to writing full-time, she was a federal administrative law judge. She has served on the national boards of Sisters in Crime and Mystery Writers of America and was a chapter president for both organizations. *DebraHGoldstein.com*

ANTHONY LEE HEAD was an overworked trial lawyer before escaping the rat race to live on a Mexican beach. After ten years, he returned to California and began to write stories inspired by his tropical adventures. His first book, *Driftwood: Stories from the Margarita Road*, was named a Best Book of the Year by Kirkus Reviews, a Best First Book by IndieReader Discovery Awards, and a finalist for the Independent Book Publisher Association's Best First Book Benjamin Franklin award. He is currently working on a mystery set during San Francisco's Summer of Love. *anthonyleehead.com*

CHERYL A. HEAD writes the award-winning Charlie Mack Motown mysteries. She is a two-time Lambda Literary Award finalist, a Next Generation Indie Book Award finalist, and winner of the Golden Crown Literary Society's Ann Bannon Popular Choice Award. In 2022, she was awarded the Alice B. Readers Appreciation award, and her books are included in the special collections of the State of Michigan Library. *Time's Undoing*, a crime novel based on her family's personal tragedy, is due from Dutton in March 2023. A resident of Washington, DC, she lives with her partner Teresa and their canine supervisors Abby and Frisby. *cherylhead.com*

EDWIN HILL's critically acclaimed crime novels include the standalone thriller *The Secrets We Share* and three novels featuring Hester Thursby. He has been nominated for the Edgar and Agatha awards and was recognized as one of Six Crime Writers to Watch by *Mystery Scene* magazine. He lives in Roslindale (Massachusetts) with his partner Michael and his favorite reviewer, their lab Edith Ann, who likes his first drafts enough to eat them. *edwin-hill.com*

REBECCA K. JONES is a criminal appeals attorney in Phoenix (Arizona) by day and a crime writer by night. Her short stories and translations have appeared in EQMM and other places, and her first novel, *Steadying the Ark*, was published in 2022 by Bella Books.

KRISTIN KISSKA used to be a finance geek, complete with MBA and Wall Street pedigree, but now she is a self-proclaimed *#SuspenseGirl*. She has contributed short stories to eleven crime anthologies, including Malice Domestic's Agatha Award-winning *Mystery Most Edible*. A member of International Thriller Writers, the Women's Fiction Writers Association, and James River Writers, she lives in Richmond (Virginia) and serves as the vice president of the Central Virginia chapter of Sisters in Crime. *KristinKisska.com.*

R.J. KORETO, a business and financial journalist, has been a magazine writer and editor, website manager, PR consultant, and seaman in the U.S. Merchant Marine. He is the author of the Lady Frances Ffolkes and Alice Roosevelt mysteries and the upcoming Historic Homes mysteries, and his short fiction has been published in both EQMM and AHMM. With his wife and daughters, he divides his time between Rockland County (New

York) and Martha's Vineyard (Massachusetts). *rjkoreto.com*

TOM MEAD is a UK author whose work has appeared in EQMM, AHMM, and numerous other places; his story "Heatwave" was included in *The Best Mystery Stories of the Year 2021*, edited by Lee Child. He is a member of the Crime Writers' Association, the Society of Authors, and the International Thriller Writers. *Death and the Conjuror*, his debut novel, was published in the US by Mysterious Press in July 2022 and is due from Head of Zeus in the UK in January 2023. *tommeadauthor.com*

JOSH PACHTER was the 2020 recipient of the Short Mystery Fiction Society's Golden Derringer Award for Lifetime Achievement. His stories appear in EQMM, AHMM, BCMM, *Mystery Magazine*, *Mystery Tribune*, and elsewhere. He edits anthologies (including Agatha Award finalist *The Beat of Black Wings: Crime Fiction Inspired by the Songs of Joni Mitchell*) and translates fiction and nonfiction from multiple languages, mainly Dutch, into English. *joshpachter.com*

RAQUEL V. REYES writes stories with Latina characters. Her Cuban-American heritage, Miami, and Spanglish feature prominently in her work. *Mango, Mambo, and Murder*, the first book in her Caribbean Kitchen series, was a finalist for both the Agatha and Lefty awards. The *New York Times Book Review* wrote that "it executes its mission...with panache." Raquel's short stories have appeared in anthologies, including the 2022 edition of *The Best American Mystery & Suspense*. *LatinaSleuths.com*

ANNA SCOTTI writes in several genres. A story from her EQMM series about a librarian in Witness Protection was reprinted in *The Best Mystery Stories of the Year 2022*, and her YA novel *Big and Bad* received a Paterson Prize in 2020. She also writes poetry and is the author of the 2021 collection

Bewildered by All This Broken Sky. In her spare time, she teaches middle-school English, a prospect far scarier than murder most foul. *annakscotti.com*

GABRIEL VALJAN is the author of the Roma, Company Files, and Shane Cleary series. In 2021, he won the Mystery Readers International's Macavity Award for Best Short Story, and he has been a finalist for the Agatha, Anthony, and Silver Falchion awards. He lives in Boston. *gabrielvaljan.com*

ANDREW WELSH-HUGGINS, an Associated Press reporter, is the author of seven novels featuring Andy Hayes, a former Ohio State and Cleveland Browns quarterback turned private investigator, and the editor of the anthology *Columbus Noir*. His short mystery fiction has appeared in EQMM, *Mystery Magazine*, *Mystery Tribune*, the 2021 Bouchercon anthology *This Time For Sure*, and elsewhere. A Finger Lakes native, he now lives in Ohio. *andrewwelshhuggins.com*

FRANK ZAFIRO was a police officer in Spokane (Washington) from 1993 to 2013, retiring as a captain, and is the author of over three dozen novels, including the River City police procedurals, the hard-boiled SpoCompton series, and the Stefan Kopriva PI mysteries. He is an avid hockey fan, a tortured guitarist, and the host of the crime fiction podcast *Wrong Place, Write Crime*. He lives in Redmond (Oregon). *frankzafiro.com*

On the following pages are a few
more great titles from the
Down & Out Books publishing family.

For a complete list of books and to
sign up for our newsletter,
go to DownAndOutBooks.com.

Land of 10,000 Thrills
Bouchercon Anthology 2022
Greg Herren, Editor

Down & Out Books
September 2022
978-1-64396-290-0

Featuring some of the top, award-winning authors in the field today—from Mindy Mejia to Marcie R. Rendon to Michael Wiley, Susanna Calkins and Erica Ruth Neubauer, and Bryon Quertermous, Tessa Wegert, Raquel V. Reyes, and Richie Narvaez—doing some of their finest work to date. Collected and curated by award-winning editor Greg Herren, with stories ranging from light to darkly funny to just out-and-out macabre, *Land of 10,000 Thrills* is one of the strongest anthologies put together by the Bouchercon conference to date.

Beneath the Black Palms

Stories by Nolan Knight

Down & Out Books
September 2022
978-1-64396-273-3

Come for the sunshine, stay for the dread.

Nolan Knight's masterful, stylistically-diverse short stories expose the nerves of lonesome dreamers, outcasts, squares, con men and have-nots. No one is spared *Beneath the Black Palms*, the most unforgettable short story collection in recent years.

Rock, Roll, and Ruin

A Triangle Sisters in Crime Anthology
Karen Pullen, editor

Down & Out Books
October 2022
978-1-64396-274-0

These twenty-seven stories reflect music in all its forms—from church choir to opera, country to tribal drums. Of course, rock & roll, the soundtrack of teen lives, predominates—in fiction about Elvis fans, record albums, and bad-boy bands.

Unique stories feature crimes ranging from theft to baby-stealing to murder, each accompanied by a soundtrack, goose bumps, and adrenaline.

Old Man Rider
A Bishop Rider Book
Beau Johnson

Down & Out Books
October 2022
978-1-64396-275-7

It's all come down to this. The past, the present, and the conclusion of man who's chosen to end so many colliding for the final time.

From an unimaginable start within the pages of *A Better Kind of Hate* to a bitter, bloody end throughout *All of Them To Burn*, Bishop Rider remains what he's always been. What a certain type of predator forced him to become. His life and struggle not only a journey of choice driven by necessity, but one decades in the making.

CPSIA information can be obtained
at www.ICGtesting.com
Printed in the USA
BVHW091426011122
650803BV00002B/142